ANGELS AND ASHES

Angels and Ashes © 2016 Avelyn Paige

Example Copyright notice: All rights reserved under the International and Pan-American Copyright Conventions. No part of this book may be reproduced or transmitted in any form or by any means, electronic or mechanical, including photocopying, recording, or by any information storage and retrieval system, without permission in writing from the publisher.

Cover Designer: The Final Wrap

Editor: Southern Sweetheart Author and Book Services

Photographer: Shauna Kruse

Model: Alfie Gordillo

This is a work of fiction. Names, places, characters and incidents are either the product of the author's imagination or are used fictitiously, and any resemblance to any actual persons, living or dead, organizations, events or locales is entirely coincidental.

Warning: the unauthorized reproduction or distribution of this copyrighted work is illegal. Criminal copyright infringement, including infringement without monetary gain, is investigated by the FBI and is punishable by up to 5 years in prison and a fine of $250,000.

BLURB

Her husband is dead. His wife should be.

One year after Darcy Kyle's husband died in a tragic accident, she receives a letter from the grave. Left with more questions than answers, Darcy sets out to find the truth and prove her husband was murdered. Even if it means putting herself in harm's way.

Michael "Raze" Sanders has always had a thing for Darcy, but his loyalty to his dead former club vice president and best friend has kept him away. But now Darcy's sticking her nose where it doesn't belong, and her life is in danger. Is it loyalty or lust that has Raze watching from afar as Darcy hunts for answers?

As the truth is uncovered, neither Raze or Darcy are prepared. And their need for each other is about to be both their downfall and their salvation.

Dedication

To Jezebel
My ride or die writing buddy. Thanks for the support and the snuggles in your thirteen years.
I miss you every day.

Chapter 1

DARCY

"DADDY'S HOME, BOYS," I call out from the kitchen. The loud pipes from his Harley nearly shake the house free of its foundation. "Colt, watch your brother. I'm going to out to help your dad bring in his gear."

Colt's muted reply echoes from their room just before playful giggles flow out of the door. Giggles typically indicate those two are up to no good, but I'll let their dad take care of any problems that occur today. It's his turn after yesterday's marker incident in the newly-painted spare bathroom. Troublemakers. All of them. Carbon copies of their father. Where the three of them go, chaos ensues, but I wouldn't give it up for anything in the world.

Reaching the front hallway, I peer out the window and find it's not my husband's bike in the drive, but club president's. Raze swings his leg over his black Harley Davidson and walks toward our front door. A sense of foreboding rushes stops me dead in the hallway. The door slowly opens with a slight creak and reveals Raze's large, muscular body. His shoulders droop and his eyes are glued to the floor.

Something's wrong.

"Where's Brent?" I ask so quietly, I'm not even sure he hears me.

Raze doesn't even lift his eyes from the floor. Almost as if he is afraid to meet my gaze. "There's been an accident, Darcy."

A gasp escapes my lips, adrenaline rushing through my veins as the mental emergency checklist unfolds in my mind. Trips to the hospital with my husband have become more of a regular occurrence the longer we've been married. I swear, the man has a medical chart the size of that clumsy tool guy on TV in the 90s. It's like a medical team family reunion whenever we breeze through the emergency room doors. I often wonder if they could put in a frequent visitor express lane for us.

"An accident," I repeat, turning to get my purse from the hallway table.

Raze reaches out and grabs my arm, pulling my attention back to him. I tear away from his grasp and glare at him for stopping me. I need to get to my husband. Raze doesn't back down, though. Instead, he lingers before releasing me.

"Which hospital did they take him to?" I ask, turning once more to grab my purse. "Kindred or San Antonio? God, I hope it's not Kindred at this time of day. It'll take hours to get there with the rush-hour traffic."

Raze's enormous form steps forward and blocks me from stepping around him. "Darcy, I need you to listen to me." His voice is filled with sorrow and pain. "Brent's not in the hospital. He's dead, darlin'."

I blink and stare up at the man in front of me. *That's not possible. He was just here in this house, kissing me goodbye in this very hallway?*

Brent had left this morning with a smile on his face and a promise to take us all out tonight to see that stupid Minion movie the boys have been driving us crazy about for weeks. It can't be true. Can it?

The world slows then as visions of my husband's body lying in a casket spill over into my mind. My body goes limp and I stumble. Raze lunges forward to catch me before I descend to the ground into a sobbing mess.

"Darcy. *Darcy.* Please answer me, darlin'. You're scaring the fuck out of me. Tell me you understand what I'm trying to tell you."

Strong arms pull me against a hard, muscular

chest. He's trying to comfort me, but even without being in the right mind, I know it's a futile action. His hands stroke my hair, and tears pour down my face.

Lifting my gaze upward, my eyes connect with his. Raze's face is tear-stained, and his icy-blue eyes are as mournful as my own must be. He's in pain, too. But the pain he feels is nothing compared to the pain writhing inside of me. I know he loved my husband, but he'll never fully relate to the pain I feel in this instant. He may have lost his brother, but I lost the one person on this Earth who understood me and helped me give life to the boys playing in the sunroom next to us.

The boys. Oh god. How do I tell them that their daddy isn't coming home?

They're so young. Too young to live without their father. Colt may comprehend that his dad's not coming back at six years old, but three-year-old Wesson won't understand at all. My eyes drop to my stomach, and another sob rips from my throat.

Neither will the small bump growing inside of me.

Brent didn't even know I was pregnant yet. I was going to make the announcement tonight at dinner that our family was going to be growing by one more. It was my anniversary surprise to him. Brent always wanted more kids, but after the difficulties we had with Wesson, our doctor had warned us our precious little boy would reasonably be our last child. Little did any of us know that a miracle was still possible. Our little miracle that Brent would never get to hold or to love.

"How?" I croak. "I want to know how."

Raze releases me from his grasp and pulls me into the living room by my wrist, sitting me on the couch. His hand falls from my wrist, and he settles in beside me, his large frame causing the couch to dip beneath his weight. He sighs loudly and grabs for my hand again, stroking his rough thumb against my palm.

"He came by the clubhouse this morning to drop off some payroll checks. A couple of the guys needed some help putting an engine back into its mount, so I didn't get a chance to talk to him before he left. I was out in the shop working with Slider when Voodoo got a call about an hour ago from the local PD. They'd found his bike wrecked about five miles from here on Mountain Avenue. By the time the ambulance got to the scene, he was already gone. We'd have never known until the hospital called you if one of Voodoo's cop buddies hadn't been working the scene. I didn't want one of the cops coming to the house to tell you and scare the boys, so I waited until I had gotten confirmation and came to tell you myself. I'm so sorry, darlin'. I know he wasn't ready to lose his family like this. He had too much to live for to die so young."

Before I can stop myself, I rip my hand from his grasp and slap him hard across the face. Raze doesn't even flinch or react as a red imprint of my hand begins grows on his skin.

"Too much to live for? Brent would have *died* to protect our family, and that screwed up fucking club of yours."

Raze's face flashes with anger. "I know you've never understood the club...," he starts, but I cut him off.

"You must think I'm stupid," I seethe, tears blurring my vision. "I damn well know he wasn't headed toward the club this morning. He told me he had some business to take care of in San Diego, and that he'd be home early for family night. Tell me the truth. Tell me how my husband died."

Raze shakes his head and shifts uncomfortably next to me. Standing in complete and utter silence, he stalks toward the door. I open my mouth to berate him further, but he stops abruptly and pivots toward me, his eyes locked on mine. "I know you're hurting, darlin', but getting pissed at me won't bring him back. I wish it could. He died on his fucking bike, and that's all you need to know."

"You son-of-a-*bitch*," I screech, leaping from the

couch with so much force I reach him in just a few broad steps. My hand flies toward his already-red cheek, ready to throw every ounce of my rage into another slap.

Raze catches my wrist in his large hands before it can connect, and his eyes narrow. Gripping my wrist in one hand, he uses the other to grab my chin, forcing me to look him in the eye. I'm powerless to move.

"I let you hit me the first time because I knew you were in pain. That won't happen again." He releases me and steps back, putting distance between us. "He wouldn't want you acting like this. You need to focus on your boys right now, and figure out how the fuck you're going to tell them."

His words only enrage me further. "My family is none of your concern," I hiss.

Raze shakes his head, frustration lining his face. "Once the funeral is over, if you want to hate me or the others for the rest of your life, that's your prerogative. But for the next few days, you put on a brave face for those boys of yours. Brent loved our club, even if you don't. He wouldn't want you at odds with us right now."

"I don't give a shit about your club or your *feelings*," I spit back. "My boys will never have a thing to do with the Heaven's Rejects. Brent didn't want that for them." The lie spills so easily from my lips. Brent wanted nothing more than the boys being his legacy some day. We had many arguments about it. "I want nothing to do with your club, or you."

Raze's face grows grim before his calm and stern everyday grimace settles back into place. His face is usually unreadable, untouched by emotion-driven gestures, but even in my grief, I can tell he's seething right now. I don't care, though. My husband is dead because of him and his club.

"If that's what you want, so be it, Darcy. But until that man is buried, you will let us take care of his family. Morton's already has his body, and he's waiting for your call to set up arrangements. The club will handle the procession to the cemetery, and I, as his president, will officiate the graveside service. You can have your religious shit or whatever you want at the funeral home, but the cemetery is ours."

"How dare you—" I snarl, but Raze's thumb presses tightly against my lips, halting me mid-sentence.

"Tell the boys and call the funeral home, Darcy. I'll have Maj come by later to get the information from you. If you need anything, contact me directly," Raze orders. And with that, he stalks out of the house, slamming the door behind him. The shuffling footsteps of Wesson and Colt grow louder in the hallway, and I can hear Raze's motorcycle starting up and disappearing down the road. Wiping the tears from my eyes, I watch as my two young sons enter the room.

"What's wrong, Mama?" Wesson asks. "Why did Uncle 'aze make you cry? Was he mean to you?"

Holding out my arms to them, I watch as they both rush toward me and encompass their little arms around my neck and torso. More tears flow as I work up the courage to tell them. I know I'm only delaying the inevitable by stalling their questions with a hug, but I can't help it. I need to feel them in my arms. A piece of their father lies inside their little bodies. As soon as I tell them, their worlds will shatter, and I'm not ready to see their hearts break. Wesson wiggles to break free of my grasp, forcing me to release them.

I stare into their beautiful faces, waiting for the right words to form on my lips. *How did we get so lucky to have such handsome boys?* Wesson's cold little hand caresses my face, and I'm snapped back to our grim reality.

"Mama, what's wrong?"

"Mama's got some bad news, boys." I whisper around the lump in my throat. "Daddy had an accident."

Colt remains silent as Wesson's confusion sets in. "Is Daddy at the 'ospital with the pretty nurses?"

Holding up his bandaged finger, he looks at me with hope. "Daddy can have one of my batman bandy-aids, but only if he doesn't cry when you put the magic meddy on, Mama. Big boys don't cry."

Wesson's sweet words shatter my heart even more.

"No, baby. Daddy doesn't need a bandy-aid where he is."

Colt's face instantly pales. He knows what I'm about to say isn't good news. He grabs for his brother, and I pull them both back into my embrace.

"Daddy's with the angels now, isn't he, Mama?" Colt's tiny voice is just a whisper against my chest.

Keep it together, Darcy. You can't fall apart right now.
"Yes, baby. Daddy's with the angels now."

We stay that way for a long time, crying and clinging to each other for what seems like hours, until finally, their bodies succumb to grief-stricken exhaustion. One at a time, I carry the boys to their rooms, settling them into their beds in a daze.

I feel numb. Empty.

Picking up the phone, I dial my parents, and once that call is complete, I call the funeral home. Morton's continuous barrage of questions about how to deal with the body of the love of my life cut me down until I have nothing left inside me.

The last few minutes of the call blur through time

as my soul shatters away, knowing that the only person who can fix my broken heart is the one I will be burying in just a few short days. This isn't fair to me, and especially not to our boys. Losing their dad so early in their life is a tragedy.

Hours later, I sit in total darkness in the room I have shared with my husband, my hands pressed against my belly, remembering our time together as a family. Sadness and grief overwhelm me, formulating not only into rage, but also a revengeful plea to the heavens to bring him back to me, no matter the costs.

They say there are five stages of grief, but to me, there is only one. *Revenge.*

I will find out the truth about what really happened to my husband. I swear it on our unborn child's life. I may be just a former biker's bitch, but those bastards will pay for what they took from me. I will crush their hearts in my hands.

I just have to bide my time. First, I need to bring this little one into the world, and make sure the boys will be safe from the backlash that may come from what I'm planning to do.

Brent may have loved the Heaven's Rejects, but they killed him. They took him from me. I'll find out why. I'll do whatever I have to to find the truth.

Chapter 2

RAZE

THE DEMON inside me is screaming for fucking vengeance, just like the rest of the club. As much as I want to light the fire under these motherfuckers, I know it's not the right time. We don't have a plan. We don't even know where their hide-y-hole of a clubhouse is at the moment. I've got the feelers out there trying to track them down, but they've come up with jack shit so far. The time for revenge will come soon enough for those Tribe bastards.

While the planning and slow action of avenging Jagger is causing tension with my brothers, today is the day we lay our brother to rest and mourn alongside his wife and sons. Just thinking about his funeral puts knots in my stomach. His boys are too fucking young to lose their old man, and it eats me alive knowing that Jagger will miss out on their entire lives. I had twenty years' worth of memories with my own father, before his lifestyle finally claimed his life, but Wesson and Colt will only have a few short memories, if they even remember him at all.

Some people might say he is watching down on them, but guys like us never make it to the pearly gates. Nah, guys like us end up in hell's furnace, paying for every sin we've ever committed. I've dealt with a lot of shit over the years, all with Jagger by my side. There's no fucking heaven for a Heaven's Reject. We'll be the ones paying the devil his due. I would never say that in front of his family, though. Not in front of his widow and two heartbroken little boys. The latter being the cause of my inability to sleep the past few nights.

Darcy had gone through the motions of arranging the services with Morton. Her sad eyes had glistened with tears while picking out his casket, their two boys clutching at her the entire time. But there was something about her has me on edge.

While some may see the outward appearance of her sadness, I see something more sinister. Brief flashes of anger and hatred radiate from her gaze every time she looks at me. Almost as if she knew the truth about his accident. I know that's not possible, but if it were, that kind of truth would shatter her existence. Ignorance is bliss in some cases, and especially in this one. If Darcy knew the truth about how Jagger had died, she'd be leading the charge to avenge him like a goddamn Valkyrie.

No. It's best she remains in the dark. Best for her and the boys. Best for all of us.

I couldn't sleep last night knowing I would have to say goodbye to Jagger today. I had tossed and turned for hours before finally giving up and dragging my ass into my office. Honoring him properly in the service looms over me like a lead balloon. I try to find the right words, but Darcy's face as I told her the news replays over and over in my mind. That face felt like a forty-five caliber shot to the heart. Her heart had shattered in front of me, and I couldn't do anything to stop it.

Jagger had been damn lucky to have a woman like Darcy in his life. I never could figure out how the old bastard had landed her, even years after the fact. She'd been barely legal when he brought her to the clubhouse for the first time. I know because I'd ID-ed her myself.

That bastard had just smiled at me as he pulled her into his lap and staked his claim. Her voice sang sweetly with each word that spilled from her lips. Her sexy southern drawl damn near killed me each time her beautiful mouth opened. It wasn't long after that he announced he was going to marry Darcy. I was happy for him, but hell, I was a little jealous, too. She's exactly the type of woman any of us would be lucky to have. And then she got a taste of what being married to a man of this club was really like. After that, shit changed.

He would come home at all hours of the night, covered in blood from beating the ever-loving fuck out of some punk or dealing with a rival club stirring shit up, and Darcy just walked away without a word. But there were a few times I saw that southern sass in her roar to life. She would lay into him in front of the entire club. Especially after he had missed some special event for their boys.

Jagger always laughed it off, saying she would forgive him as soon as they got home. He boasted that he could solve every problem they ever had in the bedroom, but there were times I knew even a good fucking wouldn't get him out of the doghouse. I'll admit, Jagger wasn't exactly the best guy on the planet, but for her and the kids, he'd paint the fucking moon purple if it made them happy.

Drumming my fingers on the hardwood top of my desk, I decide to just wing his eulogy. I'd be absolutely fucking kidding myself by thinking I could come up with the right words to say. The mess of crumpled up papers littering the floor is evidence enough. I'm not cut out for writing some bullshit speech.

Just as I toss the last of my incoherent scribbles toward the overflowing trash can in the corner, a knock comes from the door.

"Yeah?" I call out.

The knob slowly turns and in walks Hero and Ratchet. Hero looks ragged from lack of sleep, and Ratchet doesn't look much better.

"Hey, Prez," Ratchet mutters, as he and Hero slide into the chairs in front of my desk. Hero looks at the scattered mess on the floor and chuckles.

"I see your speech is going well." He quirks his lips up on one side. "Better be careful. The tree huggers will start picketing in your office."

Running my fingers over my buzz cut, I blow out a heavy sigh. "Writing something pretty isn't exactly highlighted on my resume. Popping a nun's cherry on a Sunday wouldn't be this damn hard."

Ratchet and Hero chuckle.

"Not sure waving your dick around would make a nun break her vows," Hero says. I shoot him a glare, and he raises his hands in defeat. "Jesus, I was kidding. Don't get your panties in a wad, Prez."

"You keep this shit up, Hero, and Ratchet might just get a promotion to VP," I inform him.

"Nah," Ratchet mutters. "You know I'm not the

leading by example type, Prez. Well, unless you want me to teach the prospects to be a pain in your ass."

Hero grins. "Yeah. Remember what happened last time you let Ratchet out of his cage? He 'accidentally' burned down that politician's mansion."

"Who would have thought the finer things in life would burn just as fast as the shitty stuff?" Ratchet recalls with a shrug.

Shaking my head, I can't help but laugh. He seems unaffected by the fact he had torched ten-million-dollars' worth of shit in a rich neighborhood last fall. Did the politician have it coming? Hell yeah. After what we found in that twisted little penthouse of his, he deserved to die, but his daughter was our target. The hefty fee his ex-wife had paid us to get her out made her intentions crystal clear. The house burning down was just an added bonus to them both, and a gift to keep Ratchet's dark nature at bay for a little while longer.

"And that right there is the case and fucking point of why we don't let you play with matches anymore, Ratch." Ratchet just grins. "Anyway, did you two come in here to bust my balls, or do you have a reason for the early morning visit?"

"Just wanted to check on you," Hero replies. "This shit ain't easy on any of us, but you knew Jagger the longest. Seeing him strung up there like that brought back some bad fucking memories for me. That's why Ratch and I have both checked out of the situation a bit. You didn't need the two of us darkening the clubhouse's corners more than they already have been."

"Your place is with your brothers. Both of you. We need to stand united. But I know it has to have drug up a bunch of shit after what you saw in Iraq."

"Worst fucking years of my life. I figured I'd be in the nuthouse by now, but I guess I have Jagger to thank for that," he says with a half-hearted sigh. "I'm going to miss his ugly mug."

Ratchet sits in the chair next to him, his body stiff and his face filled with pain. Ratch has never been one to show emotion, so to see him reacting this way tells me he's really hurting with Jagger's murder. Hell, half the time, Ratchet barely talks. Calling him a man of few words is a goddamn understatement.

"We all miss him. He was our brother, and a founder of this club. His lives in the walls of this place," I say.

"Until Darcy came along. That bitch changed him," Ratchet mutters.

Staring Ratchet down, I narrow my eyes and try to keep my anger in check. "I know you never understood his need for an old lady or kids, but Jagger loved having a family." That fucker was so goddamn happy when the boys were born. "He changed because he was ready to change, and it wasn't all because of Darcy."

Ratchet's expression never wavers. "He changed when she rolled into his life. He wasn't the Jagger. He was some upstanding family man. He stepped away from this club. He once said he'd die before he gave up being VP, but then he met her and they punched out a couple of kids, and he stepped down with a smile on his face. If that's not old lady bullshit, I don't know what is."

Pushing myself up from my chair, I circle around the table and stop in front of Ratchet. He stands to meet me face to face. "He stepped down because he was too sick to continue on as VP," I growl. "He had a fucking heart attack on the charity ride to Las Vegas six years ago, and he waited until he got back to deal with it. He could have fucking died on the road, but didn't want to look weak, so he powered through."

Ratchet swallows but doesn't reply.

"I don't know what your problem is with Darcy," I continue. "But that shit ends here. We are burying her husband today. Your brother. She doesn't need any of your bullshit, Ratchet. You can either go with the club, or your ass can stay behind and help the girls cook. The choice is yours." And with that, I walk straight out of my office and right into Maj.

"Everything okay, baby?" she asks. "I heard yelling."

"Yeah, babe. I'm good." Pulling her to my side, we walk toward the mostly empty main room of the clubhouse. I'm surprised we haven't had a visit from the local PD. The noise from the visiting chapters alone would warrant a disturbing the peace call, but they know not to interrupt our club's business. I had called in a couple of favors to help with the traffic on our ride to the cemetery. I want shit to be as easy as possible for his family.

Maj leads me to the bar, where a box sits on the counter. She pulls t-shirt after t-shirt out of the box, and it doesn't take me long to realize I've seen these shirts before. They're Jagger's.

"Found these in his locker. What do you want me to do with them?" She asks.

"Tear them into strips and give them to all the riders. It'll be like Jagger's riding with us."

Maj takes a black Harley shirt in her hands and rips a strip from it. She moves to my arm and ties it around my bicep. Giving her hand a squeeze, I kiss her on the cheek, and she gets to work, handing out the shirts to the club girls and the other old ladies to cut and distribute to the rest of the club.

A heavy weight presses on my chest as I realize that it's time. *Fuck.*

Heading toward the exit, I pass Ratchet and Hero as they step out of my office. Ratchet simply nods, signaling that he'll behave today. I know he's hurting, but I won't hesitate to corral him if he gets out of line with Darcy. He may see her as the reason his hero walked away from his role in this club, but that had been Jagger's decision, not Darcy's or his.

Stepping into the sun, I see Jagger's black and gray metal casket being loaded into the back of our Harley hearse trailer by the people from Morton's mortuary. Darcy got her religious memorial service last night at the funeral home, so today is for club traditions and saying goodbye. Darcy argued with me at first, but I wanted his last ride to start from the clubhouse. She was reluctant, but finally agreed after I explained to her that Jagger himself had designed this funeral ritual, she knew he would have wanted it this way.

While I button up my cut, I catch sight of Darcy holding open the door of the car that will follow me on this ride. Her face is hidden behind a wide-brimmed hat and black lace veil. She waits patiently for her sons to climb into the backseat, but I can see that she's visibly shaken.

A white handkerchief is clutched in her hand as she stops to watch me prepare for the ride. I can feel the heat of her veiled stare like a physical touch, and then her body disappears into the car and Morton closes the door behind her. As he makes his way to the driver's side, I approach the hearse holding my brother's body and lay my hand on the warm glass.

It shouldn't have been you, Jag.

Lifting my hand from the window, I move to my motorcycle and slide my leg over the warm leather seat. After a moment, I switch on the ignition and then fire the engine up. I let my Harley rumble for a few minutes, finding comfort in its familiar growl.

Turning in my seat, I look back to the hearse hooked up to my bike. This is Jagger's last time at our clubhouse. The clubhouse he'd helped build. A lump forms in my throat at the thought. *There's no time for that, Raze.*

Revving the engine, I swallow past the lump and force myself to move. Slowly, I move forward, pulling the hearse to the front of the clubhouse. The procession there is already lined up. Dozens of Jagger's brothers and their old ladies are here.

Hesitate momentarily, I inch my way to the end of the parking lot and pull out onto the highway. The car with Darcy and the boys is right behind me, followed by two neat rows of motorcycles, all here to give Jagger one final salute.

"Time for one last ride, my brother."

Chapter 3

ONE YEAR LATER

DARCY

THREE SHORT WORDS had forever altered the course of my life. I never imagined I'd be a widow, raising our children on my own at just thirty-years-old. Brent had promised me forever. We knew with our twenty-two-year age gap, he would pass long before me, but that's the kind of guy he was. Brent never worried about what tomorrow would bring, and that's one of the many reasons I loved him. He was the optimist in our relationship, even if the world looked down upon our age difference with disdain. Chuckling quietly to myself, I remember the day he overheard someone calling him a cradle robber. He had been quick to tell them the only opinions that mattered in our relationship were our own, and then cracked a joke about me robbing the grave instead.

Brent always had a way to spin the dark shit around us into a joke to make me smile.

I miss him so much.

For the past hour, I have been sitting at the vanity he had built me as a wedding present, staring at the stranger in the mirror. The woman had lost everything and gained nothing in return. My icy hands brush against my pale cheeks, while tears fall in quick succession down my face. My dark-brown hair looks lifeless and dull, just like my skin. The light in my eyes has dimmed to nearly nothing, and I know they'll never shine again. I may put on a brave face for my children, but deep down, I've been shattered inside. Thinking about Brent's smiling face only makes the darkness swell more. Every time I see his smile, I also see that damn club lurking in the background.

I have tried to keep my distance from them since Brent's death, but somehow, I keep finding myself at that fucking clubhouse. Maybe it's because I can feel my husband there, or maybe it's the familiarity of the people, but I haven't been able to walk away from the club my husband had loved so much.

Those within and associated with the MC are the only friends I have out here. Not having their support in my life has made things so difficult. I've even had to turn to Dani a few times to help me with the boys in emergencies. She has never let me down, though. Her own pregnancy is progressing, and we have formed a much deeper bond as not only friends, but as mothers.

But it's still not right. I know Raze is lying. I know he lied about Brent wrecking his bike. That motorcycle was in pristine condition, just like he'd always kept his 'other wife'. I had teased him about that so many times. No. My husband didn't accidentally die. He was fucking murdered, and his brothers know who has his blood on their hands.

Regardless, I still come around. Deep down, I know why. When I'm missing Brent the most, I always end up at the clubhouse. I need answers, and if I stay away completely, I'll never get them. My husband was stolen from me, and the motherfuckers that took him will pay for their crimes against my family. They murdered the man I love and robbed his children of knowing their father.

The moment his life was snuffed out, I put a plan into motion to protect my family if something were to happen to me. Brent's life insurance was more than enough to set us for life, and put the kids through college, but I want to make sure they wouldn't want for anything. The side business I had started while Brent was out on long runs has flourished since his death, and I'm so close to the goal I had set for myself. Soon, I can settle the score once and for all. I never thought of myself as a killer, but for the memory of my husband, all bets are off.

A soft cry from beside the bed snaps me back into reality.

"Mama's coming, baby," I whisper. Sliding the chair back from the vanity, I slowly stand and make my way to the small bassinet nestled next to the side of the bed. Peering inside, I see the sweet smile of my little girl, as she wakes from a good night's sleep. Brent always wanted a baby girl, and it pains me to know he never got to see her.

"I want a little girl that looks just like you, babe."

"A biker with a baby girl? That sounds like trouble," I tease.

"No one would mess with her, and she'd be the toughest little girl in town. I even have a name picked out."

I stare at him in surprise. "And what would that be?"

"I'd call her Roxie Belle."

And Roxie Belle she was named. She's the spitting image of her father with brilliant green eyes and black curls. She might only be four months old, but you'd know exactly who she belongs to. Her demanding and somewhat stubborn personality, which she inherited from her father, was apparent the day she was born.

Uncurling her from the blankets, I gently lift her from the bassinet and cradle her against my chest. Her little hands splay against my skin while I sway and hum a lullaby to her. I wrap one of her blankets around her and gingerly move into the kitchen to make a bottle. I make quick work of mixing her powder formula with water and setting the bottle into the warmer on the counter.

A few minutes later, I take the warmed bottle, tuck her tiny little arm under mine, and pull her close to my chest before settling into the love seat near the patio door. Much like her brothers before her, a six-ounce bottle never lasts long. She sucks away at the formula as her free hand wraps around my finger, making my heart swell. I'd give anything for her father to see her like this. His favorite time with the boys was sitting up in the middle of the night and feeding them. He told me it made him feel like the best dad on Earth when he could feed them and settle them back down without ever waking me up.

He was such a good father.

Setting the now-empty bottle on the side table, I shift her in my arms and lay her across my shoulder, patting her on the back. Just a few pats later, Roxie lets out two large burps before cooing against me.

"That's Mama's girl. Let's get your diaper changed and back into your swing before your rowdy brothers get up."

Twenty minutes later, Wesson barrels into the kitchen with messy hair, demanding his belly be filled. Like his little sister, he wakes up like clockwork, but Colt has to be dragged from his bed by his feet, kicking and screaming for five more minutes. He gets that from me. I was never an early riser until I married Brent. That man would make so much damn noise and leave every single light on in the house. I could never go back to sleep after he got ready.

It's memories like these that break my heart on a daily basis, and yet somehow, they also keep me going.

"'ancakes, Mama. I want 'ancakes," Wesson demands.

Smiling back at my boy, I reach into the cabinet and pull out the pancake mix, setting it onto the counter. "Is this what you want?" I ask with a grin. "I was sure you were going to ask for bacon and eggs this morning."

"Naw, I want 'ancakes. Can you make the shape of a weenus?"

I stop dead in my tracks. *Did he just say what I think he did?* Turning to face him, I watch as Wesson hops up into his usual seat at the island and lets his legs swing. Just looking at him, I know I must not have heard him right.

"Wes, what shape did you want them in?" I ask, hoping to hear something different.

"A weenus. You know, Mama, like what I have." He beams at me while the shock registers across my face. Setting the spatula down, I place my elbows onto the cool marble and lean close to him.

"Wes, where did you hear that word?"

His legs swing harder, knocking against the wood of the island. His eyes draw down to the counter as he stammers to answer me.

"Wes, I asked you a question," I say with a bit more authority. "Please answer me."

"I promised not to tell," he says with a sniffle. His reaction to my question sends dozens of horrific scenarios running through my head. There's no way my little boy is going to be faced with the sick and twisted shit my brain automatically went to with his confession.

"Wes, you will tell me now, or you'll be sent to your room. Answer me."

"Colt said it, Mama," he whimpers. "He learned it at school."

Casting my gaze back to the pancake box, I stifle a laugh. I swear my kids could be on *America's Funniest*

Home Videos with the things that come out of their mouths. I seriously wonder if anyone else has to deal with their kids asking for weenus pancakes. Walking over to the fridge, I gather the supplies and begin to make Wesson's pancakes. After flipping a large stack of warm cakes smothered in butter and syrup, I set them down in front of him and trudge off to his brother's bedroom to start our normal morning routine. I try to be nice waking up Colt, but as soon as I rip the covers off of him, it's game on. What should be a five-minute process turns into a twenty-minute ordeal before he finally admits defeat and gets up for school.

Colt trudges into the kitchen and deposits himself next to his syrup-covered brother before picking at his food. Today's going to be one of the bad days for my precious boy. I can tell from the look on his face that he dreamt about his dad again. I can always tell by his lack of appetite and inability to talk. Walking over to him, I slip my arm around his chest and pull him close.

"I know you miss him, baby, but you have to eat. Daddy wouldn't want you to be all skin and bones. He would want you to be big and strong like him," I whisper into his ear.

Colt only nods and picks up his fork, shoveling a cold pancake into his mouth. I press a kiss to the top of his head, check on Roxie, then quickly go to the bedroom to change. By the time I'm back, Wesson is playing peek-a-boo with Roxie, while Colt keeps his older, brotherly eye on the both of them. I honestly could not have asked for a better set of kids. From the moment Roxie was born, Colt instantly took on the role of man of the house. His level of devotion for Roxie's safety and care makes me proud to call him my son.

Scooping up Roxie from her swing, I send Wesson off to put on the clothes I laid out for him while I change Roxie and get her dressed. By the time he walks back into the kitchen, we are all dressed and ready to go to school. After Brent died, Wesson really regressed in his interaction with kids, so I put him into a local daycare and pre-school across the street from Colt's elementary school. Not only did it make it easier having them both so close to each other, but Wesson started to come out of his shell more. After six months, he finally returned to the crazy little boy I had before his dad died.

"All right, ladies and gentleman. Let's get this school show on the road."

The drive to both buildings is only fifteen minutes away and takes no time with the level of traffic on the city streets of Upland. It's one reason I like this city. It's far enough away from Los Angeles to actually feel cozy and safe, while at the same time, it's close enough to do just about anything you could ever want. Most people wouldn't classify California as cozy, but to me, it's a decent substitute for my hometown of Jackson, Mississippi.

After dropping both Wesson and Colt in front of their buildings with their curbside class monitors, I make a quick pit stop through Starbucks to grab my usual non-fat vanilla latte with an extra pump of caramel before heading home. Pulling back into the driveway of the house, I compare the other houses on the street to our modestly sized home with a much-larger-than-normal yard. It's the typical Spanish-style with a fenced-in archway surrounding the porch. Brent had always hated that Californians called a quarter of an acre a large yard, so when he saw the acre that came with this house, he snatched it up quickly.

The flowering trees blow in the early fall breeze as I step out into the dry morning heat. Unlatching the car seat containing a sleeping Roxie, I head toward the house. Before I can make it through the gate of our front sidewalk, a flash of white from the center of the door catches my eye. Setting Roxie's seat down onto the sidewalk, I find a letter taped to our front door. *What in the hell could this be? It's too early for the mail.* Pulling the tape from the door, I turn the letter over and get the shock of my life.

In bold letters scrolled across the front of the crinkled paper in a familiar script I never thought I would see again, I find one word.

Darcy

Chapter 4

RAZE

WHY THE FUCK *did I agree to do this shit?*

I knew running our legitimate security company would come with some crazy ass jobs, but this one really takes the cake. Playing scary bodyguard to the latest virginal pop princess has been like living in hell. It's like being surrounded by those screaming bitches on that housewives show the club whores like to watch. One of these days, I need to put a parental lock on those channels. Their cackling has interrupted Church far too many times since that show came back on.

I was an idiot when I volunteered to give Hero the day off to take Dani to her lady doctor appointment. I should have assigned one of the prospects. Shit, Slider would probably get off on this. But me? I've spent the last forty-five minutes watching this scrawny blonde chick with tiny tits sing the same song over and over again. If the money wasn't so damn good, I'd have walked by now.

"Thank you, everyone. I love you all. Goodnight!" she screams into the microphone over the cheering crowd below. Then the girl, who I've now named Fuck Me Barbie, takes one last bow before exiting the stage on the left. Thank fucking God this shit's almost over. I need a stiff drink and one of the club girls on her knees to wipe this shit from my mind. I wonder if Bubbles and that mouth of hers has been used tonight. Call me crazy, but other than a warm pair of lips around my cock, I wouldn't dare sink my dick into their black holes of pussy. I make for damn sure our girls are clean, but I'm not about to put my dick where my brothers dump their loads. One-night stands are a far better risk than a club whore or a cut bunny trying to become the president's new old lady. I had one of those before, and she turned out to be a traitor to the club. I'm not exactly in the market for another crazy bitch that wants to own my balls anytime soon. I have enough problems trying to raise my teenage daughter and son on my own.

Making my way to the stairs, I watch as Fuck Me Barbie grabs a towel from one of the stagehands and uses it to wipe the sweat from her body. I notice she takes just a little too long brushing the towel along her tight dancer's body. I can tell from the evil smirk that forms on her face that she's far from innocent, and a hell of a lot older than the eighteen the tabloids say she is. If I were a betting man, I'd peg her for at least twenty-three, but even knowing she's legal doesn't mean I'm interested. I don't sleep with the clients for the same reason I don't sleep with club whores. Communal playthings and little girls with Daddy issues need to stick to the men who will mistreat them the way they expect, and leave me the fuck alone.

Fuck Me Barbie rubs her fingers around her nipples that have budded with the cold air flowing backstage. She throws the towel back at the stage hand before hopping off the last set of stairs and sliding up next to me. Her hand brushes my groin before she spins for the stage crew to remove her wireless microphone. "Wanna come back to my hotel tonight?" she whispers over her shoulder, eyeing her hand that covers my still soft dick. "I'd like to see what you could do to earn a big tip for protecting my body."

Shaking my head, I laugh and remove her hand from my fly. "Sorry, little girl, but the only job I get paid to do is protect your ass. I'm not exactly interested in deflowering America's little wet dream of the month because she thinks she has a thing for older bad boys. Why don't you go play with someone your own age?"

Her sly grin falls as her tour manager, Michelle, ushers her back to her dressing room to change. I follow behind them, and can't help but admire the plump ass on Michelle. Now, *that's* the kind of woman I'd sink my dick into. She has womanly curves in just the right places, perfect tits that spill ever-so-slightly out of the shirt she's wearing, and one hell of a long set of legs. My mind wanders to how those legs would feel wrapped around my waist.

Fuck Me Barbie walks into her dressing room and slams the door, clearly pissed by my denial of her special request. Some guys might be into barely legal jail bait, but I prefer a woman who knows what to do with a man.

Leaning next to the dressing room door, I mutter a silent prayer that Barbie doesn't take nearly as long to get cleaned up as she did to get ready for the show. Her four hours of prep and war painting was a little much to sit and watch. I hear a sigh, and then Michelle leans against the wall next to me.

"Long night?" I ask, trying to keep my eyes from dropping to her those perfect tits of hers. She sighs, and they nearly pop out of her tight shirt.

"You have no idea. Cassidy is one of the toughest clients I've ever worked with."

"I don't know how you deal with little shits like her."

Michelle quietly laughs, shaking her head at my response.

"Trust me, if the money wasn't this good, I'd be back in Tennessee babysitting geriatric country music stars, but that doesn't pay my kid's college tuition."

"Damn, I wouldn't have pegged you for having a kid in college."

Michelle's tits jiggle as she laughs. "A one-night stand my freshman year of college turned me into a single mom. Been working since the day my son was born to make sure his life was a hell of a lot better than mine. Billy's a smart kid, and I don't want him to waste those brains of his. He's pre-med at the University of Tennessee."

"Sounds like a smart kid with a hard working mom. I bet you don't get a lot of downtime."

"You can say that again. The only downtime I get is when Cassidy holes herself up in a hotel room with the latest fuck of the week. It's a pain in the ass when she gets caught by the paparazzi. I don't know how many more times I can use the excuse of a late night rehearsal to the press anymore. I wish she'd just let the cat of the bag so I can get some sleep sometime."

"Ha," I exclaim. "I don't know who she thinks she's fooling with the act."

Banging and yelling comes from Barbie's dressing room, drawing our attention back to the door. Michelle leans over and cracks the door just as Barbie's naked ass flashes through the open space. Barbie needs to eat a fucking burger or something because that boney ass of hers would torture anyone who fucks her. I don't get this skinny as a rail shit that I keep seeing on the women we protect. It's not sexy to plow a twig that could snap if a big gust of wind blew.

Michelle quickly slams the door just as Barbie throws something, shrieking obscenities at her. That bitch needs a fucking time out. I start toward the door, but Michelle's small hands land on my forearm, stopping me from reaching the door knob.

"Raze, it's nothing I haven't dealt with before. Just let it go."

Michelle's eyes fall to the ground as the rampage continues inside the room. "What the fuck set her off?" I ask, watching as her entire demeanor changes with Fuck Me Barbie's tantrum.

Even if I had wanted to fuck old Boney Barbie when she offered, my dick would have retreated back inside in an instant with this childish behavior. I'd have taken a belt to her ass if I had to deal with her mouth on a regular basis. Turning away from the door, I step in front of Michelle and lean over her luscious body with my arm resting on the wall beside her head.

"She came on to you, didn't she?" she asks, her eyes pointed to the ground.

"Yeah, I shut that shit down quick. I wouldn't fuck her with someone else's dick. She's not my type."

Michelle's eyes travel back to mine as she smirks.

"That's why she's acting like a spoiled five-year-old in there. No one tells her no, and when she gets ignored, she destroys everything around her."

"Ignoring her, you say?"

"Oh, lord, yes. She fired three back up dancers last weekend because they were prettier than her. The choreographer lost his shit when he found out."

Just then, an idea pops into my head. "I think I might know of a way to get her to back off. At least for you." I wink, and Michelle grins. A curious grin.

"I just have one question for you," I say, leaning even closer. "Do you have an old man I need to know about?"

"Hell no. The only man in my life is my vibrator, which is in desperate need of new batteries. Why?"

I chuckle at that, though my dick stirs at the vision she just gave me. "You game?"

Michelle blinks, and then after a moment, she shakes her head and laughs. "You're kidding, right? Like I would even be your type."

"Babe, you're absolutely my type. And if this makes *Fuck Me Barbie* in there give you some respect, it's a job I'll do freely. Besides, I've been thinking about that ass of yours since the first time I laid eyes on it."

Arousal and amusement flash across her face before she nods in agreement. Leaning back, I remove my hand from the wall and take hers, leading her to the small space between the dressing room and the backstage storage area. I settle us into the dark and semi-private space, pressing her back against the cool metal of the dressing room's outer wall.

"We can't do this here," she whispers, her eyes wide.

I lean close, my lips brushing against the soft shell of her ear. "Who the hell is going to stop us?"

Taking her wrists in one hand, I raise them above her head, pressing them against the wall as I trace my tongue along the left side of her neck, down to the deep cavern of her cleavage. Her breath hitches as I bend lower, my mouth sucking at her nipple through the thin material of her shirt.

A moan slips from her pursed lips at the contact,

and her hips roll, pressing against my growing cock. This might not be the way I had planned for the night to end, but if it'll fuck with Barbie and give Michelle some respect, I'll do it.

Michelle's breath comes out in gasps and pants, her hands writhing under my grip above her head. My free hand glides farther down her body, then slips beneath her skirt. The tips of my calloused fingers graze her damp, silky panties, eliciting a shiver and a gasp from between her sweet lips.

Slowly, I slide the wet material to the side, eager to slip one finger between her slick folds. I find her tender nub and circle it, reveling in the moan that ripples from her. Her eyes bore into mine, and it's the hottest fucking look I have ever seen. She wants me as much as I want her.

"You a hungry girl?" I whisper, running my lips along the edge of her jaw.

Michelle moans in approval, rolling her hips and sinking her teeth into her lower lip.

Fucking hell.

Pulling my hand from between her legs, I release her wrists and spin her around to face the wall.

Dropping to my knees behind her, I slide her panties down her long, shapely legs and toss them to the side. With one hand on her back, I bend her forward just slightly and shift her skirt up and over her hips. Her pussy is glistening, begging for my tongue, and I'm not about to disappoint.

With a growl, I press forward, burying my face between her legs and sliding my tongue through her folds. Michelle gasps and lets out a little yelp of surprise before slapping one hand over her mouth. I circle my tongue around her clit, lapping and sucking as he rocks her hips, fucking my face with delicious need.

Her body trembles and her moans turn to gasps and pants, and I know she's so fucking close to coming. But she's not getting off without me. I want to feel her release on my cock.

Ripping my face away, I rise to my feet, my hands at my belt buckle just as Barbie rounds the corner. Her eyes grow wide as my cock springs from my jeans. I barely spare her a glance as I grab a condom from my back pocket and slide it on.

Positioning myself at Michelle's entrance, I lean forward and whisper into her ear, "It's going to be fast and hard, babe."

Michelle's head bobs in agreement, her hands moving to the wall to brace herself as I push my aching cock inside her.

Fuck, she's so tight and warm. She wasn't lying when she said her pussy hadn't been used in years. She surrounds me like a vice as move in and out, my hands gripping her rounded hips, pulling her back to meet each thrust.

Barbie's eyes never leave us. *That's right, bitch. See how a man fucks a real woman.*

Michelle's moans grow louder with each thrust, and she feels fucking perfect. I move faster now, holding perfect tits for leverage as I pound into her.

"Fuck," she gasps. "Don't stop, Raze."

There's not a fucking chance I'm gonna stop now. Her muscles contract, squeezing my cock, pulsing as I make one final thrust.

"Fuck," I groan, burying my face in her shoulder as her body jerks beneath me. Her release sends me flying, lights flashing in my mind as I slow my movements, sliding in and out of her, reveling in the twitching of her sweet, tight pussy.

I press a kiss to the tender place where her neck meets her shoulder and slowly pull out. Without looking at Barbie, I remove the condom, tying a knot in the end before tossing it into the garbage can to our left. That done, I pushing my very satisfied cock back into my jeans, zip them up and straighten Michelle's rumpled skirt before pulling her away from the wall.

Michelle turns and pulls my mouth to hers, her fingers twisting in my hair as she slips her tongue between my lips. I can feel her smile grow, and then she pulls away, her eyes locking on Barbie's.

In a flash of blonde hair, Barbie turns and stomps off, her footsteps echoing down the hall.

Michelle grins then and as her eyes meet mine, we burst into laughter. That bitch got an eyeful, and it serves her fucking right.

Looping my arm around Michelle's shoulders, I lead her from our little fuck nest in the hall. I'm sure half the crew here heard her moans, but what the fuck do I care? I'll never see them again. I'll never see Michelle again, but this little romp we'd just had was the best sex I've had in the past year, even if it was a quickie.

By the time we make it out to the loading dock, Barbie's already on her bus. She's as quiet as a sinner on confessional day as I walk Michelle up to the tour bus and kiss her one last time. Barbie watches from behind the tinted windows.

Releasing her, I give Michelle a firm smack on her ass and she moves to the door. I watch as she makes her way up the bus steps, then turns and smiles back at me before disappearing onto the bus and out of my life.

Without any words, Michelle understood exactly what that was and knew there was never going to be a next time. A woman like her should be fucked like that every fucking day, but I'm not the man for her.

I watch as the bus pulls away, signaling my security duty is officially over. Making my way over to my blue and chrome Harley Davidson parked against the side of the building, I throw my leg over the cool leather seat and fire up the engine. She purrs for me just like Michelle had.

Grinning at the memory, I pop the kickstand and pull away from the building, allowing the open road to clear my head. There's only one place left to go.

The Heaven's Rejects' clubhouse.

Chapter 5

DARCY

IT CAN'T BE *from Brent.*

My breath hitches as I stare at the letter in my hand. *How is this even possible? It's been a year.* Clutching the crumpled letter to my chest, I reach down to retrieve Roxie and her car seat before sliding my key into the lock and stepping inside the house. I walk over to the kitchen island, still covered in the boy's breakfast plates, and gingerly lay the letter down in a clean spot. Roxie begins to fuss, so I set her down and unbuckle the straps. Lifting her from the seat, I cradle her in my arms and move over to the love seat. It takes just a few minutes before she's asleep for her mid-morning nap. The entire time I was rocking her, I stared at the letter from a ghost, half expecting it to just vanish.

Gradually, I rise and place Roxie into the second

bassinet I keep in the dining room so I can work while she naps. She coos and cuddles into the soft blanket I swaddle around her, and then her breathing becomes steady and even again. If she sticks to her schedule, I have just forty-five minutes before she'll be ready to play and eat again. Forty-five minutes to decide if I want to open the letter or just burn it. I honestly don't know if I'm ready to read what it might contain. What if Brent had some post-death confession about an affair, or this is his version of a fucked up Hollywood romance movie?

The letter isn't why I'm hesitating, though. Brent used to write me letters all the time, while we were dating. He was always very old-fashioned and truly tried to romance me as often as he could when he was home. It was his way of letting me know how much he loved me, and to give me memories that could never fade away. I saved every single letter, and in the last year, I have read each one a million times. They've even begun to fray at the edges. Other than my children, those letters are the only thing I have left of him to preserve his memory. I'm not sure I can physically sustain another blow to my already shattered heart.

You can do this, Darcy. It's far easier to rip the Band-Aid off now than let it burn a hole in your heart out of fear.

Walking over to the dirty counter, I pick up the letter once more and just stare at my husband's scribbled handwriting for what seems like a millennium. So many mixed emotions barrel into my mind all at once, to the point I feel like the little girl in that new Disney movie. Fear, disgust, joy, sadness, and anger flourish as my fingers tremble when I flip the letter over. The envelope is sealed with a smiley face sticker I know came from one of the boy's coloring books. There are about a thousand sheets of them in my desk. The sudden realization that Brent wrote this letter in our home nearly stops my heart.

How long ago was this written?

I bring the back of the envelope to my lips, inhaling his cologne scent on the old paper. Laying a chaste kiss at its seal, I pull the letter away from my face and walk toward the junk drawer in the kitchen that houses the letter opener. It's all I can do to stop myself from ripping it open, but deep down, I know I may need to turn this over to the police, or even some of the men outside the law that I've been considering contacting.

Slipping the sharp edge of the letter opener beneath the seal, I slice open the envelope. A thrice-folded piece of paper is nestled inside it, and I quietly slip out to the covered porch to read it. I settle into the rocking chair Brent made for me, unfolding the paper gingerly while smoothing the edges on my leg. The first two words are all that I read before the tears begin to flow.

> Belle,
>
> If you are reading this, then I'm not with you anymore.
>
> I fucking hate that. I wanted nothing more than to spend my days growing old next to you.
>
> This might be sappy shit, but I still remember the first day I saw you. It was like the skies had opened up and painted you in a heavenly light the moment my eyes connected with yours. I remember wondering how the fuck I could get a girl like that, and then you smiled at me, and I handed you my heart on a silver platter right then. Even if you wouldn't have given me the time of day, I would have spent the rest of my life pining after you, because with just one look and that sexy little smile of yours, I was fucked for life. I knew from that one glance you were the only one to teach this old man

how to live again. You gave me the best life. The one I didn't know I deserved. With you and our boys, I died a very happy and fulfilled man.

You need to know I never wanted to leave you. You're probably angry at the world right now, but I did what I had to do to keep us safe. All of us. Please don't blame the club. They're innocent in all of this.

I dragged you into the life of a biker's wife, but seeing you and our family interacting with my brothers were some of the happiest moments of my life. You didn't question why I needed them, and you let them into our lives like real family. It takes a special woman to love a man like me, and I thank God every day that you agreed to give me a chance.

I love you, Belle, and will always love you. Tell the boys I love them, and raise them to be the men I know they're destined to be. Be happy for me, Darcy, and every time you feel the sun shining on *your face, that's me, covering you in my love.*

Brent

P.S.

There's a file of information hidden under the floorboard of our favorite spot. Find it. Give it to Raze. I hate to ask you to do this, but you're the only one I can trust. Promise me you won't open it. This is Raze's cross to bear now.

I love you, my sweet southern belle. I'll see you again someday.

Setting the letter down on my lap, my hands fly to my face to mute my sobs. Seeing his scribbled penmanship was one thing, but to discover my suspicions were correct about his accident brings the weight of the world down on me once more. The club killed him. Directly or indirectly, I don't know, but it's because of his association with them that he's gone.

I stew in sorrow and rage until I hear Roxie fussing in her crib. Leaving the letter behind on the seat of the chair, I hurry inside and straight to my girl, scooping her into my arms as I sob uncontrollably and seethe with anger. In the kitchen, I fix her a bottle while she continues to fuss in my arms. Roxie seems to always know when I'm upset because she fusses until I quit sobbing. Tracing my finger along her cherub face, I come to a decision that could change our entire lives. But it will vindicate my husband.

Once she's finished, I change her diaper and put her in the electric swing with some music. She coos and watches the mobile of giraffes and elephants swing as I move to my purse, retrieving my cell phone from the front pocket.

I dial a familiar number and wait. It takes two rings before her voice comes through the earpiece.

"Hey, sexy mama," Dani's cheerful voice answers. Judging by the music and noise in the background, I have a sneaking suspicion she's at the clubhouse.

"Hey. Can you come watch Roxie and grab the boys from school? I hate to ask you to do this knowing you're about ready to give birth at any time, but I had an emergency pop up."

"Sure, not a problem. It would be kind of nice to get away from Hero's hovering, anyway. Do you need me to stay the night?"

I sigh, unsure how long this task is going to take. "Yeah, that would probably be best. There's plenty of food, diapers, and formula for Roxie, and the boys will eat just about anything you put in front of them."

"Sure, no problem. Is everything okay?" she asks. I can hear the concern in her voice. "Do I need to have Raze or Hero come over?"

Play it cool, Darcy. Don't tip her off that something is up.

"No, everything's fine. I just have something I need to handle, and I don't want to take the boys out of school. I really appreciate you helping me, Dani. Especially knowing how much Hero hates you being away from home right now."

Dani laughs into the receiver. "Don't you worry your pretty little head about my husband. I know how to make him see things my way."

I laugh at that, having seen firsthand just how easy it is for her to make him see reason, whether he likes it or not. And he usually doesn't. We finish our conversation, and after quickly checking on Roxie and cleaning up the kitchen, I head to the bedroom and pack an overnight bag. It'll only take me a few hours to get to where I'm going. Unlocking Brent's nightstand, I pull out the Glock .380 automatic hand gun he gave me shortly after we got married. It's illegal to carry across the border, but I'm not going into a foreign country alone and unarmed. I'll grease some palms or flirt if I have to, but this gun is coming with me.

Once I'm sure the safety is still clicked on, I tuck it in the back of my jeans, tossing an extra clip into my bag just in case. Brent always worried about me being home alone, especially when trouble brewed up for the club, so he made damn sure I was armed. Little did he know, I was a better shot than he was. My daddy raised a true southern belle. I'm pretty to look, but deadly if crossed. Let's just hope this little adventure won't cause the other side of my upbringing to be necessary.

I grab Brent's letter, along with my passport, and zip up the bag just as the doorbell rings. Greeting Dani at the door, I go over a few things with her, give Roxie a quick kiss on the forehead, and head out of the door. For a woman carrying twins, Dani doesn't look a bit exhausted. God, I wish I had pregnancies like hers, but then again, my baby making days are over. Three is definitely enough for me.

Dani will need my van to pick up the boys, so I'm forced to take the car I have avoided driving since Brent died. His 1971 Dodge Challenger R/T he named Betty. He loved this car and his bike more than he ever loved anything in his life, besides his family, of course.

Tossing my bag into the passenger seat and

placing the gun under the driver's seat, I put the keys in the ignition and let the engine roar to life. While Betty idles, I grab my phone and say the words I never thought I'd speak again.

"Siri, get me directions to Tijuana."

Chapter 6

RAZE

THE RIDE to the clubhouse from the Hollywood Bowl takes longer than expected. Apparently, some jackass decided it would be a smooth move to try and drive in the carpool lane with a semi-trailer and jackknifed when the California Highway Patrol tried to pull him over. My one hour trip turned into three hours because people don't seem to realize shit like that doesn't fly in California.

Fucking idiots.

Rolling into the clubhouse at nearly two a.m., I notice the line of Harleys parked by the back door. Looks like most of my brothers are here late. I guide my bike into the first spot and lower the kickstand. Before I even swing my leg over, the door of the clubhouse swings open and out steps Ratchet. His entire demeanor is filled with fluid anger. *Fuck, can't*

I come home to a normal night at the clubhouse? It seems there is always someone with a bowl full of piss-covered Cheerios around here. When did this MC turn into a high school with hormone-crazed teenagers looking to score some pussy and rebel against their parents?

Sliding off my bike, I remove my leathers from my legs and stow them in the saddlebags on the back. Ratchet takes a long drag off of his cigarette as turns his face to the sky with his eyes closed. I approach him carefully because, much like Hero, Ratchet can have moments of instability, and it's best not to sneak up on him. He sees me and tosses his cigarette to the ground, grinding the cherry out with his boot.

"Sup, Prez. You look like you've had a hell of a night."

I sigh. "You could say that. Remind me to kick Hero's ass the next time I try to help him. Fucking pop singers, man."

Ratchet laughs, and shakes his head. "She the one that put her lipstick on you, or do you have a secret you need to share?"

I raise my hand and drag the back of it across my lips, only to find the bright-red stain of Michelle's lipstick there. I didn't even notice she had it on, but it would explain the smoothness of her lips.

I can't help but smirk at the memory. "Nah. Her manager went for a ride though."

Ratchet reaches into his pocket and pulls out his pack of cigarettes, then tips it forward to offer me one, but I wave his gesture off. He shrugs, then slides one from the pack and pulls it to his mouth, lighting the end before taking another long drag.

"About time you got your dick wet," he says. "Me and the boys were about to start taking bets on which bitch you'd be taking to bed. I know Maj fucked you up, but we expected you to mow through the club whores once she left."

"Let's not talk about that bitch," I growl.

Just the mention of my ex-wife's name sends rage coursing through my body. That bitch crossed the line far too many times to let her last indiscretion slide. Turning Dani in on a fake warrant to her fucking rapist step-brother was one thing, but fucking my own brothers in our bed was a step too far. The decision to not only end our marriage, but her life, was the hardest one I've ever made.

Maj planted the seeds of disloyalty in my club. There was no way I was going to risk all the hard work we'd put into making this club legitimate just because my old lady couldn't keep her legs closed. I had dragged her out into the Mojave to kill her, but when it came down to it, I couldn't pull that trigger and take the life of the woman who had given me my children. Twelve years of a semi-happy marriage made me weak, but the job still had to be done.

I waited for hours out there in the desert until my back-up arrived. Taking the gun from my hand, Trax sent me away, and just as I reached my truck, I heard the gunshot echoing off the mountain range. While he often worked against me in club politics, he always came through on orders.

"What's got you out here chain smoking?" I ask, needing the subject to change. "Something I need to know?"

Ratchet exhales a long billow of smoke from his lips before tossing his second cigarette onto the ground.

"Just some bullshit with Ricca."

Ever since we brought Ricca home from the Twisted Tribe compound, Ratchet has been glued to her side. While I wouldn't be too keen on being cozy with a Tribe's cast-off, Ratchet doesn't seem to care. She's been battling her demons from her time in their demented playroom, but he's been the one helping her back to reality. If I didn't know any better, I'd think she was his old lady.

"What happened this time?"

"She told me she wants to leave the clubhouse and move into an apartment."

"How's that a bad thing? She'd wouldn't a pain in our asses if she wasn't here."

Ratchet glares at me, his eyes flaring with anger.

"Shit, sorry I asked, man," I say, raising my hands in surrender. "I know you feel responsible for her, but hell, maybe it'll help her sort her fucked-up head."

Ratchet stands in silence for a moment, and then just turns and walks away. He knows I'm right, but for the first time in a long time, I think he might actually care about someone besides himself. I just hope it doesn't fuck up our club business because he can't let a piece of pussy go. Ricca is an unstable liability, and she would serve us better not being in our clubhouse.

I pulling the back door open and the bass of the stereo almost smacks me in the face as the heavy sound waves reverberate out from the main room.

The main room is lined with the typical man cave and pool hall shit; worn leather couches, a well-stocked bar, and a pool table that's been used far too many times as a fucking surface. But tonight, there seems to be a new attraction in the main room. In the center of the couches is a bare-chested woman swinging from a newly-installed stripper pole. She jumps and wraps her legs around the pole, then slides down. The guys hoot and holler as her tits barely brush the ground when she spins. While a nice pair of tits would usually interest me, I've seen Ruby's far too many times to even care.

Side-stepping the action at the center of the room, I saunter over to the bar and slide up next to Hero. Four empty bottles sit in front of him. He's not usually a big drinker, so it's obvious shit has hit the fan.

Slapping him on the back, I draw his attention to me.

"Thanks for the pop whore duty today. You could have warned me, you know?"

Hero's face turns from a scowl into a smirk as he chuckles and shakes his head. "Then I'd be the one looking like they begged for their eyes to be gouged out. You'd have done it either way. The money was too sweet. Fifty large to watch some pretty bitch prance around a stage singing cock tease music is easy money. Have any trouble?"

"Nah. Like you said it was easy money. The little bitch tried to get me back to her hotel room, though."

Hero wiggles his eyebrows at me, a knowing smile plastered on his face. "Well?"

"You know the rules. Dicks don't touch the clients. Besides, girls with Daddy issues are too much fucking work and a lousy lay." Hero heartily laughs, before he takes another swig of his beer. "Did you know about Ruby's performance?"

"Nah. It just sort of happened. The guys were here waiting to see if you survived the job. Then the beer started flowing, and Ruby started stripping. Not my idea of fun anymore."

"That and Dani would chop off your balls if she caught you playing hide and go fuck with another girl."

"No shit," he mutters. "Pregnant woman are dangerous, Raze. I thought she was going to kill me last weekend because I told her we didn't need to put the cribs together yet. The look I got from her could have killed a man where he stood. I'm just glad the tool box was next to me and not her."

I laugh at his confession. Dani is a tough girl, and after everything she's been through, it makes sense that she's a little demanding while carrying the spawns of Hero in her belly. If I remember right, she doesn't have long until they make their grand entrance.

"Dani pissed at you at again?"

Hero chugs his fresh beer down in three large gulps before sliding the bottle next to his empty ones. His hands rake through his hair while I wait for an answer.

"Nah, She's not pissed, but I'm fucking screwed. You know we're having twins, right? Well, we found out today what the second baby is. That little fucker was hiding for months behind the other one."

I smirk. "Well, what is it?"

Hero's bewildered eyes meet mine, and his words come out in almost as a whisper. "A girl. I'm having two fucking girls."

Two fucking baby girls. I can't contain my laughter.

"It ain't fucking funny, Raze. I'm going to be in jail before they ever turn sixteen. Some boy will come sniffing around, and I'll be in jail for breaking his fucking hands and hacking off his dick."

The visual he gives me is too goddamn funny for words and sends me laughing uncontrollably. Slapping him on the back, I continue to laugh as I stand and walk away, leaving him to wallow in his own domestic misery. All I can think of is that karma is about to make Hero its bitch.

Checking in with Voodoo and Tyson, I make sure everyone is lined up for their security work this week, then I head back outside and over to my bike. It's time to head home and make sure my kids haven't killed their babysitter today.

The ride home is short, and both kids are fast asleep in their rooms. Well, in Harley's case, locked in her room with a motion detector aimed right at her window. That girl has given me the slip far too many times to be given any freedom. I just hope I can reverse the bat-shit crazy her mother let her get away with before it's past the point of no return. I don't want my daughter to be anything like her mother, and I'll use force if necessary.

Walking into the bedroom, I strip off my cut and shirt, then toss them across the chair in the corner by the walk-in closet. After removing my jeans and boots, I fall into bed wearing only my boxers. It's been a long fucking year, and it hasn't been until recently that sleeping has gotten easier. It feels like I've been awake for weeks, but little by little I'm finding my way back to normalcy.

I'm sound asleep when my phone rings, the noise startling me awake. *Who the fuck is calling me at this hour?* Crawling from the bed, I retrieve my phone from the pocket of my jeans and blink down at the name on the screen.

Sliding my thumb across the screen, I answer. "Hello?"

"Raze?" the voice whispers, a slight edge of fear to her words.

"Dani, what's wrong? Are you and the babies okay?"

"I'm fine, and so are the babies, but Raze, I think you should know that Darcy just took off in Jagger's car with a gun tucked into her jeans."

My blood runs cold. "What the *fuck*? Where was she headed?"

"She didn't tell me, but I saw a passport tucked into the pocket of her bag. I have a feeling she's going to Mexico."

Fuck, just what I need.

Another bat-shit crazy woman hell-bent on stirring up trouble. I end the call with Dani, then dial Voodoo's number and instruct him to track Jagger's Challenger. Jagger loved that car beyond words and had made Voodoo put a tracking device on it in case it was ever stolen. His paranoia will play in our favor, since something has Darcy spooked enough to take the car. V comes through five minutes later and sends me the link to the tracking monitor.

Sending off a quick text to Slider, I request his babysitting presence at the house, then quickly shower and throw together a change of clothes, grabbing my bulletproof vest from the closet. I don't know what I'm walking into, but I will be prepared. Especially with how much the violence in Mexico has escalated in recent months.

Pulling a sheath of knives from the nightstand, I strap my shoulder holster on and tuck knives in each open slot, concealing them under my cut. Bringing a gun across the border is illegal, and would land my ass in Mexican prison. I have to stick with blades. If worst comes to worst, I can call in a favor to one of our allies and get firearms if necessary.

It will be dangerous to wear my cut in Mexico, but I need to make sure I have my club affiliation displayed for identification purposes. V will have notified the local clubs that I will be in their territory for personal reasons by the time I get down there. Let's just hope they roll out the welcome wagon and not the undertaker should I have a run-in with them.

Grabbing my things, I make my way down to the garage as a motorcycle rumbles up into the driveway. Slider glides into the side garage door while my bike idles, and I pull on my leathers. Giving him the rundown of his duties, I toss him the spare house keys and swing my leg over the seat of my bike. He disappears inside, and I retrieve my phone from my back pocket and click on V's link. The tracking software takes a few minutes to connect to the car's embedded device, but soon, a map with a moving icon appears.

Sure enough, Darcy is speeding down southbound I-5, and is already south of San Diego. Pulling out of the driveway, I give my Harley some gas and race after her. I don't know what that woman is up to, but going to Mexico alone is the worst fucking idea she's ever had. I just hope I can get there before she does something stupid.

Chapter 7

DARCY

THE DRIVE through Los Angeles and San Diego is mostly uneventful. Typically, no matter the time of day, the traffic is always backed up, but today it's smooth sailing through both cities. It's not unusual for there to be a five-hour back up at three in the morning around this part of California. Coming from another state, the traffic and the width of the highways scares me. It was nearly three years before I would venture out on the freeways on my own. Now, so many years later, I'm cruising down one of the biggest freeways in the state with carefree ease.

Just as I arrive at the Mexican border, I hit traffic. Crossing the border is going to take some time, so I dip my hand into my bag, pulling out my passport and a bag of pork rinds I had picked up from a convenience store just south of San Diego. The sign above the freeway indicates that the wait will be more than two hours to get through border patrol.

I munch on my snack, allowing my mind to float to my destination, and the significance behind Brent choosing this place to hide whatever it was for Raze. Gatito Del Diablo was just a stop on our spring break bar crawl on Avenida revolución in Tijuana. The girlfriends I had made while attending the University of Southern California went on and on about how crazy night life was in Tijuana, and back then, I was just as big of a daredevil as they were. I was there to have fun, and I had no idea that walking into that seedy corner bar would change my life forever.

"I'm going to go grab us some more tequila shots, ladies."

I make my way to the old wooden bar and lean far over the edge, exposing my ample cleavage in an attempt to get the bartender's attention. What feels like two seconds later, the bartender shoves ten glasses of Patron toward me on a tray. I flash him a grin and toss a couple of twenty-dollar bills down on the bar, then turn and ran smack dab into some drunk guy trying to dance to the music playing in the bar. The tequila glasses clank, tip sideways on the tray, and spill right down my shirt, soaking not only the thin fabric, but my bra as well. The man never utters an apology as he runs his finger through the spilled tequila and attempts to rub his thick, calloused fingers across my face.

"What the fuck, dude? You owe me sixty bucks in tequila, shit head," I screech, throwing the tray onto the scuffed wooden floor.

The drunk man laughs and turns to walk away, but there is no goddamn way I'm going to let this bastard leave without paying for the drinks he just spilled. I worked my ass off all semester at a campus bar to save up for this trip, and I'm not about to waste it on some asshole who thinks he can spill my drinks and not pay for them.

He heads for the restrooms in the back corner of the bar, and I stomp off after him. I grab ahold of his arm, but when I yank back, his right fist comes flying toward me. I try to duck out of the way, but a tattooed hand flies into my view and blocks his strike. A large man steps between us, and he cold-cocks the drunken bastard, sending him collapsing onto the floor. I sidestep around the brick wall of man standing in front of me and see my assailant flat on his ass with his hands covering his blood-stained face. Jesus, this dude has a hell of a left hook.

"Is that how your mother taught you to treat a lady?" he asks in a gruff voice. "I think you owe the lady a round of the bar's best tequila, don't you think?"

The man on the floor sputters out something in a mix of Spanish and broken English as he reaches into his pocket and throws a large wad of cash at the tattooed man, who *catches the crinkled bills mid-air, then lands a kick to his mid-section just as two bouncers barrel into the area and separate the two.*

"He bothering the lady, Jagger?"

"Yeah, man. Tried to rough her up. Take that piece of shit outside," he grumbles.

The bouncers haul him up from the ground and make their way toward the front exit. The tattooed man then turns to me and shoves the cash into my hands, bringing me out of my state of shock.

"You okay?" he asks. "He didn't get any shots in, did he?"

My eyes trail upwards from the cash in my hand to find that the man before me is sexy as shit. His chest and arms are huge, covered with tattoos, and corded with muscle. His chest is broad and stretches the t-shirt under his leather vest. His chiseled jaw is bearded, but it's his icy-blue eyes that take my breath away. Blue eyes have always been my kryptonite, but I've never seen a shade of blue so bright before.

Fuck, if he looked at me and told me to strip naked and hula-hoop, I think I would oblige him without question. Judging by the tiny flecks of gray in his beard, he's a bit older than me. He can't older than early thirties, I'm guessing.

"You mute, babe, or do you see something you like?" he asks with a sideways smirk.

"No, I'm fine," I reply, playing it cool. "Thank you for stopping him. I think the tequila has killed my reaction time. I didn't have a chance to duck his punch."

His brow furrows deeper as a look of confusion washes over his face. "You get hit often, belle? If that is the case, then I think you and I need to take a trip to see your old man. He needs a little life lesson on how to treat a lady."

I shake my head as his bright eyes shine back at me.

"No, trouble just seems to follow me when I go out with my girls. I don't know if it's me or them, but trouble is never far behind," I say, nodding toward the boisterous group of girls dancing and singing in the corner of the bar. "Why did you call me belle?"

His eyes follow the direction of the noise before trailing back to me, a laugh rumbling through his hard chest. "I called you belle because of that sweet little accent of yours, and you look like one of those southern belles from the movies. So prim and proper until you piss her off," he teases. "And it's definitely the lot of you that seem to find trouble. Every single man in this place has their eyes trained on your group over there."

"So you've been watching us, huh?"

A smile grows on his face, as I do my best to try to seem sexy. Unlike my friends, I don't exactly have a ton of guys lined up wanting to date me. Apparently, feisty bitches who can take care of themselves aren't their thing.

They want damsels in distress, and until now, I'd never had to play the role.

"Nope, just you. I've been sitting at the bar trying to decide if tonight was going to be my lucky night. That stupid son-of-a-bitch gave me the opportunity I needed to talk to you."

My mouth drops in shock. "You wanted to talk to me?"

He laughs, shaking his head. "Why wouldn't a guy want to talk to the most beautiful woman in the room?"

"You think I'm beautiful?"

"Angel, you are the most beautiful creature I have ever seen. Now, you may think I'm saying this shit to get them panties off ya, but an old man like m, doesn't usually have a shot in hell with a girl like you."

"Old man," *I repeat.* "You can't be that old."

"I'm old enough," *he chuckles.* "Now, how about we go back to the bar, and we replace those drinks you're wearing."

"Sure. I hope you like the smell of tequila, because I seem to be wearing most of the bottle."

He laughs, his hands falling to my lower back as he leads me back toward the bar. Sliding onto the stool, he sits down next to me and orders a round of tequila for me and my friends, and a beer for himself. The bartender serves us quickly, leaving a shot glass for me, and sends a bar maid over with a tray for my friends. I tip the cool glass back against my lips and let the alcohol burn down my throat. Slamming the glass down onto the bar, I laugh.

"So, what's your name?" he asks after taking a swig of his beer. "I'm betting it's something pretty like Dahlia or Rose."

Throwing two fingers into the air toward the bartender to hail him over for more shots, I turn to the man and laugh. "My name is Darcy. I know it's not very hip and cool like most names nowadays, but my parents are old-fashioned. Is Jagger your real name?"

"Nah, that's my road name. My real name is Brent. How do you like me so far?"

The memory fades as the traffic for the border eases up some. The last time Brent and I came to Tijuana, we didn't need a passport to cross, but once the laws changed, Brent had insisted I get a passport for me and the kids. I never understood his love for Mexico, but he traveled here often for club business in the last few years, always remembering to bring home my favorite bottle of tequila for those rare date nights we got to take.

The border patrol agents are very thorough in their search of the vehicle, but with a little flirting, I'm able to keep their focus on me.

Once they're done, I make my way across the border, entering into Tijuana with ease. The GPS guides me right to the bar where my entire life had changed. The streets are lined with brightly-colored lights and bars with rows of palm trees swaying in the breeze. Tourists crowd the sidewalk with drinks in their hands, as the street vendors try to convince them to lighten their wallets and buy the junk and trinkets they are peddling.

Stepping out of the car, I grab my purse and click the lock on the doors. Usually, I would be afraid of leaving Betty outside like this, but I don't intend on staying long. Within seconds of stepping inside the bar, memories my husband and I shared here hit me in the face. The place hasn't changed much over the years, with the exception of the old wooden bar being replaced with a shiny new chrome top. I take in the room as a familiar voice cuts through the fog of my past.

"Señora Darcy," the man behind the bar calls out. "I didn't know you were coming."

I walk toward him and slide onto the cool vinyl stool, laying my bag on the bar next to me. "It's good to see you again, Matteo. It's been quite a few years. I didn't know if you would still be running the place."

Matteo pulls a few shot glasses from the rack behind him and dusts them off with the white towel in his hand. "You know I'd never sell this place. It's been in my family for far too long. Like I told my wife, I want to be buried here, so I can always keep an eye on this place."

I wince at his words, and his eyes flash with an apology. His hands drop from his work, and he reaches out, placing one gently over mine. "I'm so sorry, Señora Darcy. I shouldn't speak so brazenly about death. I was very sad to hear about Señor Jagger's passing. I wanted to come give my condolences, but I couldn't get away."

Taking my free hand, I pat the top of his. "My husband knew how much you cared for him."

"I'm surprised to see you, Señora Darcy. I thought that with what this place meant to you that you would never step foot in here again."

Matteo removes his hands and pours a double shot of tequila into a glass and slides it over to me. My hands grip the smooth glass, before I set the shot to my lips and tip it back. Matteo pours himself a shot while the familiar burn slides down into my belly.

"I'll be honest. I never thought I'd be back here again, but my husband sent me a letter saying there was something in his old apartment that I needed to retrieve. It's still up there, isn't it?"

Matteo nods, bending to wash the two dirty glasses in the small bartender's sink. He dries his hands and reaches inside the small drawer next to the cash register and pulls out an old bronze key. He places the key into my hands just before he pours another beer for the man sitting at the end of the bar.

"I locked it up tight the day I heard about Señor Jagger. It hasn't been opened since, so if he did leave something, it should still be there."

Thanking Matteo, I slide from my seat and walk toward the back staircases. With each step up, my heart races in fear and anticipation. This used to be such a happy memory for me, and I'm afraid of what I will find behind that door. At the top of the landing, I pause before taking one more step closer toward the door,.

Brent needs you to do this, Darcy. It's one of his last wishes, so put your big girl panties on and do it, no matter what secrets you may unlock.

Taking a deep breath, I insert the key and hear the lock click. Gently twisting the knob, I lay my hand against the worn wooden door and push it open. Memories of our time together flood my mind, while I take in the sight before me.

You are the most beautiful thing I have ever seen, Darcy. How did an old man like me get so lucky to find himself a piece of heaven on Earth?

The room hasn't changed since the very first time I saw it. The tiny twin-size bed still sits against the south-facing windows with the shabby, blue-and-white-checkered cotton curtains. I don't know how both of us managed to fit on that thing together, but we made it work somehow. Over in the far corner rests a single wicker chair next to a tall reading lamp, and a tiny faded-blue dresser. A thick layer of dust covers everything, muting the glow of love that once beamed from this room. It's been abandoned, just as I have since Brent's death. It does surprise me that Matteo never rented it out.

I sit on the thin mattress, sending the springs creaking under the weight of my body. Being in this room brings back so many memories of a time that has become a clouded, distant memory lost in time. I know most girls would have chalked up the experience of sleeping with an older man to a drunken college spring break mistake, but for me, that night with him cemented our two lives together. He was exactly the kind of man I had been looking for, and even with his trepidations about our age difference, I knew he was the one for me.

A few short months later, I found myself married to a biker, and living the kind of life my parents had nightmares about. It took them nearly two years to finally come around to the fact that I had married Brent, and it wasn't about to change any time soon. But as they saw how he provided me with a good life and a dream of dozens of children, they relented in their disapproval and embraced him as their son-in-law. Brent worked hard to gain their approval, because in his eyes, family always came first, and without them, life is just a shell of an existence.

Wiping the tears from my eyes, I rise from the bed and begin to search the room. The mattress, dresser, and most obvious places come up empty. My husband was a smart man, and he would never hide something in plain sight. Scanning the room, my eye catches on something under the dresser. I quickly slide the flimsy wood over, and find a shiny new section of wood beneath where the dresser had been placed. Falling to my knees, I knock on the wood. A hollow sound reverberates back.

I pull at the section with my fingernails, but it won't budge. An idea strikes me, and I bound down to the bar, retrieving a crow bar from the maintenance room. I rush back up the stairs and make my way back over to the spot, raising the crow bar high into the air. Just before I swing downward, heavy boots stop in the doorframe. I whip toward the sound, and when I see him, I gasp, the crow bar falling to the floor with a clang beside me.

Chapter 8

RAZE

WHY THE FUCK did Darcy keep this little excursion to herself? She wouldn't just take off without a reason. She had obviously felt the need to arm herself, so she sure as fuck should have called me to let me know her intentions. I had made a promise to Jagger that I would take care of her and the boys long before his ticket to hell was stamped, and I still stand by that promise.

Darcy and her secrets have only piled up over the last year. Her sudden disappearance from family gatherings for the club already had me suspicious of her actions, but when she showed up with a rounded belly months later, I knew she had not been entirely truthful with me. I stewed for days in a rage-induced haze before I could calm myself enough to ask what all of us were thinking.

"What are you doing here?"

Darcy's thin frame had begun to round with pregnancy. She looked so much like the young girl draped on Jagger's arm with her added weight. Her thin, almost sickly appearance had made her beauty fade. I've always liked my girls healthy, and so did Jagger. I knew it would have killed him to see her this way.

Darcy's eyes narrowed with each step I took. Her body tensed as I stepped directly in front of her. "I came here to ask you something."

Her eyebrows arch upward, and with her arms crossed over her chest, she puffs herself up, automatically on the defensive. Even with her growing stomach, Darcy is still the spitfire I'd always known. Maybe it was just the heat fucking with me, but she was even more beautiful when she was pregnant and pissed off. Would I tell her that? Fuck no. I like my balls where they are.

"What business do you have with me that warrants you coming all the way out here? You know there's this little thing called a cell phone you could have used."

Her words are clipped and angry, which only add fuel to the slow-burning rage and arousal simmering inside of me. Jesus, that sassy tongue of hers is sharp.

"I didn't come all the way out here to fight with you, Darcy. I just need to know whose baby you're carrying."

Her eyes flare with anger, her fingers clenching tightly into fists as she inhales a shocked gasp. Just watching her heavy chest heave makes my dick hard. Angry bitches have never turned me on before, so I have no idea why my cock decides to stir at this particular moment. Darcy is still Jagger's old lady, even if he is dead, and sinking my dick into her would be trespassing on my brother's memory. Nevertheless, my dick has never seemed to have a conscience when it came to warm pussy.

"You've got some fucking nerve accusing me of fucking another man," she snaps. "I buried my husband three months ago, and for you to think I could move on so quickly shows just how much you really don't know me."

"How the fuck was I was supposed to be able to get to know you, Darcy? From the time you two got married, you holed up in Jagger's house and only came out to the clubhouse on special occasions. That doesn't exactly make you warm and fuzzy to be around, darlin'."

The tension in her body grows before her arms fall from her chest, her hands landing on her hips. God, the sass on this woman is infuriating and arousing all at the same time.

"I didn't come around because Brent didn't want me around some of the sleezeballs you call your brothers. After that prick Trax from that other chapter cornered me at the clubhouse, Brent kept me home to keep me safe."

The thought of Trax even touching her makes my blood boil. The number one rule for old ladies is you don't go sticking your hands into someone else's honey pot. We have kicked men out for less.

"Why didn't you or Jagger come to about that? I would have protected you."

"Brent didn't want to stir up trouble, and he was far more content knowing I was safe at home."

"I was his club president. He should have come to me and let me handle it. That's part of my goddamn job. Now, enough deflecting, woman, and answer my goddamn question."

Her fingers unclench, and a stream of tears roll down her face as her small hands cover her rounded belly.

"It's Brent's. I found out a few days before he died."

A heavy sigh escapes my lips as the urge to pull her into a deep embrace fills me. I force myself to stand my ground, though, because I honestly don't know what she would do if I initiated contact on that level with her.

"Why didn't you tell me?" *I ask, sadness washing over me.*

Jagger would have jumped from the rooftops knowing he was going to be a dad again. After all the medical shit that had gone down when Wesson was born, Jagger hadn't wanted to face the fact that more kids would be too risky, making his dream of a little girl impossible. Most men like us want boys, but Jagger had always wanted a daughter. He used to yammer on and on, after a few glasses of whiskey at the club, about having a baby girl. I, for one, thought he was bat-shit crazy because little girls in pretty dresses don't exactly fit into our lifestyle. But to each his own.

Her eyes trail down to her belly as fat tears drip off of her cheeks and onto the ground.

"I only told my parents about my pregnancy. Deep down, I thought if I said it out loud, someone would come take my baby away, just like they took my husband."

I walk closer to her and lift her hands from her body. She grips mine tightly, her eyes rising to meet mine. The angry and mournful sorrow behind her brown eyes nearly guts me. She shouldn't be facing this alone, and I hate that she thinks being near the club will take away the only things she has left to love in this world.

"An MC is about brotherhood and family. It's not the club whores, turf wars, or any of that other bullshit." Removing one of my hands, I gesture to the club insignia on the front of my jacket. "This patch means we pledge our lives to protect the bond we have as brothers, and that includes our families. Brent wanted you to be a part of this family because he knew we'd keep you safe if bad shit showed up on our doorstep. I think you should know that I made Jagger a promise, and I intend to keep it, Darcy. If you need anything, I want you to call me. Even if it's an extra pair of hands to change dirty diapers or an emergency babysitter, this club will be there for you. We take

care of our own, and I plan to make sure you, the boys, and this new baby will never be scared again."

The memory of our confrontation continues to linger in the back of my mind as her cherub face blurs into my vision. Darcy has always been a looker, and after three kids, her body has now filled out completely. She has curves in all the right places, and that ass of hers is one for the record books, making me wonder what it would feel like to be inside of her, that ass ramming hard against my cock.

Where did that come from?

Shaking off the forbidden fantasy that just played inside of my head, I cross the border into Mexico. Most people would never make it across this heavily-guarded border with the sheer amount of steel strapped to my body, but with a little cash and my security license, anything is possible.

Before moving out of traffic, I check the tracker link and find that the car has stopped in a popular bar scene in town.

Why the hell would she come down here to get a damn drink? She could get the same tequila or piss beer at home. Something has led her leave the kids behind, and it's more than just this hellhole.

Cruising on the bike, I make it to the bar district of town with relative ease. Down the street, I spot Jagger's car parked directly in front of a bar. Veering into the spot directly behind it, I kill the engine and pull the keys from the ignition, stowing them in my pocket.

On the sidewalk, I chuckle quietly to myself. Darcy had booked it to Mexico, only to end up in a place called The Devil's Pussy. This seems more like a place Jagger would haunt than Darcy. I peg her for more of a wine and cheese party kind of girl rather than a shitty beer and Montezuma's revenge type.

Walking through the doors, an older Mexican man stands behind the counter, wiping it down with a rag. I stalk over and slide onto the empty barstool in front of him.

"What can I get you, Señor?" he asks, his voice nervous and stiff.

"I'm looking for the woman who showed up in that beauty of a car parked outside. You see her in here?"

The man shakes his head back and forth, then turns and reaches for what I can only assume is a pistol beneath the cash register. Pulling one of the long, combat knives from my shoulder hostler, I twirl the sharp blade in my hand and slam it down on the bar top, which sends the man spinning on his heels to face me. His eyes land on my blade and his hands rise in the air in surrender.

"I don't want any trouble, Señor."

"There won't be any trouble if you tell me where I can find the woman. Your eyes automatically went to what assume is a gun underneath the bar, so you know exactly who I'm talking about, and I'm for damn sure betting she means something to you."

"Yes, I know who she is," he says, his hands still held high. "Her husband was one of the regulars here. What do you want with the Señora?"

My fingers slowly trace up the sharp edge of the blade before I stow it back into the holster. I need to show him that no harm will come to her if he gives me the information I want.

"Let's just say I was a good friend of her old man. You gonna tell me where I can find her, or do I need to get my knife back out and cut the information out of you slice by slice?"

His eyes grow wide as my hand slides back under my cut.

"She's in Señor Jagger's apartment upstairs," he says, pointing toward the back of the bar.

Apartment? Since fucking when? Jagger only owned one piece of property that I had been aware of. The house he shared with his family. Fucker had been keeping secrets even from me.

Removing my hand from inside my cut, I stand and walk toward the direction he indicated and quietly make my way up the stairs. Banging and crashing flows from a room at the top. The door stands ajar, revealing Darcy standing in a corner, holding a crowbar high above her head.

"Do you want to explain to me why the fuck you are in a bar in Tijuana with a crow bar and a gun?"

The crow bar falls from her hands and lands on the floor next to her. Darcy stands in shock as I walk into the room, bending down to pick up her discarded tool. I hold it out to her, and she glares as she snatches it away from me.

"If you needed a vacation darlin', you could have just said something instead of running away."

"I didn't run away, asshole," she snaps. "Why the fuck are you here?"

She's filled with rage yet again in my presence, and my cock springs to life in my pants. Why the hell does she have this effect on me, and why can't my cock just stay soft around the one person I can't have? I'll go so far as to admit that I've always been attracted to her, and even that sassy mouth of hers affects me, but she is my brother's widow. Crossing that line isn't exactly looked well upon in our club, and I for damn sure won't be crossing it any time soon, even if she offered herself up to me.

"Dani called and said you took off with a gun tucked into your jeans. Care to tell me why you didn't fucking call to tell me why you needed to escape to Mexico? I doubt you had an overwhelming need to get a warm beer in a town like this."

She rolls her eyes, which only makes the growing problem in my pants harder.

Calm the fuck down. She's not the pussy you want to be chasing right now.

"I came here because of you and my goddamn husband."

I gape at her, confused as she stomps over to her bag and rips a folded piece of paper from inside.

"This was on my door this morning, and before you even ask, yes, that's his handwriting." She shoves the paper into my hand.

I quickly read over the letter and stare at the faded words.

She's right. This is his handwriting. How in the hell did she even get a letter from Jagger after all this time? Dead men don't write letters.

"You know I'm right. I'm here because of that little request he made in the P.S. portion of the letter. I'm here because he asked me to come find whatever the fuck he has hidden here for *you*."

Folding the letter up, I hand it back to her and let the words of my fallen brother seep into my mind. They don't make a lick of sense, but at the same time, the need to find what he has hidden here exponentially grows. I grab the crow bar from Darcy and move her aside.

"You think whatever he's got stowed here is under the floor?"

She points to a newer section of wood directly in front of me. "That part right there. It echoes when I knock on it, so I think it's hollow underneath."

Stripping my cut off, I hand the worn leather to Darcy and kneel on the floor, placing the tip of the crowbar between the seams of the wooden panels. It takes a few tries, but finally, the wood releases from its seal and pops up. After breaking the board free on all sides, I lift it up and set it on the floor next me. Reaching my hand into the dark hole, I feel around until my fingers graze a smooth packet lying in the farthest corner.

I slide the packet from its hiding spot and pull it back into the light. The thick manila envelope is covered in dust, but remains sealed. Darcy's eyes lock on the envelope in my hand as I blow the dust off of it. Turning it over, I find my name scribbled in Jagger's familiar script on the front. Darcy steps closer, her hand stretched out to take it from me, but I pull the packet away from her grasp.

"Now, darlin', Jagger told you point blank that this isn't for you. Don't you be getting any ideas about taking it away from me."

The fire from her anger flits in her gaze like a burning log as she crosses her arms in a huff. I rise from the ground, tucking the packet under my arm and using my free hand to wipe the dust from my leathers, then I walk right past Darcy, grabbing my cut from her hands as I head for the exit.

"Where the fuck do you think you're going?" she snarls.

"Well, darlin', me and this packet here are going home. If this is as bad as I think it is, I'm not about to open it up in some shit hole bar in Mexico. Now, get pretty little ass back into that car and head home. Your part is done, and it's time you get back to those kids. If what's in here is something you need to know, I'll share it with you, but until then, this packet is club business and none of yours."

Chapter 9

DARCY

RAZE WAS hot on my tail the entire trip home. He mimicked every lane change I made, and he even stood guard while I pumped gas into Betty. Maybe his suspicions about me high-tailing it out of there were warranted, but I still didn't like his eyes following me everywhere I went. His gaze made me uncomfortable and oddly aroused, all at the same time. It's not that I'm attracted to him. Well, maybe a little bit, but that's not ever going to happen. He is my husband's pseudo-brother, and I won't cross that line, even if I have to admit that watching him ride behind me on the freeway is arousing and exciting. His muscles flexed and curled whenever he leaned into turns, and watching his shirt ripple in the wind nearly set my panties on fire.

I would have pulled over into the median and let

him take me right there in the dirt if I'd gotten a glimpse of those fucking dimples while he followed me. More than once I had to remind myself that while he looked damn good, Raze is the enemy. He is the person standing between me and my goals, and he is also the man my body had suddenly decided it wants a taste of.

Forcing myself to focus on the way he suddenly dismissed my involvement back at the apartment helps curtail the crotch fire smoldering down below. That son-of-a-bitch had the nerve to shove me out with his dismissive boy's club mentality. Anything to do with my husband is *my* business. I risked everything traveling to Mexico on my own to get that envelope for him, so you'd think he would let me in on whatever is in it. But that patch on his back is enough to keep the information from me, which gives me yet another reason to hate that fucking club. He was right. I do need to get back home to the kids, but I'm not going to let sleeping dogs lie. It's time I call in someone I never thought I'd turn to again. A Heaven's Rejects' member with a checkered past and loose morals. Especially when it comes to the right amount of money.

As the last few miles tick away, my mind wanders to the level of control Raze seems to have over his rag-tag team of misfit bikers. I honestly don't understand why the men and women of the club just bow to his will without a second thought. Well, I guess the men I understand more because he's their leader, but that's not the case for the women. Sure, he's got the looks that make most women want to rip their panties off and beg to be taken hard. His defined, strong arms, and muscled legs even make me want to climb aboard and fuck him, but my attraction to him means jack shit when it comes to avenging my husband. I need that information, and I'll get it one way or another.

Shit, if my mind keeps thinking about Raze like this, I'll need to get new batteries for my vibrator. He's the last man on this Earth I would fuck, even for relief.

I pull into the drive as the sun is rising into the sky. The neighborhood is quiet. I'm not surprised to find a familiar bike parked next to Dani's car, since wherever she goes, Hero is usually not far behind. After everything that's happened to them in just a short amount of time, I don't blame him for basically being her own personal stalker. At least she gets some good benefits out of the relationship, or so I assume.

Quietly, I sneak into the house and find Dani and Hero snuggled up on the couch with Roxie asleep in her bassinet. I wish I could have a smidgen of the peace these two have found in each other. Maybe it's jealously that Hero is still here to hold her, but it pains me to see someone so happy in this house. After just a year's time, happiness seems like it will never live here again.

I try to be quiet as I walk past the couch to check on Roxie, but Hero's eyes fly open, his hand reaching for the gun holstered on his hip. Instinctually, I raise my hands in the air, hoping he realizes it's me. His hand falls from the gun and back to his face, rubbing the sleep from his eyes.

"Shit, Darcy. You're too quiet for your own good. I didn't even hear the door open."

"With a new baby in the house, you tend to figure out how to walk quietly in and out of a room," I say, casually lowering my hands. "I've had to master ninja baby skills."

Dani mumbles and shifts in her sleep as Hero pulls his arm out from under her head. He gently repositions her against one of the cushions, before rising from the couch. I peek into Roxie's bassinet and find my little angel bundled tightly in her blankets, sleeping soundly. Hero steps up next to me and cocks his head to the side, looking down at the sweet child snoozing soundly.

"I don't know how you do it, Darcy. Raising the boys, and now, Roxie all on your own."

I turn to face him as he watches my daughter.

"It's not hard to be a mother, or in your case, a father. You just have to try your best, and if you can give them a happier and better life than you had, you've succeeded as a parent."

He sighs, turning toward me. "You make it sound so damn easy. I don't think I'm ready to be a dad yet."

I smirk at him and stifle a quiet laugh. "You can never be ready to be a father, Hero. Trust me, until you have your baby in your arms, you'll never understand the bond between parent and child. Would it make you feel any better to know that Brent was a hot mess when Colt was born?"

Hero laughs softly. "No shit. He was scared?"

I grin, thinking back to the early days of Colt being in our lives.

"He woke up every five minutes to make sure Colt was still breathing, and he refused to change a diaper unless I was there to supervise. There was one time I went to Albertson's for more formula, and he called me panicking because Colt had sneezed twice in five minutes. He was determined the baby had the swine flu, and that we needed to go to the emergency room." Hero chuckles, and I place my on his shoulder. "Fatherhood doesn't come with a guide. Just trust your instincts, and be the man they need. Support Dani through the bad nights, and the good ones. One day, you'll look back on the day the twins were born and wish they were still that little."

He sighs, then turns to face a sleeping Dani on the couch. His gaze is filled with love as he watches her rounded belly rise and fall with each breath she takes. "I just hope I don't fuck it up and put a thumbprint in my kid's head because I forget about that soft spot they'll have. I've never held something so fragile before."

"You'll be fine, I promise. I'll be here for the both of you, just like you've been here for me with Roxie. If I can handle raising two rambunctious boys, and now this precious little girl, you can handle twins. By the way, did you ever find out what the second baby's gender is?"

Hero's eyes flicker with a mixture of tension and happiness. "Two girls."

A laugh catches in my throat, and I nearly double over. He stares at me in confusion as Dani slowly rises from the couch, awoken by the sound of my muted laughter.

"What's so funny?" Dani asks.

"Oh, nothing," I reply. "Hero just told me about the twins. He's screwed, isn't he?"

Dani nods in agreement while chuckling. Hero starts to interject his frustrations, but the ringing of his phone interrupts him. He pulls it from his pocket, looks down at the screen, and immediately steps outside onto the porch. Dani and I watch in silence as he paces back and forth outside the sliding glass door, speaking angrily into his phone. The conversation is short, and he presses the screen to the end the call. Anger wafts from him when he yanks the door open and allows it to slams shut, sending Roxie's eyes flying open in fear.

"Babe, are you okay?" Dani asks. "Did something happen?"

Hero shakes his head and moves toward his wife, kneeling before her and taking her hands in his. "I need you to stay here with Darcy today, angel. Shit has gone down at the club, and you'll be safer here than at home alone." He quickly rises and looks to me. "Lockdown here goes for you, too. Raze wants everyone inside until he gives the all clear."

How dare he issue orders for me like I'm some dutiful old lady. I'm not part of that damn club anymore, and if he thinks for one second that he's going to bark orders at me and expect obedience, he has another think coming.

"Darcy, did you hear me?" Hero barks.

"I'm not an old lady anymore, Hero, so you tell Raze he can shove his lockdown bullshit up his ass. Dani is more than welcome to stay here, but I won't be kenneled like a fucking misbehaving dog. He no longer has no jurisdiction over this family."

Hero's eyes flare with anger, but I don't care. These men may follow Raze lock, stock, and loaded barrel, but that's not my life anymore.

"If I have to duct tape you to that chair, I will, Darcy. Raze doesn't issue lockdowns without a good reason, and if he thinks it might spill over into our families, he's doing this for your own good. Keep your ass in the house, and we'll all be happier for it."

He waits for me to make another comment, but I remain silent. I've learned in the years of being involved with this club that sometimes it's best to say nothing at all. It'll get him out of this house faster, and I can move freely once he's gone. I will play the good little widow role until I hear his pipes rumble from the drive. After he's gone, I have shit to do, and neither the fucking Heaven's Rejects or their bullshit is going to stop me.

He leans in to give Dani a quick kiss and rubs her belly before stalking to the door. Without another word, he slips outside, and the loud rumble of his motorcycle engine roars to life. As he speeds away, the sound fades just as Roxie cries out.

Rushing to the bassinet, I pick her up and cradle her in my arms. She wails for a few minutes, as I rock her gently, but when Dani hands me a prepared bottle, her cries disappear. Swaying her little body in my arms, I watch as she drinks, the tiny grunts of happiness like music to my ears.

"I'm going to go check on the boys," Dani says, then disappears down the hallway.

Looking back at Roxie, I smile down at her, my love for her soothing my burning soul. I pat her butt as I sway, and once the bottle is empty, she falls into a restful mid-morning snooze. Leave it to my daughter to wake up to the sound of a Harley. She'll probably grow up with gasoline and chrome fever pumping through her veins, just like her dad. As I lay her back down, Roxie smiles in her slumber. I lean down and place a gentle kiss on her forehead, then step back and watch her tiny body relax knowing her mama's home. This sweet little girl means the world to me, and knowing how much she would have meant to her father only drives my need for information about what Raze found in that packet, and why Hero left here in a blaze of hellfire and brimstone.

"Mama's going to find out one way or another, baby girl. Even if it kills her."

"What did you say?"

I whip around to find Dani with Wesson trailing quietly behind her. He runs to me, sending me falling to my knees as he wraps his arms around me and nuzzles my neck.

"I missed you, Mama. Why did you go away?"

"Mama didn't want to have to leave, baby, but she had to go take care of something for Daddy."

His face moves from my neck and, his sleepy confused at the mention of his father.

"Baby, I know it doesn't make sense, but I promise it's okay. Now, how about Aunt Dani and I make you breakfast and pick out a few movies to watch?"

His brows scrunch tighter together. "But, Mama. I have to go to 'chool today. It's my turn at show and tell."

Running my hand through his messy hair, I rise from the floor and take his hand, then lead him toward the kitchen.

"School's closed today, Wes," Dani offers. "So, you get to spend the whole day with me and your mama. Aren't you excited?"

He nods his head vigorously and bounces in excitement as I pull a package of bacon and a carton of eggs from the refrigerator.

"Well, duh, 'unt Dani."

After making quick work of breakfast, I leave Dani alone with Wesson while I head to my office. I told Dani I needed to get some invoices sent out, but that's not the reason why I'm isolating myself in here.

Sliding my dead phone from my back pocket, I plug it into the charger.

As it charges, I open my laptop and quickly check a few business e-mails.

Once the phone has enough juice to turn on, I slide my finger to unlock the screen and pull up the contacts. The one I'm looking for is at the top, right next to Brent's number. Seeing his name still in my phone makes my heart plummet into my stomach. I haven't been able to bring myself to delete his number. It would only make his absence more real.

I click on the name and the phone rings twice before a gruff voice answers.

"What?" the man answers with a grunt.

"Trax, it's Darcy. It's time you and I had that little talk about the information I asked you to get me."

"You got the cash?"

"Yes, ten grand, just like you asked. I just need a time and a place."

"We're on lockdown, but I suspect you already know that," he grumbles

"Yeah, that's why I'm calling. I can't wait anymore. I'll never get the answers from Raze."

"Meet me at the diner in Delano at noon three days from now. If shit changes with the lockdown, I'll let you know."

Before I can reply, the line goes dead. Trax may

not be the best way for me to get info, but he's my only choice. He's the only brother whose palms can be greased. I know that makes him a traitor to his club, but that's *his* problem, not mine. If he can tell me who killed my husband, I'll gladly watch him hang. In my book, all is fair in love and revenge.

Chapter 10

RAZE

I HATE myself for the way I treated Darcy at the bar, but deep down, I know it had to be done. I could smell her need to eliminate anything that stood between her and the truth. She may have acted as if she was going to give me that packet once she found it, but her eyes told another story. Darkness danced behind those brown eyes, and with each moment she lingered on that packet, I knew how desperate she was to find the truth, even if she had to kill me to get it. I refuse to hurt a woman, but I doubt she would have hesitated to hurt me.

The need to wrap her in my arms and let her cry out her frustration had wafted over me when I told her she was no longer needed. My heart has always held a soft spot for Darcy, but that's the only piece of me she'll ever get. Maj and all her bullshit ruined any chance at happiness for me, and the likelihood of Darcy changing that is slim to none. Even if we were both interested, she would always see me as the man who killed her husband, though I wasn't the one who strung him up and left him for dead.

The parking lot at the clubhouse is nearly empty, as it should be at eight in the morning. I park my bike and slide off, my muscles screaming for a good stretch. The ride back was way too damn long, including the increased wait from the lines at the border, but I forced myself to stay awake. Darcy's stop for gas outside of San Diego was my only chance for relief, but I never dismounted my bike, just in case she tried to give me the slip or take the packet from me. I couldn't let her out of my sight for a single second. The way her eyes were constantly checking to see if I was still hot on her trail told me she would do anything to shake me if the opportunity arose.

Unlocking the door to my office, I flick on the light and enter the room, slapping the packet onto the desktop. Plopping down into the chair, I hope a chance to relax will ease my back ache. The pain sucks, but it's worth it because I know that Darcy arrived home safely. She is so hell-bent on digging into her husband's death, I think she forgets that her kids need her more than Jagger needs avenging. I know all too well that revenge can cloud your best intentions, and it takes someone like a child to bring you back to reality.

I stare at the packet on my desk for several minutes before grabbing it and ripping open the seal in a swift movement. I dump the contents onto the desk and find five more envelopes inside. The smallest envelope catches my eye because my name is written across the front.

With a sigh, I run my finger under the seal and rip it open, exposing a folded piece of paper. I unfold it slowly, knowing my life is about to explode. Jagger was the kind of guy who never sugarcoated the truth, and having a personal letter from him means the news inside is probably the worst kind you can deliver to a man.

Raze,

Before you even think about busting my balls, yes, I wrote you a fucking letter. I could start with the "If you are reading this, I'm gone" bullshit, but we both know that I'm long dead and buried by now, so why sugarcoat it? There are some things you need to know, Raze, and fuck me, they are not easy to write down.

It wasn't my ticker that made me step down from being VP of the club, but your lying, cheating bitch of a wife. I've had my suspicions about Maj for a while now, but it wasn't until the last lockdown that I realized how deep her betrayals ran. She's been playing you, and the entire goddamn club, since the day you two met. She's in bed with the cartel, Twisted Tribe, and your own fucking brothers. Maj has been bringing guys from the cartel into our ranks across the other chapters.

There is a file that Darcy should have brought with this letter that has everything I've been collecting. I know you're probably pissed I didn't tell you about this, before I handed the reigns over to Hero, but I needed to find proof before I accused the woman you love of treason. I'm not the kind of man to break up a marriage without a good fucking reason.

Go through the file, Raze, and for fuck's sake, when you confront her about it, take someone with you, or at least a gun. I know she's the mother of your children, but that bitch needs to die for what she's done. Your kids would be far better off without her in their lives.

Stay safe my brother, and kill that bitch for me.

Jagger
P.S.

Protect my family, Raze. Darcy and the boys will need the club more than ever, and if I know my wife, she'll fight you tooth and nail before she lets the club intercede. Should she move on, I'm entrusting you with another task. Enclosed are two more letters I need you to give to her and her new old man when the time is right.

P.P.S.

If Darcy even starts looking in Slider's direction, crush his balls.

"Fuck."

My wife is the fucking reason for everything that's gone down in this club, and I didn't even know it. First, turning Dani in to her killer stepbrother. Now, this? How was my vision so clouded by my feelings for her? Was I that fucking stupid to believe my wife truly loved me? How could someone bring children into this world, knowing their relationship was all a fucking sham?

My hand slides across to the second and third envelope, each with my name. The other two envelopes I leave undisturbed, and they will stay that way until the time is right, just like Jagger asked.

After ripping my envelopes open, I spill the contents out onto the desk. Photo after photo of my ex-wife with known members of the Manuel Cartel stare back at me, quickly followed by a stack of pages filled with bank transactions between an account in Maj's name and an unknown account in Mexico. How in the fuck did she accomplish all of this? How did I not see it?

My mind wanders back to all of the new brothers we've welcomed with open arms over the years. How many of them have betrayed us? Thinking through the ranks of my own chapter, I know I can trust each and every one of them with my life. Jagger had recruited almost all of them. If one of my closest brothers were suspected of being a traitor, Jagger would have told me. My wife was too smart for her own fucking good, and I'm betting these men are in the other chapters. My thoughts shift to the actions that will come to pass with this information, and how our numbers may fall. We'll need to be at full strength in order to take on the cartel, all while protecting our families at the same time. Their reach is far greater than ours, and it may come down to making a deal with the devil to come out of this alive.

Grabbing my phone, I send a quick text out to my brothers requesting them to come immediately. I make sure to leave Hero out of the message, though. He's still with Dani at Darcy's house, and I don't want to rile her up any more than she already is. Within twenty minutes, motorcycles come rumbling into the parking lot, followed by my brothers barreling through the door like their asses are on fire.

"What the fuck is going on?" Voodoo asks, filing into Church. Right behind him is Ratchet, Tyson, Hot Shot, Dirty, and two transfers from a disbanded chapter, Thrasher and Irons. The tension in the room is heavy, and I know that one false move will trip the hair trigger, sending the room exploding around us.

Once everyone is seated, I place the open envelopes in the center of the table, dumping out the contents. Each man grabs a photo and studies it. Voodoo instantly goes for the stack of bank transactions, his eyes moving back and forth across the information on the page. The silence in the room is deafening as I slide the letter from inside the pocket of my cut. I read it aloud, leaving out the personal note from Jagger. That information will stay with me for the time being, since it doesn't involve the club. It is simply a last request from a man who knew his time was limited.

"You've gotta be fucking shitting me, Prez," Ratchet snarls. "You're telling me your old lady was a fucking cartel spy and none of us knew it? This has to be some bullshit trick. Sure, Maj was a bitch for what she pulled with Dani, but a murderer and a manipulator? Come on. She was barely here. How did you even find this shit?"

Rubbing my hand against my bald head, I sigh. "Jagger wrote a letter to Darcy with instructions on how to find this. She took off on her own, and Dani alerted me to her leaving. Found her in Tijuana in a shit hole bar, along with that packet."

"Shit, he involved her in this?" Ratchet asks, his brows knit together. "Doesn't that seem fishy to you? He never had that bitch here while he was alive."

My fists slam onto the table, and every set of eyes snap to me. "If you ever call her a bitch in front of me again, I will beat your ass myself. Darcy could have burned that letter, and we'd never have found out about any of this bullshit. Not until the cartel overran us and killed us all. She's saving your ass, while you're condemning your dead brother's widow." I hold my hand up to silence Ratchet before his hate-fueled tirade continues. "Listen, Ratch. I know it seems so fucking far outta left field, but the evidence is there. It's not like we can dig Jagger up and ask him for more proof. He's fucking dead, and from what I see here, my wife was the fucking reason."

"What do you need us to do, Prez?" Hot Shot asks.

"For the time being, we're on lockdown. I need someone to bring in all the women and children, or at least make sure they all get out of town safely. Have Ruby fill up the storeroom, and prepare for at least a week or two. I need two men to collect my kids and take them to Darcy's. Make sure they have all the shit they need to keep up with their school work."

"Ratchet and I will go get them," Dirty volunteers.

"I'll get cracking on this unknown bank account and see if I can track it down. I'll search for any bank records that may pertain to Maj, and see where the money trail goes. It might take me a couple of days to hack into the banks, but I can do it."

"What about Hero? Where is he in all of this?"

"He's over at Darcy's with Dani and the kids. I'll be bringing him in as soon as we're done here. I need a volunteer to watch Darcy's house. The cartel may not know where she lives, but with the new baby and Dani being pregnant, I don't want any of them within throwing distance of the club. It's safer there for the time being."

"I'll go," Irons says. "I'm new enough that none of these Spanish fuckers will know who I am. I can blend in."

"Thanks, man."

"Anything you ask, Prez, but what about the other chapters? Are we bringing them in?"

"I think we need to, but we should limit them to just the men we've known for a while. I want to limit the information that may leak to the spies amongst us." Turning to Voodoo, I call his attention back to me. "V, I need you to run background checks on all the new guys from the last twelve years. Start with the farthest chapters and work your way closer to home. Maj would have brought them in at a distance, until she knew she could get away with it."

"Sure thing. I'll pull the membership records right now."

I look to each of my brothers before rising from my chair. "I know this is the last thing we wanted to come knocking on our door, but we need to take care of this now. This club was meant to be a brotherhood, not a fucking means to an end for the cartel to clear their path farther into California. The shit's about to hit the fan, and I need to know you're all on board with me."

Each man nods his head in agreement, and a sense of pride falls over me. My brothers are willing to stand beside me while we attempt to clean up the mess left behind by Maj and her family's cartel. Killing Twisted Tribe was one thing, but facing an entire cartel will be so much more. Ties and bonds will be tested, and our families and friends are going to be right in the crosshairs until we put this shit to rest. There are things we have to do and plans we have to make to ensure everyone will be taken care of if this shit goes south. My priority now is my own children's safety, as well as the added responsibility of Darcy and her kids. Jagger will haunt my ass until my last breath if I leave them unprotected, but there's no doubt she's going to fight me every step of the way. Too bad for her I'm a hard man to say no to, and I don't really give a shit about her opinions on my methods. One way or another, the kids will survive, even if we don't.

"Prepare yourselves, my brothers. We are at war."

Chapter 11

DARCY

"YOU'VE GOT to be fucking kidding me. That bastard sent his kids over here?" I growl at Dirty, as he unloads Harley's suitcase onto the driveway. "I'm not Raze's halfway house for wayward children and pregnant women. I have my own kids to take care of. Not to mention the fact I don't have enough beds for everyone."

"Prez's orders. I don't like being locked down any more than you do, but buck up, buttercup because this shit's happening whether you say yes or no."

Dirty slams a second suitcase on the ground and shoves the tail gate of the Ford pickup truck closed with a boom that echoes off the neighboring houses. He reaches down for the suitcases without a word and heads toward the door, placing them inside. As I follow him, I hear Harley's protests at her new confinement with Ratchet.

She sounds like her mother. This will be like going to Disneyland when the admission is free. Crowded, hot, and every single person is grumpy as shit.

"If he seriously thinks I'm going to babysit his wild child daughter, he's delusional. Dani is one thing because she's a friend, but I have never even met his kids. I have no idea what to expect from them."

Dirty's hazel eyes narrow on me before he brushes past me on the sidewalk with Ratchet right behind him. He heads toward the unloaded pick-up before turning around to answer me. "You're a mom, Darcy. I'm sure you can handle two more kids. Besides, Dani can help you."

I scoff . "Dani is ready to pop at any second. She needs to be off her feet, not on them, chasing after his kids. How do you expect me to feed all these mouths?"

Ratchet steps up on the running board and puts one foot inside the cab of the truck. "I'd stow that fucking holier than thou attitude, if I were you, Darcy. If something were to happen to his kids, there'll be hell to pay." After delivering his threat, Ratchet slides into the cab and slams the door behind him. "The club will see to whatever you need."

What a fucking asshole. I knew he didn't like me, but he seriously needs to start wearing a hat, because no one likes to see a dickhead.

Dirty shakes his head again and opens the driver's side door, a cock grin spreading across his face. "Aren't you a southern girl, Darcy? I thought you all could garden and shit. I'm sure it's in your debutante handbook or something."

"The closest thing to a green thumb I have is buying lettuce from the friendly man down at the farmer's market," I snap, flipping him the middle finger.

That only makes him laugh harder. "Irons is watching the house and will bring over supplies. If you need anything else, tell him, and he'll relay the information to someone at the clubhouse. Just behave and this will all be over soon." Dirty jumps into the cab of the truck and shuts the door just as the engine roars to life.

"Who the hell is Irons?" I yell out, throwing my hands up in the air in exasperation.

He rolls the window down before heading out of the driveway. "One last thing. Harley's a bit of an escape artist, so if you have any duct tape or chains, you might think about strapping her down to a something that can't be moved, like a safe or some shit, so she doesn't sneak out." Dirty snickers as he throws the truck in drive and peels out of the driveway.

Just what I need. A house full of kids, a pregnant woman, and a goddamn Houdini teenager. Fuck. My. Life.

Turning with a huff, I stalk back into the house, stomping like a spoiled child mid-tantrum. Is that necessary? Fuck no, but it makes me feel a little bit better about my new domestic situation.

Once inside, I slam the door behind me, and everyone in the room jumps. "*Listen up*," I say, my voice loud enough for everyone in the whole house to hear. "This isn't exactly an ideal situation, but we're going to make the best of it. This house isn't built for this many people, so we have to bunk up. Dani, you'll be in my room, while you two," I say, pointing to Raze's kids, "will be sharing Colt's room."

Harley stamps her foot in disapproval, glaring at me with teenage angst and anger. Just by looking at her, you can see her teenage bitch fit rising up into her throat, ready to spew sass and hatred.

"I'm *not* sleeping in the same room as my little brother. I need my own bed," Harley demands, bringing her arms across her chest.

"Well, you have two options. You can sleep in the same room as your brother, or you can pop a squat on the floor in my room with a four-month-old and a pregnant woman who will have to pee every twenty to thirty minutes."

Her eyes grow wide at my proposal before her brows furrow back into a teenage, angst-ridden scowl. I have no idea how kids master the death stare at such a young age, but Harley has it down pat. I'm betting it comes from her mother.

"You can stop that little glare anytime now, Harley," I say. "That shit doesn't work on me. And before you try to pull a disappearing act, I want you to know I've been warned about your tendency to wander off. So, if you think I'm going to leave you to your own devices for even a second, you have another think coming, sister."

Her anger reaches the boiling point, and I can almost see the steam rolling out of her ears. Well, that or one of those Looney Tune characters I used to watch growing up. Just picturing Harley's face as an infuriated Wiley Coyote's brings a smirk to my face. Her glare intensifies, and I know that little smirk just tipped her over the edge.

This should be fun.

"If my dad knew how you were treating me…" she begins.

Holding up my hand, I silence her rampage

before she can even get started. "Your dad may call the shots at the clubhouse, but this is my house, and I do not give a flying fart in space what he has to say about my rules. If you're going to be under my roof, and in the sanctuary of my home, it's my way or the highway. Do you understand me?"

Harley's defiance lingers in the air as she mumbles to herself.

"You might want to speak a little louder, Harley. It's not polite to mumble."

"I'll stay with Ky," she says, chagrin reverberating in her voice.

"Good. Now that it's settled, Colt will show you both to your room. Dinner will be at five, and you're to be in bed by nine."

Both of Raze's kids sigh.

"Dad lets us stay up until eleven," Ky says, his voice not much more than a whisper. "But I understand, Mrs. Kyle."

It shocks me how different Raze's kids are, not only from each other, but from their parents. Harley seems to have inherited her mother's need to stir the shit pot and cause as much havoc as she can. Ky, on the other hand, is quiet and fiercely loyal to whoever is in charge of him. Their looks are also startlingly different. Harley looks so much like her mother's side of the family with her tanned skin, dark hair, and dark eyes, but Ky is fair skinned, with bright-green eyes, and dirty-blonde hair. While you can't tell now with his shaved head, once upon a time, a dark mop of hair used to reside on Raze's head. If I remember correctly, Brent once told me that Raze's family is Italian, so Ky's light coloring from a Hispanic mother and an Italian father doesn't make sense to me, but sometimes rare familial traits only pop up from time to time in kids.

Colt interrupts my internal inspection of Raze's kids when he leads both of them down the hallway with their luggage scraping across the floor of the living room. As much as it will cost to buff those scuffs out of the hardwood, the sweet silence that lingers is worth the hassle and money. But that silence only lasts a moment before a slow clap begins from the couch in the center of the room.

"Damn, girl. I didn't know you had that in you," Dani chuckles. "I've never seen Harley back down like that. Not even to Raze. I think you could show him a thing or two about how to parent his kids. Hell, I want you to teach me how to keep these twins in line."

"I hate that I had to lay down the law with them, but Dirty warned me about Harley. I can't let her get the impression that I'm a pushover."

Dani laughs, her hands running over her large

belly. "I think the twins even straightened up inside here at your so-called laying down the law. They were kicking and moving around like kids on a sugar high until you started yelling. I think you missed your calling as a drill sergeant."

I flash a sideways smile at her before stepping into the kitchen to take stock of my groceries. I take notes of what I will need to feed my new family of six and a half people, counting that extra half for Dani. Hell, I don't even know what these kids like to eat. If Harley's defiance from the first five minutes of being in my home was a sign of how well this will go, I'm sure if I feed them something they're allergic to, it will skyrocket this arrangement from nails on a chalk board to walking over hot coals, and then a nice salt in the wound rub.

How am I going to survive this without pissing off Raze and killing his kids?

Reaching back, I pull out my cell phone and shoot off a text to Raze.

> I'm not your personal babysitter. Why do I get the honor of watching your kids?

His response is nearly immediate as my phone chirps with the incoming message.

> Because I trust you to keep them safe. Plus, Harley needs a kick in the ass, and I think you're the right woman for the job.

I can't help it. I feel a jolt of happiness from his statement, and his declaration that he can trust me. Yet, his entrusting me with his kids doesn't mean shit when it comes to him trusting me with Brent's information. The club and trust aren't exactly a two-way street, when it comes to someone outside of the brotherhood. Especially when you have a pair of tits.

> I'll keep them safe, but you owe me.

He responds almost immediately again.

> Like what? You have something special in mind?

I know this will set him off, but I can't help it. A fair trade is a fair trade.

> The information I gave you, and the truth about my husband's death.

The quickness of his responses end, and it's several minutes before my phone chimes again.

> Raze: Brent died from a bike accident, Darcy. I'll take them off your hands soon.

The bastard may have thought he shut me down, but that's about as far from the truth as you can get. I'll get my answers, whether he helps me or not. He's a charmer for sure, with his muscled body, and strong, chiseled chin, but I won't let myself fall for his tricks. He has every other woman in the world fooled with his good looks and flirtatious ways, but not this one. I know when he's bullshitting me, and right now, the bull is full of shit.

Over the next two and half days, everything is peaceful with the minor exception of finding Harley smoking in my spare bathroom. I've worked hard to keep my kids away from second-hand smoke, to the point that I nearly have a sixth sense when it's near me. After I ripped the lit cigarette out of her mouth, I forced her to watch me take each one from the pack she had in her hand, and I ripped each one in half and flushed them down the toilet one by one. The look of horror on her face was enough to know that I had just moved from bitch to tyrant in her mind, but frankly, I don't give a shit. A girl her age shouldn't be smoking at all, and it shows the kind of absentee parenting she has grown accustomed to with Maj being out of the picture.

Settling back into my rocking chair on the patio, I drink my afternoon tea and think about Raze's ex-wife. The whole things sends a chill spiraling down my spine. Her disappearance has never sat right with me, but that's Raze's bed to lie in, not mine. The rumors of her leaving him and heading back home to Mexico seemed to satisfy everyone else. So, what's the point in questioning her leaving her own flesh and blood behind without a second thought? It seems fishy to me, but like I said, it's none of my business. I'm not the one married to the bitch.

My thoughts shift to the other half of that marital equation, and what prompted this lockdown. Could it be the packet I found in Tijuana, or did someone piss in his Cheerios? Heaven's Rejects is a legitimate club now under his command, and according to what little Brent could tell me, they always seem to toe the line between the good and the bad.

Which reminds me... I have an appointment today with one of the brothers in Delano. How the hell am I going to get out from under the watchful eyes of the man stationed outside my house? It's not like I can stroll out to the garage, throw open the door, and nonchalantly leave without him tipping off

Raze. I wouldn't get to the corner of our block without someone catching wind and reporting my escape. Knowing him, I'd probably end up in chains next to Harley if I tried that. Hell, he would probably like that, and in a different situation, I might have even volunteered as tribute.

How in the hell am I going to pull this off?

Suddenly, a muted scream comes from my bedroom.

Shit. Dani.

My cup falls from my hand and shatters against the cement patio as I bolt from my chair. Softer cries bellow from my room, and I run down the hallway, busting through the door, only to find Dani lying on the floor at the foot of the bed, gripping her belly as she pants. I rush to her side, sliding my knees across the carpet. Her skin is covered with sweat, and she's gritting her teeth against the pain.

"The babies," she whispers. "It's too soon."

My hands fly to her stomach, fighting back the panic building inside me. I'm not a medical expert, but even I can tell something is wrong. I've got to get her to the hospital before she delivers these babies pre-term.

"Stay here, and try to stay calm," I order. "Just keep breathing slowly, and make sure you exhale when the pain is bad. I'm going to call Hero, and an ambulance. We need to get you to the hospital."

Dani nods just as another round of contractions hits her. She grits her teeth, trying to hold back her scream. Rising from the ground, I charge down the hallway in search of my cell phone that should be lying on the counter. I fumble, trying to grab it from the counter top, my hand shaking as I to search my contacts. Harley and Ky rush down the hall, their eyes are both filled with panic.

I fumble to dial Hero's number, anxiously tapping my foot as it rings.

Pick up, Hero. Your wife needs you. Come on. Come on. Pick up!

"Yeah?"

"Dani is in labor, and I need you to get to the house. Now. I'm calling an ambulance," I say, the words tumbling out of me in a rush.

He doesn't even respond. The line just goes dead.

After punching in 9-1-1, I give the operator my address. The woman on the phone assures me that it will only be a few minutes before the ambulance arrives. Slamming my phone back down on the counter, I rush back to Dani, ordering Ky to go out front and tell Irons what is going on, and to watch for the ambulance. Harley takes Roxie, and keeps the boys in their room. I don't want them seeing their Aunt Dani like this. Especially if I have to help deliver the babies. Back in the bedroom, Dani clutches her belly, inhaling and exhaling, trying to force herself through the pain.

"Hero?" she asks.

"He's on his way, and so is the ambulance."

Dani nods, just as another round of contractions hit. They are coming far too close together to be anything good, and I hope she makes it to the hospital before she delivers. She grabs my hand and squeezes, and for a moment, I just hold tight until the wail of an ambulance pierces the air.

"The ambulance is coming, Dani," I whisper. "Hold on."

A few minutes later, two men burst into the room with large medical bags, and right behind them is Hero. He dives onto the ground next to his wife, and I scoot away to give everyone room.

"It's going to be okay, angel. It's going to be okay," he says, not only to comfort her, but himself. The paramedics ask Hero and Dani questions as one kneels beside her, taking her vitals. The second man leaves and returns with a stretcher.

As they slide the back board underneath her, Hero and I both grab a corner and help lift her onto the gurney. The men strap her down, and Dani's hands reach out for both Hero and me when they wheel her out of the bedroom, her eyes wide with fear. I try to hold her hand, but maneuvering though the house is difficult with her joined to me. When they exit the front door, I have to let her go and watch as they wheel her toward the ambulance. In the blink of an eye, she is heaved through the rear door of the ambulance, and Hero climbs in behind her.

"I want Darcy to come with me," Dani begs. "Please, Tyler. I need her with me."

"You heard her, Darcy. Get your shit and follow us," Hero grunts, yelling for Irons to move into the house.

"Are you sure he's qualified to watch four kids and baby?" I ask, just as the paramedic moves to close the doors to the ambulance.

Hero scoffs at me with narrowed eyes. "He's all we have, and my wife needs you, so fucking deal with it."

After he barks his orders at me, the last door is locked into place, and the ambulance pulls out of the driveway with a wail of the sirens. I spring into action and run back into the house, grabbing my purse, phone, and keys, all while barking orders to the man I'm entrusting with both Raze's children and my own.

"I have a two-year-old, a six-year-old, and a teenager, Mrs. Kyle. I think I can handle this motley crew. I've already got a call over to the clubhouse for some reinforcements, so you put rubber to asphalt and help our girl bring those kids into this world."

I race out the door and slide into Brent's car. Throwing the car into reverse, I zip down the streets, taking care not to go over the speed limit. California police cars have this unique ability to blend in and catch you completely off-guard, and because of their stealth, I had four tickets under my belt in the first year I lived in Upland alone. Slow and steady is the way to win the traffic jam race around here. Just as I turn into the hospital's emergency room parking lot, a text beeps on my phone. Parking as close to the doors as I can, I reach into my purse and grab my phone as I push down the lock on the driver's side door.

> Trax: You here? I ain't waiting all fucking day.

Shit. I can't leave Dani to meet him, but an idea pops into my head, and I rush to type out a response as I hurry toward the rotating emergency entrance.

> Dani's in labor. Meet me at San Antonio hospital in a couple of hours, and I'll get your money.

Leave it to Dani to give me my opportunity to seek the truth. I just hope both of us are as lucky as I hope we are.

Chapter 12

RAZE

"WHAT THE FUCK do you mean you haven't found anything yet?" I yell at the men surrounding my table. "It's been two goddamn days, and you haven't found a fucking thing? How can there be no evidence? She's not that fucking good. There has to be a paper trail. A bread crumb. Something!"

The men sit in silent solitude as I pace the front of the table. Anger flows through me like a flooded river seeking a new place to wash over the shore. The men around this table are some of the best trackers in the security business, and they've found jack shit on my ex-wife. I knew she was smart, but there's no fucking way she was this careful. She couldn't even hide her string of lovers, so how the hell did she hide her connections to the cartel so well?

"Prez, I know. I looked at every account in that

stack you gave me and came up either empty-handed, or on a money trail so long, even an army of hackers would take months to get a pin on the money's location," Voodoo says, drumming his fingers on the table. Large bags have formed under his eyes, and even someone from the outside could see that he hasn't slept since I gave him his orders. I can't fault him for this being outside of his skill set, but it still pisses me off that we aren't any closer to finding out where the fuck that money is, or the reason behind their infiltration.

I rake my hands over my head in frustration and let out an exasperated scream. The tension in the room continues to rise with each passing second, and the boiling point will soon be reached.

"Does anyone have anything to share? Hero? Tyson? Ratchet?"

Each man's eyes are downcast onto the table, and their lips never utter a word.

"Jesus, how did this bitch cover her tracks so fucking well?"

"Short of riding down to Mexico and finding the Cartel walking down the street, we've got nothing to go on at this point," Hero says. "I wish we had better news, but even the police chatter about the Manuel Cartel isn't giving us any leads."

A knock comes on the door, and Slider's head

pokes through the opening. I glare at him, and a look of fear flashes over his face.

"What the hell do you want?"

"Prez, there's someone here to see you. I know better than to interrupt Church, but I thought you'd want to know. It's Trax. Says he has some information for you."

I frown and motion for Slider let our guest enter. Slider steps out of the way as Trax pushes past him. His heavy boots stomp on the hardwood of the meeting room, and he trudges straight toward an open chair, plops down into it, and throws his muddy boots on top.

"To what do we owe this unexpected appearance, Trax?" I ask. "Last time I checked, lockdown meant your ass wasn't to leave your clubhouse."

He pulls out a knife from the holster on his thigh and grates it underneath his dirty fingernails, tossing the dirt onto the floor. "I figured with your on-going domestic problem, you might want to know some of the intel I have, since one of my men fucked your ex-wife. The limp dick bastard squealed during his punishment for touching something that didn't belong to him."

There are less than five people in this entire world that know about Maj's infidelity, and he just announced the issue to every one of my brothers. So much for keeping that part of the story on the down low. It's not that I didn't want them to know, but it doesn't exactly fill my heart with pride knowing that I couldn't keep my wife's pussy where it belonged.

"That true, Raze? Your old lady run out on you with one of the brothers?" Hero asks.

I sigh. "Yeah, man. Found out right after we got Dani back. I wanted to keep that part to myself, but apparently shit for brains over here, doesn't know how to keep his fucking mouth shut."

"Shit, Prez. I can't believe she'd do that."

"Yeah, there are a lot of things I didn't think she was capable of doing, but it took Jagger dying to find out just what kind of woman she really was."

Nodding appreciative thanks to Hero for his concern, I turn my focus back to Trax and his declaration of knowledge.

"What did the cocksucker have to say?"

"Oh, not much. Just that your old lady has loose lips in the sack. He kept going on and on about Tijuana, and how she told him that's where she was headed to when her job was finished with the club. Brute also mentioned that Maj had a blue cell phone she carried at all times. She guarded that phone like her life depended on it."

Maj was always on her her phone, but it was in a red case. Never a blue one. That bitch had a second phone. That's how she hid her communications with the cartel. A fucking different cell phone. God, I hope it's not a burner phone because that will add a whole new level of complications if we find it. The damn thing must be back at the house, because before our little trip out to the desert, I made damn sure she didn't have a phone or anything with her.

My actions that day might make me sound like a cold-hearted son-of-a-bitch, but I did what was necessary for this club to survive. I only wish I had known all of this bullshit before, so I could have kept her alive. Then I could have punished her ass for all of her wrong doings before I killed her. I don't think I would have had quite the same problem pulling the trigger and ending her life if I had.

I tell my brothers the suspicions of the phone still being at our house before I adjourn Church. As we exit the room, I instruct Ratchet and Hero to follow me out to the house and help me tear it apart. We can cover more ground if I have two extra sets of hands helping me.

Just as we make it outside, Hero's phone rings. He stops to answer it, and the look on his face changes in an instant. Something is wrong.

"Dani's in labor," is all he says, before jumping on his bike and flying out of the parking lot.

Ratchet and I stand in the blowing dust he'd left

behind, frozen in silence, neither of us knowing what to say next. This kind of news is never easy to hear, and I know Ratchet is fighting the urge to take off after him.

"Shit. I thought she wasn't due for a couple of months," is all Ratchet can muster, before looking to me for orders. He knows where he needs to be, but his loyalties and friendship with Hero are ripping him up inside.

"Ratch, tell Slider to head over to the house to help out Irons. You and I will head to my house to see what we can find."

"What if Hero needs us?"

"The last thing that man needs is for us to be butting into his business. If shit goes south, he knows to call me."

Ratchet nods before heading back inside to give out the orders. I'm far from a religious man, but I say a silent prayer for Hero and Dani anyway. Losing a child is far more damaging to a man than anything else. If things go bad, he risks losing everything he worked so hard to get this year. He deserves the chance to hold his children in his arms and watch them grow up. It would be a cruel twist of fate if something were to happen now.

Ratchet stomps out of the building a few minutes

later and slides onto his bike, with Slider right behind him.

"Irons called, Boss. Dani wanted Darcy with her, so Irons and I will be in charge of the kids."

It doesn't bode well with me that Darcy isn't there, but Irons is a family man. The kids should be fine under his watch. I make a note to swing by on the way back from my house to check on them.

I love my kids, but having them at Darcy's has given me a well-deserved break. Trying to run the club and our security business has always taken time away from my kids, but it has been a learning curve to balance out my life now that I'm a single dad. Maj may have given birth to them, but they were raised by the other women in this club than by her. I can only hope they're both learning from the experience of being around a real mother like Darcy.

As her name flickers to life in my mind, her smiling face pops into my vision. I've said it a thousand times, but she's such a beautiful woman. The way her dimples flare to life as she smiles or laughs is enough to make any man come undone. There's an air about her that screams confidence and loyalty. It's a damn shame she's had to face so much turmoil in the last year, but she could have a calm life now, if it weren't for her constant need to meddle in club business. It took everything I had at the apartment in

Tijuana not to throw her over my lap and beat her ass for the sass coming out of her mouth. My cock stirs at the thought of my red handprints on her creamy white skin.

Jesus, Raze. Get ahold of yourself. This is not the time to be thinking about smacking Darcy's ass. You need to get laid.

Shaking the idea from my head, I straddle my bike and flip on the ignition before rolling out of the parking lot to the south. The ride to my house is almost relaxing, though I know shit may hit the fan if we do find that fucking phone of Maj's, but Darcy immediately comes back to my mind. I recall memories of seeing her on the back of Jagger's bike, and how her hair used to flow in the wind like it was dancing.

Shut it down, Raze. Shut it the fuck down.

Pulling into the drive, I notice the sun setting behind the house. I've always loved this house because it seems so simple compared to the rest on the block. The red brick stands out from the more traditional style homes, and I like being different. It doesn't hurt that I got this house for a steal in California real estate terms, for three-hundred-and-fifty-thousand dollars. I walk my bike toward the side of the house and unlock the side entrance of the garage.

My search begins in the most obvious places; in

our bedroom, the office, and Maj's home salon where she worked when we were on lockdown. Ratchet tore through each room in destructive precision, while I thumbed through our personal files and our family's laptop.

Apart from cutting open all the couch cushions and mattresses, I'm nearly at my wits end when an idea pops into my head. Maj loved to cook and never allowed me or the kids in the kitchen, when she made dinner. Throwing open the cabinet doors, I shake and toss every single can and box in them. One can rattles just a little bit differently than the others. Grabbing a knife from the butcher block, I place the tip of the blade under the lip of the can and systematically pry open the sides until the seal finally pops. Reaching my hand inside, I pull out the phone I've nearly destroyed my house looking for.

"Time to find out what exactly you were hiding," I mutter, as I tuck the phone into the inside pocket of my cut.

After giving Ratchet orders to secure the house and clean up the mess, I ride swiftly back to the clubhouse, knowing the key to all of this might very well be sitting in the pocket of my cut. Trax's intel will prove to be valuable if this pans out.

After parking my bike, I jog into the clubhouse and nearly run over one of the girls as I slide into

Voodoo's work/play room. Computers, laptops, and screens line the southern wall, emitting a nearly blinding light from their luminescence. The rest of the room looks like a nerd's paradise with tables covered with the newest and best technological gadgetry. Voodoo does love his toys, and they often come in handy on hard security cases, so we keep letting him play.

I scan the room and finally find Voodoo passed out on top of an open laptop's keyboard. When this is over, I need to send him on a long vacation to catch up on sleep and just relax. V has become invaluable to the club. His hacker skills helped us save Dani from that sick motherfucker she called a step-brother.

Rest in pieces, asshole.

I make my way around the table and gingerly pick up one of the thick programming books lying next to Voodoo, before letting it slip through my fingers to slam down on the table.

Voodoo's eyes fly open, and his weight unsettles the base of the chair just enough to tip back, sending him tumbling onto his ass. A laugh escapes my lips as a pissed off Voodoo glares up at me from the floor seething in startled anger.

"Rise and shine, sleeping beauty," I tease. "I have a present for you."

He wipes the sleep from his bagged eyes and

pushes himself off of the ground, dusting off his clothes and righting the chair once more.

"I'm not exactly a fan of your wake-up method, Prez. You could do with some etiquette lessons. I prefer a warm pair of lips and a tight pussy for my morning rise and shine."

"Yeah, so do I, but we don't always get what we want, do we?"

Voodoo smirks, crossing his arms over his chest.

"A present, huh? You know it's not my birthday for another month. Besides, the entire Denver Broncos cheerleading squad wouldn't fit in your breast pocket."

I reach into my cut to retrieve the phone. Voodoo's eyes grow wide, and he snatches it away from me. Within a matter of a few seconds, the phone is hooked up to his computer via two cables, and numbers and letters flash on the screen.

"This is better than the Broncos cheerleaders, Prez. You've brought me the holy fucking grail."

"That so? Anything useful?"

I step closer to his screen and lean next to him, craning my neck to see information, but it all looks like chicken scratch me.

"It won't take me long to jail break this ancient thing. It doesn't even have a touch screen, so the tech on it is easily hackable."

"How soon will you know anything?"

"Couple of hours max. Why don't you go see those kids of yours while you wait? Might be good to get out of here for a bit."

Rubbing my hand across my brow, I feel the exhaustion wrap around me. Sleep hasn't exactly been a hot commodity for me lately, but Voodoo is right. I need to see my kids before we head straight into this shit storm.

"Any news from Hero?" he asks. "I know some of the guys are itching for news."

"He texted me about an hour ago saying things were progressing toward surgery, but that's the last I heard from him."

"Keep us posted, Boss."

"Sure thing," I reply, making my way toward the door. It doesn't take me long to check in with the others, and then I head out for Darcy's house. It may not be the best place to rest my head, but at least the kids will know everything is okay if they see me in one piece.

Chapter 13

DARCY

"THEY'RE BEAUTIFUL, DANI," I coo at the two pink bundles cradled in their father's arms. The pale color and soft blankets contrast so much with the tattooed hardness of Hero, but he beams a megawatt smile while he watches his daughters sleep. Though he tried to play off his emotions about becoming a father, a glimmer of a tear still lingers on his cheek. Dani watches from her hospital bed as their daughters stake their claim on their father's heart. I had thought Hero would look so awkward and uncomfortable, but he seems at ease.

"Have you decided on the names yet?"

Hero nods for me to take one of the girls into my own arms. Gently cradling her little head, I tuck her swaddled body into the crook of my arm. She is just as beautiful as her sister, with a thick mop of dark hair and dark eyes. They both take after Dani's Hispanic genes. A familiar feeling of want and disappointment wafts over me as I note how precious new life truly can be. What is it about the way a new baby smells that makes you want to have more all over again? *Shut up, ovaries. You have a new baby at home.* The little one stretches her mouth open in a wide yawn, squirming in the confines of her swaddle.

"I've had my children's names picked out for so long, Hero didn't have a chance when it came to naming them," Dani jokes, while Hero places their other daughter into her arms.

"Why even try? I knew every one of my suggestions would get shot down." Hero shrugs his broad shoulders, and Dani stifles a quiet laugh.

"Hero, girls are brought up from a young age to be mothers. It's only natural Dani had names planned out already. While you boys get army guys and guns, we get baby dolls, fake diapers, and bottles. It's not exactly an even ground when it comes to kids."

"I would have still liked my names to be considered," he grumbles, with just a hint of gruffness to his voice.

"Our daughters are not going to be named Brandy and Whiskey, so just stop where you're going right now. Don't even start about Thing One and Thing Two either."

"What? I thought it was funny."

"Ignore your father, girls," Dani says to both babies. "He's an idiot. Now, back to Aunt Darcy's questions. This beautiful angel is Embry Rose," she says with a look of sheer, unbridled, blissful happiness plastered on her exhausted face.

I pad toward Dani, taking care to not wake the unnamed baby in my arms. "What about this little beauty?" I ask, slipping her tiny body from my arms and nestling her against Dani's chest.

"Monroe Isabella, after my mom's favorite movie star, and my grandmother, Izzy."

"Such beautiful names for two very beautiful little girls. You will both have your hands full when they get older." I chuckle as a grimace momentarily flashes over Hero's face.

"Tell me about it," he mumbles. "They won't even know what a boy is until after I die. I'll make damn sure of that."

A soft knock interrupts our laughter, and in steps her obstetrician, Dr. Bextor. The middle-aged man seems worn out, and that feeling is very warranted with how difficult it was to bring the twins into the world. Once Dani got to the hospital, her contractions were only two minutes apart, and she was beyond the point of stopping her labor with medication. She was dilated to far.

Dr. Bextor assured her that he would do everything within his power to make her delivery easy, but the threat of an emergency caesarean lingered, not only because Dani was carrying twins, but her blood pressure had skyrocketed. She was monitored closely for roughly an hour before Dr. Bextor delivered the news that she needed to be prepped for a C-section. Because they didn't have time to give her an epidural, they were forced to sedate Dani, while Hero paced the halls with me. His eyes were filled with terror and panic. I tried to reassure him as much as I could, but words and a pat on the back couldn't soothe the pounding of his heart while he waited for news. Thirteen minutes after Dani was taken back into the surgical suite, the nurse rushed into the hallway and escorted Hero back to the maternity ward.

His heavy steps alerted me to his approach, and when my eyes trailed up from the floor, a smile was on his face. That smile melted away all my worries, and I noted the swagger in his step. His news of two healthy babies and a very tired Dani was the sigh of relief we both needed. He asked me to come back into the room with him while we waited for Dani's anesthesia to wear off, and for her to return to the room so she could meet her girls. The nurses soon stripped off his shirt and had him fill in for the skin to skin contact they now recommended for newborns. When Dani finally arrived, love filled the room as her eyes locked on the girls, and she saw her newly-expanded family sitting in front of her. The whole experience melted my soul.

"Hey, Doc," Hero says. "I can't thank you enough for what you did for my family."

Dr. Bextor waves his hands dismissively, and stepped closer to the bed, admiring the girls. "They're by far the most beautiful twins I've ever delivered."

He admires the girls once more before two nurses walk into the room. "While the girls seem to be in good health, and have a relatively strong pair of lungs, I would still like to place them in the neonatal intensive care because of their low birth weights. I think it would be best if we monitor their progress a little more closely to make sure they're fully developed despite their premature birth."

Dani's eyes well with tears as she looks to the tiny girls in her arms. "How long will they have to stay, Dr. Bextor? I was hoping to take them home with us."

"I know you would, Mrs. Tobias, but while the delivery age of the most sets of twins are thirty-five weeks on average, your girls were between thirty-three and thirty-four weeks. This is only as a precaution, to make sure they are both ready to go home, and that their lungs are fully developed. I'd also like for them to be closer to the five-and-a-half pound mark to ensure they are growing at the right pace."

Hero moves his hands to Dani's shoulder. "I want my girls to be healthy, Doc, so if they need to be in a hot box, let's do it."

"Mr. Tobias, it's best for both girls, and the quickest route to getting them home. My nurses will take the girls down now and get them settled. You and Mrs. Tobias are more than welcome to visit as much as you would like, and that goes for after you're discharged as well."

"Thank you, Dr. Bextor," Dani mutters.

Dr. Bextor sidesteps while the nurses walk around him to collect the girls. "I'd like to monitor you for a few extra days as well, Mrs. Tobias. Your heightened blood pressure is a disorder we call pre-eclampsia. Ten to fifteen percent of pregnant woman show symptoms early in their pregnancies, such as higher than normal blood pressure and increased headaches, but in your case, its onset was rather late. I will say that had your friend here not called an ambulance, we might have lost both you and your children."

"Will this happen again if she has more children, Doc?" Hero asks, his brows creased with worry.

"While your wife will run a higher risk for it to happen in subsequent pregnancies, we will know to monitor for it more closely, and to educate you both on the signs and symptoms, but no, it will not prevent you from having more children."

Both Dani and Hero sigh at the doctor's encouraging words, and the nurses begin to exit the room with the girls.

"Give the nurses a while to get the girls settled before you come down to the unit. Take this time for both of you to get some rest because you'll both be very busy and exhausted when you do these get two home."

Dr. Bextor shakes both Hero and Dani's hands before exiting the room behind the nurses, and then my phone vibrates in my back pocket. *Shit. I completely forgot about meeting Trax here with the excitement of Monroe and Embry's arrival.* I excuse from the room, saying I need to get back to the house and the kids, leaving the new parents to likely get what is likely to be their last night of good sleep for a very long time. I then head toward the atrium on the fourth floor, where I instructed Trax to meet me.

Inside the elevator, I whisper a silent prayer that Trax has come through for me. I know it's a risk trusting someone associated with the club, but Brent always told me how Trax was the type that would sell his mother to the highest bidder if it would benefit him. My only fear is that he'll sell me false information, or worse, take it back to Raze. That's a calculated risk I will take for answers and justice though. The elevator jolts to a halt, and I anxiously tap my foot, waiting for the doors to open.

Just breathe, Darcy. Pay the bastard, get your information, and deal with the aftermath later.

Stepping through the elevator doors, I exhale the deep breath I've been figuratively holding since I came up with this idea to use him. It's now or never for the truth. I can't live with never knowing, so this is a necessary evil I need to handle for myself and the kids. Peering around the corner, I don't see a soul on this portion of the floor.

I picked the atrium because I knew it mostly houses the offices of the administration and charge nurses. Someone behind me clears their throat and I whip around to find Trax walking toward me. His scruffy face is hard-locked on me. His worn and holey jeans are paired with a simple white t-shirt covered in grease. That, along with his cut makes him appear so painfully odd in this beautiful space. He smells of gasoline, cigarettes, and stale bar nachos. He's like a hobo amongst the beauty of this room, giving off a feeling of foreboding and wrongness.

Just get the information and get the fuck out of here, Darcy. The sooner you're away from this asshole, the better.

"Hello, doll," he drawls, his gravelly voice cutting through the pristine silence surrounding us. "You got my money?"

Reaching into my back pocket, I pull out the money order for ten thousand dollars I had retrieved from the locked safe at home and slap it into his greasy, calloused hands. He unfolds the piece of paper to verify the amount before sliding it inside of his cut. He then pulls out an envelope and smashes it into my outstretched hand. My eyes narrow on it in confusion.

"This is what ten grand bought me?" I ask. "You've got to be shitting me, right? An envelope isn't worth that kind of cash."

Trax laughs with disdain, shaking his head . "You haven't even opened the damn thing yet, and you're already bitching. You don't want it then give the fucking thing back to me." He reaches for the envelope, but I jerk out of his reach, pressing it tightly to my chest.

"You wanted that information, and I got it for you, even though I could be killed for the shit I had to snoop through. What's in that little envelope will set you on the right path," he says, poking his finger roughly against the envelope on my chest, sending a rush of fear and disgust shivering down my spine. "I'm gonna warn you, doll. It's not something you should be dipping your dainty little hands into. It's not a place for ladies to be. Especially mothers."

I hold his gaze, struggling to remain calm and unaffected. "You have no idea what I'm capable of, Trax."

"Not even God Himself could take on what you're facing, but I'll say something nice at your funeral if you decide to go through with it." And with that, he slips by me and heads toward the stairs. "At least I got paid beforehand. You can't collect from a dead woman." Trax pulls open the door and lets it slam behind him.

This man doesn't know me, and his insistence to keep my nose out of Brent's murder infuriates me more than Raze stealing my only lead thus far. I'm not a pretty little doll that sits on the shelf, hoping someone will come along to dust me off and play with me. I could rival any one of the Heaven's Rejects' men. They say cornering a mama bear with her cubs can be a dangerous situation, but they haven't seen what happens when you take something, or in this case, some*one* I love away from me.

Unfortunately for Raze and his band of mindless followers, I make a mama bear look like Winnie-the-fucking-Pooh on a honey hunt.

Trax's words about the envelope that is now safely tucked into my bra reverberate in my mind as I slip back into the elevator and out to the parking lot. Darkness enshrouds the deserted parking lot, telling me I've been at the hospital far longer than I had originally thought. I've never been one to be fearful about being on my own so late at night, but a shiver of unease churns in my stomach. I hurry to my ca and quickly lock the door once I'm inside.

My hands curl around the leather-bound steering wheel as I take my first breath of freedom in several days. I know this is only temporary. Soon, I'll return to the watchful eye of whichever brother is guarding my home under the false pretense of safety, but I revel in the quiet surrounding me now. Leaning down, I press my forehead against the chilled leather and breathe deeply to soothe the racing of my heart. Closing my eyes only destroys the semblance of peace though. Horrible visions of my husband's bloodied hands flutter though my imagination.

What if I never knew the real him? What if the side of him I saw was only an act he put on for me?

Nausea churns in my belly. *What if there's another woman? Or several of them?*

I'd be a fool to think the temptation wasn't there, but Brent had always told me he was faithful. That he was mine and mine alone.

I shove those images to the back of mind. I could be dead wrong, and it's a waste of my time worrying about something I can't change now. If it's as bad as it sounds, I honestly don't know how I will handle this on my own. I'll be damned if I'm going to turn to the club for help, but I may have to cash out a few certificates of deposits to bank roll some hired muscle if it comes down to that.

Jesus, I sound like a fucking mob boss.

My pulse races. I have the information pressed against my clammy chest right now, but it would be stupid to linger here any longer. I don't have much time before someone notices that I'm missing. I can only hope that as exhausted as Hero was when I left, he may not have alerted my watchers that I was heading home yet. *Please let that be the case.* I need a few minutes to myself before the entire world bears down on my shoulders again.

My hands tremble against the steering wheel as my stomach churns. I move to pull them from their vice grip on the wheel, but they don't move. *Why am I so scared to open this?*

Maybe I should justread this at home. At least there, I won't have to worry about surviving the drive home should the news be as bad as Trax foreshadowed.

Just go home. It may be a home filled with lies, but you will be safe there.

Making my decision, I turn the keys in the ignition, sending the engine roaring to life. My mind bounces from one bat-shit crazy assumption to the next while I make the short drive home. It's not until I park in the driveway that I realize how much the contents of this envelope could change everything. It would kill me knowing that my husband and our relationship was all a lie.

I know I did this to myself. Even now, having the information I need pressed against my skin, I'm wavering on if I want to read this. With a sigh, I shove open the door and slide off the seat, my shoes hitting the cement drive with audible pops and clicks. I lightly push against the door until I hear the soft sound of the locking mechanism clicking shut. Staying quiet is the name of the game, because waking up the kids and anyone else inside would be the worst possible thing right now. I need to be alone.

I make my way to my husband's home office, and lock myself inside. My hands tremble as I unfold the papers, and then a gasp escapes my lips as tears drop one by one onto the pages before me. My eyes scan each piece of information, but it's the two photos of my husband that crushes my heart and breaks the dam holding back my tears. My heart falls as I study a photo of Brent with his arms wrapped around a mystery woman in a loving embrace, and the other is of him exchanging cash for what looks like a saran-wrapped package of drugs.

Trax was right. This is far worse than I ever could have imagined, and the worst part of it is, I may have been married to a complete stranger.

Chapter 14

RAZE

I GET AS FAR as the back door before a small hand wraps around my forearm, dragging my attention back into the clubhouse. My eyes turn to see a visibly shaken Ricca standing behind me, shivering where she stands.

"What's wrong?"

Ricca takes two quick steps and wraps her thin arms around my neck, sobs escaping her lips and tears soaking into my shirt. Ricca and I have never exactly had a friendly relationship. Not with how she became a part of this club. That makes her death grip on me all the more surprising.

Shit, what's happened?

I use one of my hands to remove Ricca's grip as her chest heaves with sobs. Her face is covered in smears of tear streaks from her mascara. I've never understood why women wear mascara. One sad story or emotional moment leaves them looking like Elvira after a dip in the despair pool every single time.

Gently, I pat her shoulder, an awkward attempt comfort her, but Ricca is nearly a stranger to me, making the situation more awkward.

"I asked you a question, doll. What's happened?"

"The babies," she whispers. "The babies are here."

"Thank, fuck," I breathe. "Everything okay with them? Two sets of ten fingers and toes?"

Ricca nods, hiccuping out another sob.

"Doll, you need to work on your delivery of good news. You damn near gave me a heart attack."

Ricca's eyes rise to meet mine before she sobs once more and takes off down the hall. *What the fuck was that all about?* That has to be one of the weirdest interactions with a woman I've ever had, and I was married to a fucking nutcase.

Shrugging, I head out the back door and make my way to Darcy's house. With Hero's kids delivered safely, Darcy will be coming home soon, and I can get my men back. It's not that I mind monitoring the house, but she doesn't want us around, and frankly, I don't blame her. Had I been able to make the choice between Jagger or me, I would have been the one hanging from the rafters, not him. Just like my father before me, a happy life hasn't exactly been a dream of mine. Heavy are the shoulders of those who lead, and that's how I prepared myself for the future. Having kids of my own was an unexpected bonus, but even I know that old grudges or new ones could end my life just as easily as an accident on the highway. It's all part of the life we live, and I've come to terms with that.

My mind wanders the entire drive to Darcy's, and it doesn't shut off until I quietly slip in the front door. Ky and Darcy's boys are huddled around the TV playing a video game, while Harley makes faces at a cooing Roxie. Not a single set of eyes look up to see who just walked in except Slider and Irons, and that is both a scary and happy thought. It shows that my kids are comfortable here, and while that's usually a good thing, it's also unnerving. Our home doesn't hold the same sense of calm and peace like Darcy's. Maybe I should cleanse their mother's influence over us and sell the house, but that's a step I'm not ready to consider yet.

I plop down on the sofa next to Slider as he watches the boys play their game. Bending down to unlace my riding boots, I pull the boot from one foot and toe the other one off, letting them hit the ground with a plop. Propping my feet on the top of the coffee table, I settle in to watch too.

Slider's attention turns to me. "You heard the news?"

"Yup, it's good news. Also means that Darcy will be home soon. Why don't you and Irons head on back to the clubhouse? I can handle things until she gets home."

Slider looks at me quizzically, as if he's expecting there to be a laugh at the end of my statement. "You sure about that, Prez? You look exhausted, and I don't mind watching the kids."

"I've got this," I assure him, slapping him on the back. "Besides, it's nearly time for the kids to hit the sack anyway, then I'll get some shut eye myself. You two go on and rest up."

Slider grins and stands, motioning for Irons to follow him out of the door. Over the next hour, Darcy's boys begin to yawn and head off to bed on their own. *Damn, she's got these kids trained better than a prizefighter.* You don't even have to ask them more than once, or in this case, at all. Harley and Ky are a little harder, but they both relent, leaving just Roxie and me awake. I figured she would be the first one to pass out, but she's still going strong after Harley deposited her on my lap.

"Well, my little princess, what do we do with you?" I say, watching as a toothless smile takes over her face. She looks so much like her father, but has her mother's pert nose and high cheek bones. "You are going to be a looker just like your mama, Roxie, and that doesn't bode well for the entire clubhouse full of uncles who will have to scare all those little shits away from you."

Roxie smiles again before her mouth opens in a wide yawn.

"That's right, my little princess. It's night-night time. Let's see if this old man still has it."

I lay her down on the couch as I strip off my cut and pull my shirt over my head, laying it on top of my discarded boots. I pick her up and turn, leaning back against the arm of the couch as I press her warm little body against my chest. It doesn't take long before her tiny chest rises and falls in a methodical rhythm.

I lean my head back over the arm and close my own eyes, but every few seconds, they fly open at the slightest movement from Roxie. I know it's not recommended sleep with your baby, but both Harley and Ky slept on my chest when I was home, and both of them lived, though I'm taking more precautions because Roxie's not exactly my kid. It doesn't help that I know her mother would flip her shit if she caught us like this. I'll admit, I miss when my kids were this small. More cute and cuddly, and less sassy and defiant. Closing my eyes one last time, I slip into the peaceful darkness of slumber.

A few hours later, I startle awake at the sound of my phone ringing from inside my cut. As I push off the couch, I note Roxie's missing from my chest.

"Yeah," I grunt, rubbing my free hand over my brow.

"Prez, I cracked it," Voodoo says.

A sudden sense of awareness jars me fully awake, and I stand from the couch and head toward the patio door for some privacy. It's still the middle of the night, but I won't take the chance of waking up the rest of the house.

"This better be fucking good, V. I was finally getting some shut eye."

"Oh, it's good. We've hit the mother load. I've got texts between Maj and several other people, plus a list of calls from the last time it was turned on."

"Can you trace them?"

"I have the numbers running through a mobile phone database, but so far, nothing is coming up."

"This is the big breakthrough? A couple of texts and phone numbers? That's not exactly solid evidence," I grumble.

"Don't get your big boy panties in a bunch. I saved the best for last. I have two addresses."

My heart picks up the pace. Addresses we can work with. We can trace ownership through government records.

"Where are they?"

"According to Google Maps, one is a vacant lot out in Death Valley, but the other is a residence in Tijuana."

Fucking Tijuana.

It can't be a coincidence that Jagger was spending so much time down there, and that's where Maj's phone is leading us. The cartel has footholds just about everywhere in Mexico, but maybe Tijuana is their base of operation. Either way, it's a good place to start.

"Good work, V. Send a call out to the guys who went home and round them up. Call in the San Diego club and have them on standby. It's time we take a little trip south of the border."

"Can do, Boss, but there's something else you need to know. It concerns Darcy. There are photos on this phone of her and the kids with Jagger, all taken outside of their house, and various other places around town. These bastards were tracking Jagger's family, and he probably didn't even know it."

"Shit."

These fuckers *do* know where they live, and we are all sitting ducks if we start stirring shit up again. We've got to get everyone out and hidden somewhere else. I rack my brain, and only one thought comes to mind—my mother's house in Arizona. Mom and I haven't seen each other as much as I would have liked, but her house is in a populated retirement district of Phoenix. Even if they knew where she lived, they wouldn't have a chance to snatch the kids without being seen. Mom has been bitching about not seeing the kids, so this would be the perfect opportunity to get them out of here, but that leaves Darcy and her kids. I think her parents are out in Arizona somewhere as well, so this could work. We can get them all out of the state until we get shit settled.

"V, I need you to have Slider and Ratchet take one of the pick-up trucks to my house and gather a couple of suitcases for my kids, then head over here. We need to move the kids. Now."

"You got it, Prez. I'll have them over soon."

My kids will be easy to move, but getting Darcy to agree to this will be next to impossible. The house will be loud soon, so it's better to rip the Band-Aid off now than wait until we have an audience. I tip-toe down the hallway until I see a light illuminating the floor through the crack of a door. My heart stops when I see Darcy clinging to a sleeping Roxie, pacing back and forth. Her face is coiled in a look of sheer heartbreak and rage, with tears streaming down her face. I continue to watch her for a few minutes before I give myself away by knocking a photograph off of the wall. As the frame falls to the floor, Darcy jumps and immediately moves her body into a protective stance over her child, her eyes locked on the door.

"I can hear you out there."

I nudge the door open with my shoulder, as I step into the room with my hands in the air. Darcy gently sways with Roxie in her arms, then lays her down in the bassinet beside the bed, then turns to face me with her arms folded over her chest. Her face is still awash with pain, and it kills me to have to bring more of the same to her now with my request.

"Do you always eavesdrop on women in their own bedroom, or is that a newly-acquired skill?"

I blink, her questions catching me off guard. "I wasn't eavesdropping. I came down here because we need to talk."

She narrows her eyes. "Talk to me about what? Your lack of clothes in my house?"

I look down and realize I never thought about putting my shirt back on. Darcy's eyes trail downward, while my cock begins to throb at her notice. Being shirtless is natural for a guy, but being shirtless around her is a completely different story. It feels so wrong, yet so right.

"Shit, sorry," I say, spinning back toward the door. "I can go grab my shirt if that makes you more comfortable, but I need to talk to you, and it's not like my cock is hanging out."

Darcy's eyes snap up at the word 'cock', and her cheeks flush. *Shit, smooth move, asshole. Way to make this situation easier to deal with.*

"I ... um ... no," she stammers. "I wasn't checking you out, if that's what you think."

"I didn't say anything, darlin'. Besides, I never pegged you for a woman that didn't appreciate a good view."

She rolls her eyes and sits on the end of her bed, uncrossing her arms as if forcing herself to relax. "You're so full of shit. You know that, right?"

"That's not exactly a secret, darlin'. Can I ask why you're so upset? Baby fever?"

She may not like what I'm about to do, but I won't stand in front of her like a damn dictator. I want to be on her level when I make my request about moving the kids, so I sit down next to her and bite back a chuckle as she huffs at my invasion of her space.

"Baby fever?" she chuffs. "Hero and Dani's girls

are gorgeous, but I'm lacking a couple of requirements; working ovaries and a man."

I frown, not sure I understand.

"I had my tubes tied after Roxie," she explains. "It's not like I'll be using them again now that Brent's gone."

As his name leaves her lips, her voice quivers and the tears begin to fall again. I don't know what to say or even how to console her. I have a feeling there's something more going on here than simply missing her husband. I wish I had time to ask more, but time is of the essence. Ratchet and Slider are likely on their way.

But there's one question I can't help but ask. "You haven't slept with anyone since Jagger?"

Even through her tears, she still manages to scowl at me. "That's a little personal."

"Maybe it is, and I apologize. I know you miss him, darlin'. I sure as fuck do, but he'd want you to be happy."

Her shoulders straighten as she wipes away her tears. It's time to drop the bomb, and I hope to God she doesn't shoot me for it.

"I came in here for a reason," I say, eager to change the subject. "I know what I'm about to tell you will probably piss you off, but I need to just get it off my chest before you cold cock me. I need you to send the kids to your parents in Arizona."

Shock flares to life on her face, her hands balling into tight fists. Fuck, she's so hot when she's pissed. I'm about one glare away from being rock hard and seriously uncomfortable.

"What? Why the hell do I need to send the kids away?" she snaps. "You're kidding me, right?"

"There is a massive shit storm headed this way. You and the kids would all be safer away from it all."

She studies me, her eyes scanning mine as if looking for answers she knows I won't reveal. "So, this is about protecting my family and not covering your own ass? Let me guess, this has to do with what you found in the Tijuana packet."

I rub my hand across my face. Why does she have to ask so many fucking questions? There isn't time for this right now.

"You know damn well I can't tell you shit, darlin'. This is the safest route for your kids. A couple of the guys are headed here now, and they'll take you all to your parents' house. They're also taking Harley and Ky to my Mom's in Arizona. It'll be easier to handle this without any of you in the crosshairs."

Her eyes drift out into the hallway as if looking for the right answer. My gaze follows her, but all I see is darkness, and the cracked open door of Jagger's office.

Finally, she turns her gaze on me. "I'll take the kids to my parents', but if this concerns me, I want in on it."

"No fucking way," I snap. "That's not happening. Your ass will be planted in the hot Arizona sun, sipping fancy drinks by the pool. This is your chance at a free vacation. I'll make sure nothing falls on you, and that you and the kids are safe."

Darcy stands from the bed and steps in front of me. This must be her attempt at establishing dominance over me, and I have to admit, it's hot. My cock strains against the zipper of my jeans as she stares down at me.

"Even if you drop me off, I'll be right back here, and all up in the club's business. The choice is that you either know I'm here, or you're constantly looking over your shoulder to see if I am. Take your pick."

Fucking hell.

"Fine," I say through clenched teeth. "You want to put yourself in harm's way, that's your prerogative, but you're staying at the clubhouse where I can keep an eye on you."

Surprisingly, she doesn't argue. Instead, she looks smug, like she's won a prize or some shit.

This has to be the worst idea in the history of ideas though. Having her so close to the club isn't exactly the most ideal situation for my brothers or me. I need to make sure that my cock and I both stay as far away from her as possible. Dealing with the cartel sounds easier than the temptation of her.

Chapter 15

DARCY

TWO DAYS into my self-imposed prison sentence at the clubhouse, I'm about to lose my fucking mind. Between the whores, the old ladies, and Slider, I'm one smartass comment or sideways glare away from burning this place to the ground. Sure, it pissed me off when Raze ordered me to stay here, but it served a purpose other than safety for me. It gave me a chance to infiltrate the club and investigate the photos Trax gave me. Most people seemed to have been taken outside of the club, but within the walls of this place lies the beginning of my answers.

I'll admit, sneaking around this place with so many watchful eyes isn't easy, but once the booze starts flowing, my watchful keepers pass out and leave me alone to snoop around the offices. So far, I've managed to break into Voodoo's office with all it's computers and gadgets, as well as my husband's old office, but I've come up empty. Not a single shred of confirmation or evidence to support Trax's intel. To say I'm frustrated is the understatement of the year.

The only one room left on my list is Raze's office, but trying to break into it is like trying to break into the treasury at Fort Knox. After a relatively quiet afternoon, I sneak out of my temporary quarters and slink my way toward the office, only to be cut off by Dani.

"Hey Darcy," Dani smiles as she crosses into my path.

"Hey," I force out, trying like hell to keep my tone even and cool. No need to alert the masses that I'm on a mission. "You doing okay?"

"I suppose so. Missing the twins."

"I get it. Once you have kids, you never want to leave them. That's the hardest part. Especially when they're so vulnerable."

"It really is," Dani frowns.

Being away from the twins must be killing her, especially since she can only go and visit for a few short hours a day, all under Slider's watchful eye. After two failed attempts to see them, the doctor had all but barred her from being there outside of visiting hours until she fully recuperated. I can relate to how she feels. Even knowing my kids are safe where they are, it takes everything I have not to go to them. I guess that's one reason Dani and I get along so well, We're bonded by our lack of taking shit from anyone.

I should have expected her to be cheery today after her morning visit with the girls. The doctors had given her the good news that both girls are rapidly gaining weight, and could be home as early as the following week.

"Do you maybe want to hang out? I'm feeling a little cooped up, and I need to get out of our room for awhile."

"I don't know," I stall, but she flashes those sad eyes of hers at me. Dani's husband may be a part of the club, but I shouldn't punish her for the club's decisions.

"Slider is getting a deck of cards."

"You know what. Sure. A distraction sounds good right about now." It's not like I am going to get into the offices with so many people here anyway.

Worst. Fucking. Decision. Ever.

"Full house," I squeal, slamming my cards down onto the makeshift poker table made from a car hood and cinder blocks. You'd think this clubhouse would have an actual poker table, but apparently, Raze isn't one to play cards. The girls and Slider groan while I clap and bounce with excitement.

"Whose idea was it to play strip poker with her?" Ricca grumbles to Slider as she pushes her jeans down over her long legs. *Oh, shit.* Ricca picked the wrong day to be commando.

Throwing my head back, I laugh and wolf whistle as she tosses them over on the couch and tries to use use her short shirt cover her naked lower half. She smirks a me, extending her middle finger as my laughter grows louder.

Ricca's body is riddled with scars from her stint in the Twisted Tribe torture chamber last year. Each cut shines under the lights of the room, and the sheer number of them fills me with sympathy for her. I don't know how she's so comfortable in her own skin right now, but I'm betting the four shots of *Jose Cuervo* may be the culprit.

Fucking tequila.

"I'm not drunk enough for this bullshit," Ricca declares, plopping back into her chair and crossing her legs to keep Slider's eyes from wandering any farther south than they already have. I get the sneaking suspicion that Ratchet will kick Slider's ass for seeing her like this if he finds out. Even though the two of them act like whatever the fuck is happening between them is nothing, everyone knows it's just that. A fucking act.

"At least you can drink," Dani mutters, stripping

off her t-shirt and adding it to the growing pile of clothes on the floor around us. "The doctor won't let me touch the stuff so soon after my C-section, plus I've been pumping for the girls. Give Darcy another shot. Maybe she'll forget what we're playing, and we can get out of this."

A devilish grin takes over my face before I can stop it. Everyone of these fools are one hand away from losing everything, while I still have my t-shirt, bra, and panties.

"It was your fucking idea, D," Slider mutters. "If Raze comes back and sees this shit, I'll lose my prospect rocker. Distract her so we can end this before it gets any fucking worse."

That just makes me laugh even harder. "Oh, no. You're not getting out of this. If I have to be holed up here against my will, I'm going to have a little fun. It's not my fault y'all suck."

"There's no fucking way you've won three hands in a row," Slider grumbles. "I think we need to check her for cards stashed up her sleeves."

Rolling my eyes, I motion with my hands at the lack of clothes on my body. "Where exactly would I hide them, jackass? In my pussy?"

Slider's eyes grow wide and drop to the area between my legs. "I wouldn't mind checking."

"Yeah, you check my pussy for cards, and Raze will be punching you a one-way ticket to hell."

"Yeah, probably," he say with a shrug. "But it would be worth it. Who knew older chicks could be so fucking hot?" His hand falls into his lap as he adjusts himself under the table.

I don't know what comes over me, but I lean over to him and tracing my hand across his hardened bulge. "Hmm, ladies. Slider here is a shower, not a grower." He shivers at my touch, then removes my hand and places it back into my own lap.

"Not gonna happen, Darcy. I've got strict orders to keep my hands, and my dick, away from you."

I can barely control the laugh flying out of my mouth. I know damn well who issued the no touching order, and that son-of-a-bitch and I need to have a chat when he rolls in from wherever he is. No one tells me—sober or drunk—who I let into my pussy. That bastard may think he has control over me, but he doesn't have a chance in hell of stopping me from taking what I want. My mind may be clouded, but a good fuck would certainly help me drown out the demons that have taken permanent residence in my mind. Slider may not be my first choice, but he'll do.

"Stop being a pussy about showing off some skin, Slider," I say, adding a flirtatious lilt to my voice.

"You'd walk around here naked if it weren't for the guys. Besides, I won the hand, so it's time to pay the lady. Off with those clothes, big boy."

Slider slips his cut off his shoulders and lays it across the back of his chair, then reaches for the bottom of his shirt. He strips it off in one fluid motion, exposing his chiseled, tanned abs. *Jesus, how do guys get ripped like this?* Every damn man in this club looks like a fitness model. Especially Raze. If I wasn't sure I was drunk before, I am now because all I can think about now is doing a body shot off of Raze's rock hard abs of perfection. I wonder what tequila salt would taste like against his skin?

Shit fire. My brain has a hard-on for him.

"Raze is gonna fucking kill me," Slider groans again.

That's the second time he's mentioned Raze and his rules, and I'm about to lose my shit. That motherfucker isn't even here, and he's still ruining my fun. Well, as much fun as I can have being imprisoned against my will. That part's not exactly on the higher end of my fun scale.

"I don't see him around, do you? And since when did you have to turn over your balls to get a cut," I say with a smirk. "Why do you let him boss you around all the time? Aren't you a man, Slider?"

Slider's shoulders tense , his eyes growing dark

and intense. All sense of humor is gone when he slams his fists down onto the table.

"You're starting to cross the goddamn line, Darcy," he warns. "I know you're pissed to be under the club's protection, but you need to slow your goddamn roll. Raze is trying to keep you and your kids safe, and all you do is bust his fucking chops about it. He's my president, and when he says jump, I'll fucking ask how high."

I gape at him a moment before a giggle escapes my lips. Slider scowls, slumping into his chair. "Oh, you big baby," I tease, knowing I need to stop, but unable to keep the words in. "I was just trying to ruffle up those pretty feathers of yours. I was married to the former VP. I know how the club works. That doesn't mean I understand it, but by all means, die for your cause, just like my husband. At least you won't be leaving behind a family that needs you."

"Darcy, I think you need to stop," Dani says, standing from her chair. "Let's get you into bed, before this gets any worse."

Dani reaches for my arm, but I pull away from her grasp.

My laughter is long gone now. Instead, all I feel is anger and resentment at the man in front of me, and the club he represents. "No," I snap. "Someone needs to fucking tell him what he's signing up for. Do you honestly want to hand over your life to them, Slider? Have you thought about the fucking consequences that come with being in this club?" Every cell I'm made of is vibrating with rage. "This *fucking club* is the reason my husband is dead. The reason his children are growing up without him. Do you want the same thing to happen to you?"

I stumble toward Slider, but he remains silent, snatches up his discarded clothing, and heads for the exit. No. Not happening. This is the best advice he'll ever get, and he's going to listen, whether he likes it or not. He has no idea what the MC life will do to him and his future family, and he needs to hear it from the one person to experience the brunt of what it means to be in a MC.

"Hey," I call after him. "I'm still talking to you." I have to nearly run to catch up to him, but when I do, I grab his shoulder, jerking him back to face me. "Are you ready to lay down your life for these men, knowing you're risking your entire future and family? The best thing you could do right now is pack your shit and burn that cut on your back before it's too late."

Slider pushes my hand off of his shoulder, his glare boring into me. The fiery heat of his anger prickles against my skin.

"Darcy, you are either too fucking drunk or too

goddamn stupid to realize what Jagger did for this club. He saved every single man, woman, and child that make up this family. Get your fucking head out of your ass and realize that he sacrificed it all to save you and the kids. He may not be here, but none of us would have been if he not followed his instincts. I may not know the details, but I know damn well he loved his brothers enough to die for them. That's all the fucking explanation I need."

My blood is boiling as I try to understand his words through my anger. "What the fuck are you talking about? From what I've found out, my husband wasn't exactly a saint."

His words sting directly into my vulnerable, heartbroken core. How dare he say that my husband died to save us all. He needed to live for me and the kids, not die for this fucking club. We needed him more than anything. It's not fucking fair that they can just go on with their lives day after day, while I sit in mourning for the one man that completed my heart and soul.

"You are just as big of a fool as my husband was," I spit.

"I'd rather be a fool than the poor bastard who married you. You have no sense of loyalty, and that's fucking sad. I just hope your kids take after their father because they won't survive in this world if they are anything like you."

The sound of my hand smacking against his cheek cracks through the silence following his words. "You son-of-a-bitch," I seethe through gritted teeth. "Don't you *ever* speak about my kids like that. You can hate me all you want, but my kids are none of your concern."

Slider glares at me, so many unspoken words shooting out of them like arrows aimed directly at my heart. "You think you can bring down the world to make yourself feel an ounce of what it was like to be alive again, but the only thing your kind of justice will get you is a hole in the ground next to your husband." And with that parting blow, he turns and stalks toward the exit.

I move to charge after him, not willing to let this go, but a deep voice stops me in my tracks.

"What the fuck is going on here?" Raze bellows from somewhere across the room. The anger lacing his voice stops me mid-step, frozen in place. I know the look that will be on his face, but stupidly, I turn to face him. Raze's eyes are dark and filled with anger as he takes in the scene in front of him. His posture is stiff, his hands balled into fists as he stands at the entrance of the clubhouse door, Hero and Voodoo flanking him on either side. Hero's eyes fall directly onto Dani's partially-naked body, and he just grins as he shakes his head.

Ratchet shoves his way between his brothers, and before Raze can stop him, he rushes toward Ricca and drags her back toward the rooms of the clubhouse. *What in the hell was that all about?* A door slams a few seconds later, snapping me back to the reality that I'm in deep shit.

"I asked you a fucking question, prospect."

A cold chill cascades throughout my body, and goosebumps race across my skin as fear of Raze takes hold. The goosebumps disappear and make way for a slick layer of sweat that is now pumping from my pores as my heart attempts to beat out of my chest.

Slider's shoulders slump, instantly submissive to Raze and his wrath. I don't know what Raze does to his prospects to gain so much power over them, but Slider went from raging bull to cowering kitten with just one sentence. How does one man wield so much power over dozens of others that are just as hardheaded and strong as he is?

A bevy of ideas float through my semi-sober mind. Potential methods that Raze could use to subdue his brothers. This allows my imagination to picture being bound by him, and fucked into submission. Raze is oblivious to my erotic thoughts though, and continues to stare at me, waiting for a response from either of us. What would it be like to be tamed like that by him? A warm heat settles between my legs.

First, I was cold. Now, I'm sweating and aroused. Fuck, I've had too much to drink.

"Nothing, Prez," Slider mutters. "Darcy's just had too much to drink, and decided it was time to lecture me about her thoughts on our club."

Tension quivers through Raze's shoulders as his eyes set back on me. "That so?"

I can't even form words as the heat from his gaze sears into me. The only thing I can do is nod.

That's all he needs to make his next move. Before I even know what's happening, Raze stalks over to where I stand, bends at the waist and throws me over his shoulder. His rough hands grip my thighs tightly as I squirm, desperate to wiggle out of his grasp.

"Put me down you, bast—" I stammer, but his gruff voice shuts me up.

"Party's over, ladies."

Heavy boots stomp across the hardwood as Raze heads out of the room and down the hallway. He kicks the door of his room open and carries me inside, right over to his freshly-made bed, were he throws me on top of the thick blankets.

I gape up at him in shock as he jabs one finger in my direction. "You stay in this fucking room until you sober up. We'll settle this bullshit in the morning."

"But, Raze, I—" I try to stammer out, but the only response I get is the sound of the bedroom door slamming and being locked from the outside. I listen to Raze's footsteps travel down the hall, back into the main room, before fading completely.

I'm so fucking screwed.

Chapter 16

RAZE

DARCY HAD FILLED my thoughts the entire ride down to Mexico. Her refusal to stay out of harm's way is pissing me off to no end, but I can't deny the nagging desire that befalls me every time I'm in her presence. The rise and fall of her gorgeous tits in anger is one of the hottest fucking things that I have ever seen. When her arms fold over them, a lightning strike shoots straight to my cock. I shouldn't want to touch her. Not like this. She was my brother's wife, the mother of his children, but deep down, the feelings are there, nagging at me constantly to take what I want. I want to know what she feels like beneath me as her pussy takes my cock, or to see her riding out her orgasm on top of me. Maybe it's the dry spell from sex talking, or that everywhere I turn, things seem to point in her direction, but I can't get her out of my head.

Her husband was my brother, and that alone should curtail my need for her, but lately, it doesn't even register on the fucked-up-o-meter. Even the timing is off. Jagger's only been dead a little over a year and so many new things have come to light about my wife in the recent weeks, but damnit, my thoughts only drift to her. To those tits. To that mouth I want to fuck.

Would it be so bad? Neither of us have anyone. Not anymore. Could we make an arrangement?

I shake my head to wipe away that thought. She'd never go for that. I think back to the look she gave me last night. Her face was turned up in furious anger, but beneath that fiery gaze lingered something else. Something more primal than I think she even realizes. She needs relief herself. Who the hell knows? Maybe we can make some kind of mutually beneficial agreement to scratch our itches and fuck it out of our systems. The only way to know is to ask and hope to hell she doesn't kick my teeth in for suggesting it.

My thoughts are still on her when we cross the border and head toward the address Voodoo had tracked down. Hero, Tyson, Ratchet, Thrasher, and I ride our bikes, while Voodoo and Irons follow in the

SUV fully loaded with Voodoo's toys. You'd have thought it was fucking Christmas when he started loading up some of his newer technology for this run.

We pull into a shady remote hotel on the outskirts of Tijuana. This will be our home base for however long it takes. One of the club's former suppliers delivers the weapons we'd stowed here, and after unloading the SUV, we all separate to our rooms and begin prepping for our mission. As I strap on my double-sided bulletproof vest, I go over my mental checklist of weapons. I want to make sure I have everything I need should this shit go south.

After strapping on two calf holsters with knives, I shove two more sheathed knives down the inside of my boots. Guns are more efficient, but when it comes to self-defense, having a knife or four hidden away is never a bad thing. I pull my shirt back over my head and grab my shoulder holster. After clicking the straps in place, I pull out my two Glock .45s and tuck them into their sheaths, then grab a couple of extra clips and throw them into the pockets of my jeans.

Just as I finish up, someone raps on the door.

Outside, Hero and Ratchet look as armed as I am.

"You ready for this?" Hero asks.

"I'm ready to bury this shit and move on, if that's what you're asking."

Ratchet and Hero both nod, and we make our way down to the waiting SUV with Voodoo and Irons. Although the motorcycles would be faster, they're not exactly inconspicuous. The name of today's mission is re-con, and we need to look like any normal tourists, minus the guns and knives. I slide into the front seat, while Voodoo loads his drone in the back. When I asked him to pack it back at the clubhouse, you would have thought you were telling a kid that you were taking him to Disneyland. I don't understand his obsession with technology, but maybe I'm too old school for it. If it wasn't a necessity, I doubt I would even have a cell phone. Being off the grid is far more appealing to me than being connected twenty-four hours a day.

He slides into the vehicle just as Tyson and Thrasher walk out of their room in plain clothes and head for their bikes. I elected to keep Tyson and Thrasher behind to search for information from some of the club's former drug contracts down here. Even if the club is legitimate now, I still keep tabs on our former business partners, just in case shit were to go south. Some might call it stalking, but to me, it's self-preservation. Insurance that the status quo won't be changed.

Rolling down the window, I motion for Thrasher and Tyson.

"You both know the drill," I say, once they're close enough. "If the situation isn't ideal, high tail to the meet point. No need to draw any unwanted attention. Make sure to check in with me or V every hour, and we'll do the same. If shit goes radio silent on either end, drop everything and leave. Got it?"

"Yeah, Prez. We're good."

"Be safe, my brothers," I plead.

Voodoo turns on the ignition, as Thrasher and Tyson roll out of the parking lot. The GPS comes to life on the dashboard, and V punches in the coordinates of our destination. The screen flashes, and then a route pops up on the map. He puts the SUV into gear and follows the robotic male voice barking out instructions.

"Is it just me or is the female voice less annoying than the dude's?" Hero asks from the back.

"Nah, man. You're just used to being bossed around by your old lady," Irons chimes in with a laugh. "Do your balls like living in her purse now?"

I hear a whack from behind me and turn to see Irons clutching his shoulder. Hero just smiles as he shrugs at my glare.

"Do I need to come back there and separate you two?"

Hero continues to smile as he turns away and

faces the window, and Irons just shrugs. "He punches like a bitch anyway. My arm is already fine."

"Cool it, Irons," I warn.

"He makes too easy," Irons replies. "Like taking candy from a fucking baby."

"It's your funeral," I say. "Tell me, Irons. Are you a black casket with a priest kind of guy, or do you want one of those viking funerals? Might as well get that out of the way now if you're going to keep this shit up."

Irons throws his hands up in the air. "The fuck, man?"

Hero doesn't even blink. "He'll never see it coming."

I laugh as a horrified look forms on Irons' face. He has no idea that Hero is fucking with him. It's too goddamn funny to let him in on the joke, so I let him stew. The car and its occupants hush to a silence as the miles go by. Fifteen minutes later, the GPS gives the warning that we're coming up on our destination. Suddenly, Voodoo veers off next to another boarded-up building just south of our target and parks behind it.

"What the fuck? Robo dick says we have a half a mile left to go," Hero grumbles, his hand gripping the oh shit bar above the window. "Could we get a little warning before you peel off toward a goddamn building?"

Voodoo puts the SUV in park and swivels to face Hero. "Did you piss in your frilly panties there, VP?"

"You wish you could get into these panties," Hero replies, his face not even cracking a smile. "Now, what's with the brake first, explain later?"

Voodoo turns and points up the road.

"There's some cars parked across the road. We'll hide out here and watch from a distance. Once they leave, I'll fly the drone in to check the exterior of the building and monitor for motion before we go in to check it out."

"So, James Bond shit?" Hero asks, his brow raised.

Voodoo chuckles. "Yes, James Bond shit. Would you rather go in there guns blazing and hope no one's home?"

"Damnit. I've always wanted to do a stake-out, but I'd hoped to have a sexy blonde partner instead of you three. I could have passed the time quicker with her," Irons says.

Laughter fills the small space as Voodoo grabs his binoculars and watches the cars on the other side of the road. We sit there for hours, sweltering in the hot desert sun, until finally, the parked cars begin to pull out one by one.

"It's show time," Voodoo announces once the last car is out of sight. He pulls up the latch and hops out of the car. The back hatch is open before any of us make it back to him. Voodoo's hands fly while he fusses over the hunk of flying metal is currently taking residence in the back. He slowly lowers it to the ground, then reaches back inside for the remote control. Stepping away from the drone, he motions for us to follow. Methodically, he flicks a series of switches, and the propellers of the drone begin to rotate, kicking up puffs of dust around it.

"Time to earn your keep, Rhonda."

Hero, Irons, and I quickly look at each other in confusion.

Jesus Christ. He named the fucking thing.

Slowly, the drone lifts from the ground and ascend higher and higher into the air. Voodoo walks beside it, guiding it along with the controller away, sending it away from the building and toward our target. At the very edge of the building, he flicks on the camera screen.

Together, we huddle around him and watch as it flies over the dry, dusty sand. Within just a couple minutes, the drone hovers outside of what looks to be an abandoned building. Voodoo expertly maneuvers the device, pausing at each window, trying to get a visual of the interior. It doesn't work. The windows are too dirty to see through. Giving up, he continues to hover, scanning the grounds around the outside of the building before returning the drone back to us.

After it's safe return, Voodoo tucks it away, and we form a circle to decide our next plan of action.

"Place looks empty, but looks can be deceiving," Voodoo says. "How do you want to do this?"

"There's a backdoor," I reply. "It will be the easiest place to disguise our entry point. Hero, you take the front. I'll circle around back, and Voodoo, you be on the look-out for unexpected visitors. Irons, I want you to stay behind we check this shit out."

"You got it, Boss," Irons grunts.

V adjusts his vest and draws out his weapon. "Let's go break down a door. Can I at least kick it in? I've always wanted to do that. Stallone makes it look so easy in the movies."

"Fine, you can kick it down, but for fuck's sake, stow the cheesy action movie lines. I can literally see them running through your head."

"You ruin all the fun," he quips.

Slowly, the three of us move from our hiding spot and head toward the building. Voodoo darts and ducks behind cacti and other objects, as if he's the guy from *Mission Impossible*. He really needs to get out of the tech room more. I think those action movies he's constantly streaming are taking away his grip on reality.

As we get closer, Hero signals something, moving his hands, pointing and waving in different directions. Voodoo and I both stop, our heads tilted as his hands fly in a flurry in front of him. Once he's done, Voodoo shrugs his shoulder and throws up a middle finger in response. I grab the back of Voodoo's shirt and shove him in the direction that Hero had indicated.

We stalk toward the back door, and I point at Voodoo to live out his life's dream of kicking down the door. He smiles like a crazy man as he steps back and throws up his leg in a high kick to the center door. The rotted wood shatters on impact.

"Chuck Norris ain't got shit on me," Voodoo grins, but I shove him out of the way and head straight into the building with my gun drawn.

The light in the room is muted by the layers of dust that have gathered on the walls. Broken furniture litters the space, along with piles of trash. The wallpaper is peeling away, confirming our assumption that this house hasn't been occupied in quite a while. I scan the room once more, watching for movement before moving on to the next room. Three rooms later, Hero appears, holstering his gun.

"Clear up front and upstairs."

"Same for the back," I reply, holstering my own weapon. "You see anything up there?"

"Nah. It's the same as this room; trash and dirt everywhere."

Wiping the sweaty layer of dust from my face, I release a frustrated sigh. Why the fuck would Maj's phone lead us here if there isn't anything to find? It doesn't make any goddamn sense.

Voodoo's face pops through the back door and smiles. "This place is in need of a serious deep clean and remodel. You find anything?"

"Just a fucking dead end and dust mites," Hero grunts.

Voodoo nods. "Well, if you ladies are finished playing in the dirt, I found a door out here that you might want to see."

Hero and I glance at each other, then hurry out of the door after V. He leads us to the northern side of the building and leans down, pulling up on a heavy metal door partially covered with dirt. He yanks on it, and it pops open, a cloud of dust migrating into the air around it. As the dust settles, my eyes land on a rickety set of stairs leading down into a darkened hole.

"Shall we draw straws to see who gets to go down there?" Voodoo asks.

Retrieving my gun, I push Voodoo out of the way.

Hero pulls a flashlight from his pocket and tosses it to me. With a thankful nod, I click on the light and take the first step down. Each board creaks under my weight, and I pray with each step I take that they don't break. Finally, my feet hit the solid floor at the bottom with a thud. The beam of my flashlight scans around the room until something shiny reflects back at me.

Shine the light on the walls, I search for a light switch of some kind, and after a moment I see the switch near the stairs and flick it on. Light illuminates the room, and the breath is nearly sucked out of me. Several tables covered in traces of white powder and silver scales are scattered inside.

Shit. This is a drug packaging room.

Running my finger along the top of the table, I collect some of the white powder on my finger. Judging by the look and feel, I'm betting this is fucking cocaine. Besides the drugs, the tables hold no more information, but my eyes catch the flicker of something else in the corner of the room.

Stalking over to it, I shove a table out of the way, and a folded up piece of paper flutters to the ground. Reaching down, I pick it up, dust it off, and unfold it. *Holy shit. This is it.*

The map of Mexico has intersecting lines drawn all over it in pen. With a grin, I stuff the map into my cut and move the table back to its original position before heading back upstairs.

Voodoo and Hero are pacing near the door when I ascend the steps and slam the door back down.

"Find anything useful?" Hero asks.

Dragging the map out of my pocket, I slap it into Hero's hands. His face flashes with surprise before he passes it off to V.

"We've found the golden ticket, boys. Let's get this shit back home so V can work his magic."

Chapter 17

Darcy

Morning comes far too early when the rays of light set off a pounding explosion in my head. I groan and roll back over, trying to force myself back to sleep through this hangover, but it doesn't work. While I lie here, trying to force my head to stop spinning, flickers of scenes from the night before run through my mind.

A sense of guilt and the need to apologize for my drunken rant to Slider coils in my stomach as nausea hits me hard and fast. I bolt from the bed and realize I'm not in the room I've been staying in. *Oh, God. Where's the bathroom?*

But it's too late. I can't hold it in, so I end up spilling my guts into a discarded baseball cap I find on the floor. Wiping the vomit from my mouth, I take in the room around me, noting how much bigger it is than mine. There's a lounge area with a couch and a television lining the wall opposite of the large king-size bed. My stomach falls as my gaze falls on a photo of Raze and his kids sitting on the dresser next to me.

How the fuck did I end up in here?

"Did you just hurl in my hat?" a gruff voice asks from the direction of the couch. A large hand shoots up in a stretch.

Fuck.

Raze lifts his body from the couch, his defined muscular back stretching as he moves. Even feeling as awful as I do, just watching those hard muscles contract sends a heated vibration to my core. He stretches his arms out once more, then turns and stalks his way toward me wearing only a pair of basketball shorts.

Double fuck.

A blush creeps across on my cheeks as I watch him draw closer. I don't know why those V muscles are so hot, but I'm starting to think V stands for vagina fire starters. Jesus, I just want to run my tongue across them.

Get ahold of yourself, woman. He's just a man with a nice body. Well, a really nice body. Fuck, the best body you've ever seen. Goddamnit. This isn't helping.

A shit-eating grin forms on his face as he brushes past me and heads into what I can only guess is the bathroom, picking up the puke-filled hat on his way. As soon as the door closes, I rush to the mirror above his dresser and peek at my appearance. *Oh my God.* My hair is a fuzzy rat's nest with flyaways going in every direction. Smeared mascara encircles my eyes like a fucking raccoon. Mortified, I lick the sleeve of the large t-shirt I'm wearing and desperately try to scrub off the dark mascara ring of shame, but it only makes it worse.

As soon as the toilet flushes and Raze exits the bathroom, and I rush past him, shutting the door. Quietly, I search for some soap to clean off my make-up, and a brush to tame this wild beast atop my head. A soft knock comes at the door, and before I can answer, it opens. Raze's large hand inside, clutching my small make-up kit. *How the hell did he get that?* Without even taking the chance to ask, I rip it away from him and close the door again, making sure to lock it this time.

I make quick work of cleaning myself up, without the luxury of a long, hot shower, only because my clothes are still in my room, and I will not risk walking out of here in just a towel. My mental willpower may be strong, but the urge to climb him like a tree is growing by the second. The next time I get some alone time, I need to get this shit sorted out with my ovaries because they seem to be in overdrive. Sure, it's been over a year since I've had sex, but the idea of popping my widow's cherry with Raze doesn't settle well with me.

"You okay in there?" he calls out from the other side of the door. "You didn't fall in, did you?"

"No," I quickly reply back. "Give me like two more minutes and I'll be out of your hair."

I handle my business, and as I'm washing my hands, a smell wafts from beneath the door. My stomach groans and churns at the same time when I recognize the delicious aroma of freshly-cooked bacon and eggs. Cracking the door, I see Raze leaning over in front of the couch, setting something down in front of it.

"You hungry?" he asks without ever looking up. "Best cures for a hangover is either eat food or drink more, but I figure you might be more of a food kind of woman."

Hesitant, I pad over to the couch and peer at his offering. Raze has not only brought a breakfast big enough to feed the entire clubhouse, but he has also thrown together a makeshift table from a piece of plywood and two blocks. The smell of freshly-fried bacon wafts into my nose, and my stomach grumbles again. Without a word, Raze grabs a plate and piles two huge heaps of bacon and eggs onto it, then hands it to me. Next, he reaches back and retrieves a bottle of hot sauce.

"You like hot sauce on your eggs?"

I gape at him. *How does he know how I like my eggs?* Somehow, that both delights me and frightens me at the same time. *How closely has he been watching me all these years?* My own husband never remembered the hot sauce on the rare occasions he cooked me breakfast in bed.

Accepting the bottle in his had, I shake it, adding five drops to my eggs before handing it back. "How do you know about that?"

Raze chuckles softly as he begins to fill his own plate. "Don't all southern girls like hot sauce?" I study him carefully, not buying this little fib. Finally, he concedes. "I saw you pull a bottle out of your purse a couple of times you were here."

I lift a forkful of eggs to my mouth and moan as the flavor hits my tongue. I don't know why, but food nearly always tastes better after a night of drinking. Even the shittiest pizza or burrito place seems like a five-star restaurant after a round with *Jose Cuervo*. Raze adds what looks like a half of a pound of bacon to his plate before he plops down next to me and digs into his meal. I stifle a giggle as the vision of the beast from that Disney movie pops into my head. Raze could totally play him in a live-action version with his table manners.

I must be smirking because he stops mid-bite and just stares at me, his brow furrowed. "What?" he mumbles, a piece of bacon hanging out of his mouth. "I'm hungry."

"Nothing," I whisper, then turn my attention back to my own plate.

We eat in silence, but as good as it is, I mostly just move the food around on my plate. A lingering question takes hold of my mind. Eating breakfast together like this is intimate, and I feel so comfortable with him. The whole thing is disconcerting. As badly as I've behaved toward him and the club, and especially after what all I had spewed out last night in my tequila rage, my body is gravitating toward his. Maybe it's the pull of two people both mourning and seeking out the truth.

"Why am I in your room and not my own?" I whisper.

Raze tenses, then lays his empty plate on the table, before turning to face me. His blue eyes sparkle with intensity as he takes the plate from my hand and lays it on top of his. My heart clenches and jumps into my throat. *Am I sweating?* Trying to keep calm, I rub my hands on my thighs.

"How long has it been since you've been on a ride?" he asks.

I frown. Where did that come from? "A ride?"

"Yeah, a ride," he replies. "You know what? Never mind. I know the answer."

Raze rises from the couch and gathers up the dirty plates. "How about you go get dressed and we'll go out on a ride? I think the fresh air will do us both good, and we can talk in private."

I hesitate. The last time I'd been on the back of a motorcycle had been just before Brent died. I have to admit, I've missed the feel of the wind, and the excitement of being on the back of his Harley. To feel him reach back and grasp my thigh gently when we were about to take a sharp curve.

I missed that, but more, I missed him. Riding with Raze seems so wrong, but I'd be kidding myself if I said I didn't want to embrace that feeling again. It would be almost like he was still here with me.

"Um, sure," I say slowly. "Give me about twenty minutes."

Raze nods and steps out of the room with our plates, leaving me in dumbfounded silence on the couch.

Nothing about today makes any sense to me. His softness, my unrelenting need to be near him, or my need to touch him. Something is stirring inside of me, and I don't like it. Not one damn bit.

But this ride… it could change everything. I don't really have choice. Raze has what I want, and the only way I'm going to get it is from him. Brent had taken his secrets to the grave. Maybe Raze could shed more insight on why he did that. Maybe I didn't know my husband as well as I thought I did, but a man wrapped up in drugs and whores wouldn't have come home to his family every single night with a smile on his face. That type of man wouldn't have come home at all.

Slipping into the bathroom, I quickly shower and throw my hair up in a loose, wet bun. Back in the bedroom, I find a fresh set of clothes laid out neatly on Raze's bed. I don't know what bothers me more; the fact that Raze rifled through my clothes and picked out something I would have chosen myself, or the fact he made his bed. Shaking off the confusion, I fasten on my black bra and slip the Harley tank top over my head. I grab the jeans and yank them up my thighs before slipping on a pair of thick, black leather riding boots sitting at the foot of the bed. They aren't mine, but damn if they aren't the right size for me. The tank top will keep me cool enough, but the thick jeans and boots will shield my legs from being burned by the pipes.

A sigh escapes my lips when I realize something is missing from my ensemble. My cut with Brent's property patch is safely tucked away at home. The feel and smell of the leather was as soothing to me as his road name branded on my back. Call it being anti-feministic, but I liked knowing I belonged to someone, and that I was cherished and protected. Now, I'm nothing more than a faceless nomad playing biker girl and thinking about how life used to be. I may not have fit in here like the other hard-as-nails women, but I do miss pieces of the club life.

A motorcycle revs outside, and I know my trip down memory lane has to come to an end. Snatching my sunglasses off the bed, I pop them on the top of my head as I hurry out of the room. The clubhouse is quiet today, which is surprising for a weekend, but I'm thankful I don't have to face the eyes of everyone after what transpired last night. There's probably rumors of me warming the president's bed flying around right now, and I don't want to deal with any of it. Not when I'm so close to getting my answers.

Outside, Raze is already sitting astride his bike, talking to Slider. A pang of guilt punches me right in the gut when Slider's angry eyes lock onto mine. He doesn't even acknowledge me before walking away. From what I can remember, the things I had said to him were cruel and unwarranted, but how do I apologize for something I truly believe? The club has a lot of black marks against it, but even I can't deny that sometimes you have to live the way you know. Everyone has sins staining their souls, but it's what you do to redeem yourself and wash them away that means something in the end.

I approach the bike and Raze scoots up on the seat, extending a plain, black helmet to me. Before I take it, I take down damp bun and pull the extra elastic band from my pocket. I weave my hair into two braids on either side of my head before putting the helmet on and safely securing the strap.

Raze chuckles as he straps on his own helmet. "Nice braids."

I swing my leg over the back of the tank and haul my body over the warmed metal. Placing my feet on the pegs he had popped out for me, I settle against the soft back of the bitch seat. It took me three years to convince Brent to get a bike that was more comfortable for me. Raze had clearly bought this bike with the intention of having a partner to ride with him, yet I can't remember the last time I saw Maj on the back of his bike, or any other woman for that matter.

Raze pops the kickstand and balances the both of us on two tires. Once balanced, he reaches around and pulls my arms around his hard stomach. I jerk my away at first, but he just chuckles and tugs me harder against him.

Being this close is just for safety, Darcy. It doesn't mean a thing.

Once I settle against his wide, muscled back, Raze pats my leg, pulls back on the throttle, and sets the bike into motion. We cruise down the Pacific Coast Highway for several hours before stopping at a mom and pop café near Pismo Beach. The wind in my hair feels like an old friend circling me in their embrace. To be honest, I never thought I'd be on the back of a bike again. The trips Jagger and I had taken were some of the best moments of my life, but after he died, I didn't expect to ride again. But with Raze, my love of riding is coming back. He parks his bike near the building, and helps both me and my stiff legs off the bike. I stretch, trying to relax my groaning muscles. Raze slides off the motorcycle with ease. *Of course he does.* He leans against the seat, watching as I fidget and shake, trying to wake up my muscles.

"Shut up and quit laughing at me," I snap. "It's been a while, okay?"

Raze raises his hands in surrender, not even bothering to hide his chuckle. "I didn't say shit, darlin', but a seasoned rider like you should know to move your legs more on a long ride. We wouldn't want you throwing a blood clot, now would we?"

I reach up, unfasten my helmet, and toss it right at him. He catches it just before it smacks him square in the face, and his smirk morphs into a frown.

"What the hell was that for?"

"For laughing at my misery and pain, jackass." I smirk back and stalk toward the door.

A sudden flash of heat hits me, and I swear I can feel his eyes trained on my backside as I walk away. Not that it bothers me that he's possibly checking me out, or that I can feel his eyes on me without even looking back to confirm. When I reach for the door, his large hand pushes mine aside, and he sidesteps in front of me, holding the door open like a gentleman. Well, in his case, a tattooed, rough-looking gentleman capable of sweet-talking his way into any woman's panties with just a few words. Butterflies erupt in my belly while I try to put my raging hormones on ice.

Raze and me? Yeah, that's not going to happen. Take a chill pill, hormones.

Raze's hand falls to the small of my back, sending a sensation of warmth prickling all along my skin. He falls in line behind me, leading me to an open booth facing the beach. His large frame struggles to fit into the tiny seat, but he forces himself in, his knees pressed snugly against mine. he looks hilariously uncomfortable, and I can't help but chuckle. He gives me a warning glare, and I press my lips together.

The waitress comes and places two worn, plastic-covered menus in front of us, her gaze never leaving Raze. I roll my eyes as she fumbles over her words as she attempts to recite the specials.

"Today, we have... the um... spicy fish tacos, and the um... steamed crab panties. I mean, shit, the steamed crab platter," she stammers, her cheeks staining a deep crimson.

"Well, Mary," Raze replies, "while I do like my panties steamed, I think I'll have an order of the fish tacos with an ice-cold beer, and the lady will have whatever she wants."

I bite back a laugh. "I'll have the same, except I'd like an extra sweet tea, please."

I hand the menus back to Mary, who just stands in frozen silence until the man in the kitchen yells her name. It takes three times before she snaps out of her daze.

"That happen often?" I tease, dragging my eyes to Raze.

"Only with women I don't find attractive. The ones I'm actually interested in seem unfazed by my charm and wit."

I stifle a laugh as Mary and her steamed panties sashay back to our table with our drink order. She lingers just a little too long, leaning across Raze to slide his drink on the table, her tiny boobs right in his face. Jealousy festers inside me when I see Raze smirking at her as she pulls away.

Why the fuck am I jealous of the little waitress tart flaunting her tits in his face?

I unwrap my straw from the paper and sip on my tea as I watch little miss steamed panties nearly flitter back to the kitchen.

"Charm and wit, huh? Looks like your little friend there is far more interested in the D than the charm and wit part of you."

Raze laughs. "Well, I'll let you in on a little secret. I may have a good-looking mug, but my charm and wit reside somewhere a bit farther south, if you catch my drift."

I spew out my drink in surprise, my cheeks burning. Raze fists a handful of napkins and wipes his tea-covered face.

He smirks. "I didn't know you were a spitter, darlin'."

Snatching the napkins from his hand, I scrub the tea from my lips, then ball them up and toss them on the table. Just then, Mary slinks over with our food and sets the plates down in front of us. The spicy seafood smell radiating from my plate makes my stomach groan. Without a word, I grab one of the tacos and nearly shove the whole thing in my mouth.

Raze watches in horror as I devour it in just two bites.

"Fuck me sideways, Darcy. I had no idea you could fit that much in your mouth at once."

"Food is the only thing going into my mouth," I say, giving him a pointed look. "So you might as well stow that knowledge into the useless information portion of your brain."

Raze smirks and takes a bite of his taco. A drip of sauce sits at the corner of his mouth, and his tongue flicks out to get it. Watching his tongue swipe along his wide lips makes me bite my own. What makes matters worse is that he does it again, knowing damn well I'm watching. Shifting uncomfortably in my seat, I drop my gaze to my plate and focus on the food in front of me.

Two tacos later, my stomach is nearly past that uncomfortable full point where one more bite may make it explode. Taking the paper napkin that came with my silverware, I wipe the corners of my mouth only to see Raze staring.

"You know, darlin', napkins aren't exactly environmentally friendly. Should have just used your tongue, or let me use mine."

How has he gone from a pissed pit bull to a cheesy, line dropping, college frat boy in the last twenty-four hours?

"You'd like that, wouldn't you?" I quip. "This tongue is also staying in my mouth."

"Too bad." He smirks. "I can think of far better uses for that tongue than just sitting in your pretty little mouth."

I shrug my shoulders, pretending to be indifferent to his off-the-cuff flirtations. Uneasy about what is transpiring, I place my elbows on the table and cradle my face in my hands. Me doing this serves two purposes. Shutting off my mind, and hiding my face from his heated gaze.

"Don't hide that pretty face, Darcy. I see that little smirk of yours through the cracks between your fingers. You ain't fooling anyone, darlin'."

Pretending to be offended, I lift my face from my hands just in time for Mary to come along and clear our plates. She hands Raze the bill, and he takes a few bills from his wallet, telling her to keep the change.

"How about a change of scenery?" he asks. "Maybe something a little more comfortable than this seat built for skinny bitches so we can talk. How about the beach? I have a towel in my saddlebag."

I nod and slide from the vinyl-clad bench with ease, while Raze fumbles to break free. Once he stands, his hand falls yet again to the small of my back as he ushers me back out of the door. We walk back to the bike in silence, and when he walks past me to retrieve the blanket, his hand brushes against mine, sending another jolt of heat straight to my belly. He hesitates only a second at our momentary contact before grabbing the towel, a pair of sunglasses, and ushering me to the beach in front of the café.

We walk twenty or so feet before Raze stops and selects a secluded spot in the sand near the water. His large form plops to the ground as soon as the towel is laid down. He reaches up and pulls me down, making me land right in his lap. I try to scramble away, but he holds me there for a just a second before letting me go.

"Sorry," I mumble.

"Nothing to be sorry about, darlin'. I didn't mind having you in my lap, even if it was an accident."

"Why do you do that?" I whisper. "Why do you flirt with me?"

"It's just how I'm wired, darlin'. I think it helps lighten the mood."

Raze grins, and that's when I know he's lying out of his teeth. My accidental slip into his lap wasn't an accident at all. He may not own up to it, but I can tell his intentions were far from pure.

I roll my eyes, and decide for a change of subject.

"So, what do you want to talk about that required a trip all the way up here?"

Raze sighs and adjusts his sunglasses to the top of his head. His eyes are glazed over with an unreadable emotion, and even under his shirt, I can see the muscles filled with tension. "I needed to get away from the club and everything going on lately. Figured you did, too."

"That doesn't answer my question, Raze."

"You're right. I'm stalling. I don't know how to just talk and not demand shit. I've been in charge far too long to just shoot the shit with someone," he admits, fumbling over his words. Then he turns and locks his eyes on me. "We need to talk about what I walked in on last night between you and Slider. Did you really mean that shit about the club? About what happened with Jagger?"

A lump forms in my throat. "I'll be brutally honest with you. I don't remember half of what I said, but judging by the look I got from Slider this morning, and now these questions from you, I can only imagine it's bad."

"You told Slider to get out for the sake of his future family and his own life. Do you really think being a part of this MC signs away your life?"

My heart hammers inside my chest. The next words to come out of my mouth need to be well thought out and meticulously planned if I want to keep being in this club to search for confirmation of Brent's wrongdoings. "Do you ever feel like the one person in your life that you should be able to trust whole-heartedly may not be the same person everyone else sees or knows?"

Raze winces, and I know he's thinking about his ex-wife.

"Think about having the happiness in your life ripped away in an instant. Ripped away so quickly that no matter how hard you pray, cry, or fight, there's nothing you can do to change the past. That's what happened the day Brent died."

"You aren't the only one that feels that way."

I nod. "Maybe, but I'm alone. Not your or your club. My kids don't have a father. My daughter will never know her father, and do you know why? Your club. Your club took away my family."

Raze reaches over and takes my hand from my lap. The zing of the connection instantly snaps my eyes to his face. Pain and sorrow swirl within the crystal-blue pool of his eyes.

"That's where you're wrong, Darcy. An MC is a family. We support each other when shit hits the fan, and we laugh when things actually go right for fucking once. Brent wanted you to continue to be a part of this family, and this is where you need to be."

"And that's why I shut myself off from this world," I insist. "At times, I feel like I barely knew him. He kept so many secrets from me because of the club. Being a woman in this world isn't exactly easy when you can't express your fears the one person who is literally on this Earth to help you battle them. It's been a year, and even though I miss him with every fiber of my being, I feel like I didn't even know him at all."

Raze squeezes my hand. "Darcy, Jagger loved you. You have to know that, right? Just because he couldn't share everything with you doesn't mean he didn't trust you. It was to protect you and the kids from anything blowing back on you if shit hit the fan."

"But that's the point," I say, my frustration growing. "I couldn't help him any more than I can help you because my place isn't in your meeting room. It's outside of it, hoping that when you walk out, I still have a place in finding the answers."

"The answers aren't for you to find out, darlin'."

Ripping my hand away, I scramble to get away from the heat radiating off his body. The ache between my legs is nearly at its boiling point, even with the grim topic of our conversation. The need to flee overwhelms my sentences, as the words I'm about to say fly out of my mouth uncontrolled.

"That's where you are wrong. He was my husband, and I deserve to know what really happened. I deserve to know how he died, Raze. I know it wasn't an accident."

"Don't," he growls.

"Don't what? Seek the answers? Seek revenge?"

"Don't call me that name," he bites out. "To you, I'm Michael."

Micheal? His words hit me like a bucket of ice water. "Wait. What? I've always called you by your road name. Why can't I call you that anymore?"

"Because that's what I want you to call me." His eyes flare, and I know with just that look he's serious about this.

"That doesn't answer the question, Raze. Why should I call you by your given name now, after all this time?"

"Michael, Darcy," he insists. "My name is Michael. Raze is for the club. Michael is only for you and my mother."

I know he is trying to throw me off this line of questioning, but I will not relent. I need to hear it from his own lips. "Stop trying to distract me with this name bullshit and just admit that Brent was murdered. That's all I want to hear. Please, give me the absolution of knowing the truth."

Raze, or should I say Michael, shoves himself

away and stands, and I do the same, making damn sure I'm face to face with him. I square my shoulders and purse my lips, ready to fight this one to the grave. Michael begins to walk away before whipping around and grabbing me by the shoulders. I push my hands against his hard chest, trying to keep some distance between us, but he pushes against me and moves his body closer.

"You want the truth?" he seethes, his heated breath warming my face. His lips are only inches from mine, and I suck in a breath deep, the smells of warm leather and clean ocean breeze filling my senses. "Brent *was* murdered for his involvement with the club. Is that what you wanted to hear?"

"Yes," I cry. "That's what I've been asking all along. But it's not enough. I need to know why."

"You got your answer," he snaps. " And that's all I'm prepared to give you. I shouldn't have even told you that much."

"But that's not—" I say, but before I can finish my sentence, his hands slide from my shoulder to the back of my neck, and his lips crash down onto mine. He cradles my head in his hands, his rough lips foreign against my soft ones, but they draw me in, my hands gliding up from his chest and around to the back of his neck. He grips the braids on either side of my head as he draws me closer, sealing our bodies together until my breasts are smashed against his hard chest.

Each moment our lips are intertwined, I can feel his heart pounding in his chest, matching its rhythm to my own. His lips part, and his tongue breaks my pursed seal, invading my mouth. His tongue caresses mine, but suddenly, he rips himself away and takes a few steps back, leaving us both breathless and panting.

His face is twisted with guilt, and I can only assume it must mirror in my own. My fingers brush against my swelling lips, and my guilt is soon replaced by a sense of betrayal of my husband's memory. How could one man that leads so many others wear his heart on his sleeve like this?

Michael has always had a presence of power, but standing in front of me right now is a broken man who had needed something as simple as a kiss to ground him. I doubt Maj would ever realize how much she destroyed this man, and in that process, the heart and soul of this club. All along, I've thought the loss of my husband would be Michael's undoing, but I see now that it was the betrayal of his wife that dealt the killing blow.

"Michael?" I whisper. "Is Maj dead?"

His eyes lift to mine, then his shoulders slump as he releases a heavy sigh. His one momentary show of weakness is instantly wiped away when his shoulders square off and his face grows hard. "My ex-wife is none of your concern, Darcy. It would be best if you'd leave the ghosts of my past buried."

"But Michael, I—"

"I said leave it alone, Darcy," he snaps, then he snatches up the towel and stalks toward his bike.

Standing alone in the blowing ocean breeze, I realize he'd just slammed the walls between us right back up, shutting me out once more.

Only one question remains.

What has he done with his wife?

Chapter 18

RAZE

I BERATE myself the entire trip back to the clubhouse with her warm body pressed tightly against mine. In one moment, I lost the control I had on my desire to feel her, and look where I ended up; riding home with her at my back, forcing myself not to lick my lips and relive the taste of her tropical fruit lip gloss. Fuck she smells so good. I've never noticed a woman's scent before, but Darcy smells like sunshine after the rain. Maybe it's the type of lotion or shampoo she uses, but it's fucking intoxicating.

I thought for a split second that maybe our kiss would be the turning point in my attraction to Darcy, but all hopes of that was obliterated as soon as she muttered my ex-wife's name. I know it was a heat of the moment question, but feeling what I did, my lips pressed against hers, and then hearing Maj's name from those lips had killed the mood for me. Who am I kidding? Darcy is still in love with a ghost, and frankly, that alone should deter me. Jagger was my fucking brother, and I shouldn't feel these things I feel when I see her and that perfect ass walk in and out of a room. I shouldn't want to watch her every move, or feel her writhe beneath me as I fuck her senseless. I damn well shouldn't want to know what it's like to feel her brand of love.

Get a grip, man. I know you thought this was a good idea, but hit the fucking abort button while you can.

It's late evening by the time we pull into the clubhouse parking lot, and as soon as the kickstand is down, Darcy bolts off my motorcycle like her hair is on fire. She rushes in through the clubhouse door, leaving me alone with my dangerous thoughts. I sigh and swing my legs over the bike. A slow clap echoes off the building, and I jerk my head toward the noise, only to find Hero and Ratchet with shit-eating grins plastered on their faces as they clap.

"I take it things didn't go well out there, Boss," Hero prods.

"No fucking shit," I mutter. "What was your first clue? How pissed off she looked, or the fact that she ran away from me like I was Typhoid Mary?"

"I was going to go with the sprint to the door, but I'm thinking that you being in a relationship patient zero seems more likely," Ratchet chimes in, snuffing out his cigarette. "You do look a little pale and sickly."

"Keep cutting up, assholes. I see some bikes that need polishing, and two officers that look like they're in need of a prospect crash course."

Both men just laugh, not giving a damn that I'm as serious as shit on a hot summer day.

"Relax," Hero says. "No need to take out your pussy-whipped frustrations on us. Seems to me, You have a couple of options to go with."

"And what would those be exactly?"

"Fuck her out of your system, or just fuck her."

"You go from one end of the spectrum to the other, don't you, Hero?"

He shrugs as Ratchet offers him one of his smokes, but Hero waves him off. Ratchet pops one out and sticks it in his mouth before retrieving the lighter from his pocket and lighting the cigarette.

"He has a point, Raze," Ratchet says, taking a drag. "I mean we can tell from a mile away you got a hard-on for that angry bitch. Either stick it in her, or stick it in someone else. Seems to be the only cure."

"Why the fuck should I take advice from a guy who can't seem to keep the girl he wants from trying to flee to another state?" I growl.

Shit. I shouldn't have said that.

Hero winces, and Ratchet grimaces and storms off into the clubhouse.

"Low blow, Raze. You know he doesn't know how to deal with his shit with Ricca."

"I know. I feel like an asshole now," I mutter. Guilt stabs me right in the fucking gut. Ratchet is far from a stable man with normal relationships, and it's not for me to judge how he manages his love life. "I need to go talk to Darcy. I'll make it up to him later."

"Mend the fences," Hero warns. "Don't let the club fall apart because you don't know how to handle your shit." And with those parting words, he heads for the garage at the back of the property.

I yank on the heavy back door and step inside. Music rattles the walls. The fact that a party is going on right now isn't a surprise. The guys need to cut loose while we have some down time.

I pop my head into Voodoo's lair, and find him feverishly typing away on his computer. "Anything new to report?"

Voodoo jerks back with a start and rips the headphones from his ears. "For a big man, you sure are a quiet fucker."

"A skill you learn when you have kids and naptime, brother. What do you have for me?"

He returns his attention back to his computer and clicks on a few icons. Two live video feeds on the house we raided in Tijuana pop up on the screen. The place looks quiet, and the motion detectors aren't registering any movement.

I frown. "When did you put up surveillance cameras?"

"When you were downstairs playing hide and seek. Figured it would be easier to watch it ourselves instead of relying on questionable information from our snitches."

I walk into his room and clap him on his shoulder.

"It's been quiet since we've been back. A little too quiet for a cut house in the basement."

"Maybe they've got the federales on their tails," I offer.

"Nah. I don't think that's the case." He spins around in his chair, narrowly missing running over my foot with the wheel, then slides the unfolded map from the house and smooths it out on the table behind us. "See here," he says, pointing to a space on the map. "According to Google maps, this is just a wide open space, but on this map, it has a house drawn on it. I've looked at all the locations on this baby, and this is the only one where I can't find an actual structure on the satellite map."

"You think it's their base of operations?"

"It's got to be something important if it's not

showing up on a satellite map, and according to online records, it was just updated a few months ago."

Studying the map, I mentally trace the lines and estimate the location in question to be about two hours east of Tijuana, near El Diablo. The name sure does fit if this is their hideout.

"I'll send a couple of guys down to check it out," I decide. "See what they can find."

"Sounds good, Boss. I'll keep digging into what I can find in Mexico's shitty land purchase records."

I smirk and raise a brow. "Do I even want to know how you accessed those?"

Voodoo just smiles and turns back to his wall of computer screens without saying a word. Remind me not to fuck with him. Leaving Voodoo to his work, I pop my head out into the main room and call for Thrasher and Irons to follow me to my office. I give them their marching orders on the way, then send them off to V for additional briefing on the equipment he's sending with them. These are some of the best men we could have picked up from a disbanded club. They're loyal, they're tough, and they don't ask questions. I wish I had more like them.

Just as I'm about to continue on my quest to apologize to Darcy for the kiss we shouldn't have shared, I walk past my office and hear rustling. I step closer to the door and notice that the once locked door is now cracked with light scuffs on the wooden frame from being forced open. I inch the door open slightly, only to find Darcy rummaging through a filing cabinet behind my desk. Her tight ass sways in the air as she thumbs through the files. I slip into the room quietly without disturbing her search.

"Can you explain to me why the fuck you broke into my private office?" I ask, anger bubbling in my veins.

She jumps with a start and quickly slams the filing cabinet door shut. As she turns to face me, her features are racked with fear. Her eyes are wide knowing I caught her red-handed, snooping in my office.

"Michael, I—" she stammers, but I raise my hand and hush her pathetic excuses. I know why she's in here, and it pisses me off that she's going behind my back to steal the information I have tightly locked in the floor safe. Stealing from a man is one thing, but stealing from an entire MC is punishable in far worse ways than she could ever imagine. Had she pulled this shit at another club, she'd have died for it.

"Don't give me some bullshit answer, Darcy."

I step closer, watching as she backpedals and circles around to the front of my desk. I keep moving, matching her step by step until I make it to my black leather desk chair, and take a seat. Her eyes are worried, but her face is unreadable as she steps to the front of my desk, laying both of her hands on the wood and staring me point-blank in the face.

"We need to talk," she states matter-of-factly.

"I'd say we do. How about you park that sexy ass of yours down in the chair behind you? No need to ruffle your feathers in a dominance display you're not going to win."

Her eyes narrow, but she stays where she is.

"Stay standing then," I say. "Gives me quite the view. Nice tits, by the way."

Her hands tighten into fists as she jerks away from the table and slams down into the chair. Her arms fold over her chest, blocking them from my sight. I make her stew in silence while she waits for me to say something. With each passing second, the tension and temperature of the room rises, only making the situation more intense. Her huffs and puffs make the hair on my arms stand at attention, along with my dick. Each glare stiffens it further, and it's almost to the point of being uncomfortable.

"You gonna talk, or am I going to be waiting here until I figure out? I'm not a good guesser, darlin'."

"Why?" she asks through gritted teeth.

"Why what? There are a lot of things that could

be involved in that answer, and one in particular that I should be asking you in return."

Her gaze never wavers. "Why didn't you tell me my husband was murdered, and that he was a cheating bastard?"

I nearly choke on her words. *Jagger? A cheater? No fucking way.* That man was loyal to her like she was a fucking goddess who demanded his worship and tokens. I never saw him take a single look at another woman after he met her. Why the fuck would he cheat on her, and where the hell did she even come up with that cock and bull idea?

"I already told you, Darcy. Just knowing he was murdered is about as far as you're going to get with this discussion. Now, for the second part of that, you have to be fucking crazy to think he'd cheat on you."

Her eyes soften momentarily before she returns to the cold resting bitch face. "I have proof of his infidelity."

I blink. "That so? Like what?"

"Much like you and that packet, I think I'm going to play that information a little closer to my chest."

I shrug, playing it off like I'm not curious at all. Whoever fed her this information sure as fuck didn't know the man she was married to. I stand from my chair and circle the desk, stopping right in front of her. She seems so small as I tower over her in the chair, but just when I think I might be winning the dominance fight, she puffs out that chest of hers like a fucking proud peacock. Goddamnit if that doesn't turn me on more.

"Listen, Darcy," I say, keeping my voice calm and relaxed. "I get it. I dropped a bomb on you that Jagger didn't die in an accident, but that doesn't give you the right to break into my office. You're still mourning his loss, and I get that more than anyone else in this place, but I'm not the one who ordered him to do what he did that got him killed. I was just as blindsided as you were."

"Blindsided, my ass," she hisses. "You're just trying to cover your fucking tracks because whatever bullshit the club got him involved in got him killed. You're too much of an arrogant asshole to admit that this is your fault."

In one swift movement, I push off the desk and jerk her from the chair. She pulls back, her face twisted with rage, but I grab the back of her neck and slam my mouth against hers. Her hands push against my chest, but her lips crush back against mine. Her arms become slack as I whip us around and shove her ass against my desk.

Suddenly, she pulls her lips from mine and lands a slap against my cheek that makes my head whip to the side. Her swollen lips open to give me another load of shit, but I jerk her face back to mine.

"Just shut the fuck up," I mutter, then take her mouth again. Her lips part, and her tongue slide inside my mouth.

Her hands glide down my chest until I feel her fingers fumbling against my belt. She pops it open and pulls the belt away from my jeans, tossing it behind her. Her fingers begin to unzip my fly, but I use my free hand to stop her. As much as she's been fighting this, she wants it just as badly as I do.

"You sure this is what you want?" I ask, my gaze boring into hers. "This isn't something you can take back after you drop my fly. As soon as my dick is free, I'll be sinking it into that wet pussy of yours, and I won't stop until we're both finished."

Without a word, she unzips my jeans and kneels, sliding them down over my thighs, along with my boxers. My cock springs to life in front of her face, and her eyes grow wide. Maybe she hasn't seen a ten-inch cock before, because she's analyzing it like a fucking engineer on how it's going to fit. Then, she licks her lips and moves her face forward, but I pull her up and spin her around, pressing her stomach down on the desk.

I hadn't even noticed until now that she had changed her clothes after the ride. Her perky little ass is covered in a brightly-colored pair of those legging things woman seem to be into these days. While on most women they aren't flattering, on Darcy, those fucking things are a second skin. They're also easily removable. Fisting the waistband of her leggings, I peel them from her body and slide them down to her knees before positioning myself between her legs.

A hiss escapes my lips when I discover her bare pussy beneath the leggings. Maybe these fucking things aren't so bad after all. Her pussy is gleaming from her arousal, and I can't help myself as I run a finger through her wetness. Darcy jolts at my touch, her hips rolling, wanting more.

Her body is ready, and right now, that's fucking hot as hell. Foreplay is overrated in this kind of situation. Grabbing a condom from the back pocket of my jeans, I slip it on and position my cock at her entrance, then sink myself deeply inside of her. Her walls tighten around my cock, and she feels so fucking good, I know this won't take long.

Her hands grip the edge of my desk, and I reach up and grab her hair, wrapping it around my fist, as I drive myself into her over and over againn.

"Fuck," she moans. "Holy fucking shit."

"You feel so fucking good, darlin'. I've never felt a vice grip pussy like yours."

Her head swivels back, her brow furrowed with

confusion, but I thrust into her again and her confusion melts into pure, relentless pleasure. The desk moves with each thrust, as our moans fille the room.

"Just shut up and fuck me harder," she begs.

She arches her back and grinds her hips into me, taking my cock deeper inside of her. I can feel the vibrations of her impending orgasm begin to build, her walls clenching down. She's close. So fucking close.

I release her hair and grab her hips, slamming her back onto my cock. It takes three more thrusts before she comes undone. Her body bucks, her moans long and low as she rides out her orgasm. The sounds she's making sends me over the edge, and I find my own release, my cock still reveling in the feel of her around me.

When I'm finished, I fall over her as we pant, trying to catch our breath. It only takes a few minutes before she begins to squirm.

I pull away, and she reaches down, pulls up her leggings, and steps around me, walking right for the door. She hesitates when she reaches for the knob, and I can see the guilt on her face.

"We didn't do anything wrong, you know," I tell her, pulling my jeans back up and tucking my dick inside. "We're consenting adults that needed a release."

"That wasn't exactly a release," she says, her body straightening. "That was a hate fuck."

I blink, her words hitting me like a sledgehammer. "A what kind of fuck?"

"It's when two people have a spur of the moment fuck, even though they hate each other."

What the hell is with the trend of naming everything these days? Maybe I'm older than I think, but why can't things be what they are without some fucking label attached to them?

"Well, darlin'," I reply. "I'm not sure that term applies to what just happened here, but if that's what you want to brand it so you sleep better tonight, you go ahead. We both needed a release, and that's what we got. No need to brand it as anything. It felt good, and it served a purpose. End of story."

"How could something that felt so good feel so wrong?" she whispers, then she opens the door and slips away.

Fuck, this is going to be harder than I thought. Fucking her out of my system just flew out of the goddamn window. Now that I've had her, I want her even more.

Chapter 19

DARCY

WHOEVER SAID that ignorance is bliss deserves to be dragged into the street and shot. Ignorance is far from bliss. Actually, it's more like the elephant in the room. It's been three days since my escapade in the office with Michael. Three days of hiding in this room, which has become like a prison cell, because I don't have the guts to face him again. I tried to push the experience we had from my mind by drowning myself in books and Face timing with the kids, but nothing could erase the things I felt as he fucked me over his desk. The ferocity and animalistic nature of what we did is something I thought only existed in books. No imaginary book boyfriend could have prepared me for him. Or how my body ignited and burned from his touch.

The only time I sneak outside of these four walls,

is to find food. Then I rush back here to the safety of my solitude of shame. The moment he pulled out of me, everything felt wrong and right all at the same time. My body hummed for hours afterward, trying to come down from the high of it all. My heart is shattered at my own betrayal. I had fucked someone my husband had called brother. My mind was littered with imaginary conversations with Brent, apologizing for betraying his memory. Where Brent was gentle and loving, Michael was rough and intense. My body continues to betray me, though. It wants more. More for Michael's touch. More of him.

It was a one-time thing, you idiot. No more, even if you want to know if the second time around is as intense as the first time, or if that was a fluke.

Several times over the last few days, I have cowered, listening as heavy footsteps stop outside the door and stand silent before just walking away. My heart fluttered every time I heard him, and my stomach churned into a tightly-wound knot. My feet froze in place, as my hands tried to detach from my body to throw open the doors and let him take me again, because even I know if I opened up that door, I wouldn't stop it from progressing further. Fuck, my life has spiraled out of control. I had intended on being here to get answers, and I still ended up in

Michael's arms. My stupid fucking curiosity and that last attempt to find that packet were my downfall.

Today has been quiet, and so far, there have been no visits from Michael. After taking a quick shower, I throw on one of my old t-shirts and a pair of panties before curling up into bed to read myself to sleep. It doesn't take long, before my eyes begin to droop.

"Darcy?" a voice calls from outside of my door.

I freeze, instantly awake, hoping and praying he just moves on like the last few times, but I could never be so lucky.

"Darlin', I hear you breathing like you just ran a marathon in there. Just open up so we can talk."

Shifting from the bed, I quietly creep to the door and lean against the wall beside it. I can feel the gravitational pull from him through the wall, my body screaming at me to just open it up to him, and the possibilities that come with him. My hand starts for the door knob, before a thud reverberates from the door with what I can only assume is his head hitting the door.

"I'm not a begging man, Darcy, and I'm making a fool out of myself standing out here day in and day out, just hoping you'll open the door. Can you please help me save some of my pride and just open the door? I promise that's all I want," he says. "Well, that's a lie, but I'll keep my hands to myself, if you'll just let me in."

With a sigh, my needs overrule my wants, while I watch my hand, nearly on auto-pilot, go for the knob again. I twist it open, and Michael nearly falls into my room as the door falls away. He stumbles and catches himself before he face-plants the floor. His startled gaze moves from the floor to my face. He studies me for a few seconds, before taking two large steps and wrapping me in his arms. His face nuzzles my neck, but I remain stiff in his arms, fighting against myself to place my hands on his body. Touching him would be like the last step before falling into the pits of hell. I need to stay on this side of the spiral staircase, away from the amazing sex and darkness as long as I can.

"Shit, sorry," he mumbles, pulling away. "I guess I didn't keep my hands-off rule, but you can't answer the door dressed like that and not expect a man to respond."

I arch one brow upward before I realize how much I don't have on. I squirm under his gaze, suddenly embarrassed, but I can't show him my unease and still maintain the level playing field. I just need to play it off, and hope he won't notice how nervous I am to have him in my room.

"What do we have to talk about, *Raze*?"

Calling him by his road name makes him wince. "I thought we've been over this before," he growls.

"If it's okay for me to call you by your given name, why do you insist on everyone else calling you *Raze*? I can distinctly remember your ex-wife even calling you by your road name."

"Because Raze feels so wrong coming off those beautiful lips, and I don't feel like the club president with you. Just a normal man, fighting to keep his life and his business in order."

"But that doesn't make any sense," I argue. "We barely know each other—"

He presses a finger to my lips, silencing me as he traces them before his hand falls and takes mine so he can lead me to the edge of the bed. He sits, and pulls me down next to him. His hand doesn't leave mine as his thumb absently strokes my palm.

"We know each other far more than you think. We've been in each other's lives for nearly eight years, and even though we didn't talk, I know so much about you. I know that you hate roses, and prefer wildflowers, and that you hide when things get too serious. I know that you live for your children, and that you take far better care of them than you care for yourself."

My eyes grow wide at his admission. He talks like we've been intimate for years, rather than just acquaintances through my husband. It both excites and makes me uneasy to know how much knowledge he has about me.

"How do you know about the flowers, or hell, any of that?"

His eyes fall from mine and focus on the floor. "I know because of Jagger. I've seen the things he did for you. I watched your face light up with a smile when he surprised you with flowers he'd picked up on his way home from a run."

I shake my head. "Why would you pay so much attention to little things like that? You had your own wife and family to focus on."

He sighs, before dragging his eyes from the floor and looking to me again. "Because I wanted what you and Jagger had. Stability, great kids, and love."

My heart breaks as I realize he's spilling to me how unhappy his marriage was to Maj. Until the last few years, they appeared happy, but her absence in his life now proves that not everything was what is seemed on the surface.

"Don't get me wrong," he continues. "I loved her at first, but as one year faded into the next, I saw an entirely new side of her that wasn't the woman I met. She changed, and maybe so did I, but I've wanted out for a while."

"Why didn't you just leave her?"

He shrugs. "My kids. I didn't want them growing up without a mother, but even now, I think it would have been for the better. Them not having a mother would have been better than the traitorous bullshit that came with her."

I frown. "The what?"

Michael purses his lips, as if realizing he'd said more than he should have. "Nothing. Just the drama and bullshit that came with her departure."

"You sure about that?" I prod. "Because it sure didn't sound like nothing when you said it."

"It's not worth rehashing. It's in the past, and that's where it's going to stay," he mutters. "I didn't come in here to talk about my ex-wife. I want to talk about us."

"What us?" I snap. "What happened in your office was a spur of the moment mistake, and it won't happen again."

In one swift movement, he's off the bed and leaning down in front of me. His arms press down on either side of the bed, bringing his face directly in front of mine. His hot breath burns my skin, regardless of the chills rolling down my spine from his closeness.

"That's where you are wrong," he says, his words like a warning. "It will happen again, and you damn well know it will. Once wasn't enough for me, and from what I can see, it isn't over for you, either, as much as you try to fight it."

My breath hitches under the intensity of his gaze. His muscled arms are tense, the veins becoming more pronounced with each passing second. I shift nervously as he studies me.

"It can't happen again," I whisper. "It feels so wrong. I can't do that to my husband's memory and still be able to live with the after effects. I'm not ready to commit to something new so soon."

"I'm not asking for forever, darlin'," he says, his voice low and husky. "We've only fucked one time, but guilt be damned, I want to see where this goes. I've never felt n like this before. It's all hate, aggression, and fighting for dominance, and I'm into it. Just give it a chance, will you?"

He's right. I know he's right, but that still doesn't make it *feel* right. I inch my hands to his broad chest, splaying my fingers against his hard muscles and inhale deeply, my core flaming with need.

"What about the kids?" I ask. "We have to think about them. What if we get involved, and shit goes south? I don't want them in the crosshairs."

"Until we know for sure what this is, the kids don't have to be involved. I don't want to hurt them anymore than you do, but this is just a trial. I want a chance to see what this is, and if it doesn't work out, we'll walk away knowing we gave it a try."

My heart softens at his proposal. He seems so sure he could walk away so easily, but what if I can't? What if my heart breaks all over again, and this time there's nothing left of me to rebuild? What if he hurts me or cheats on me? It's not like he doesn't have access to plenty of other women, and with the secrecy of the club, I'd probably never know. The thought of cheating brings me back to those photos of Brent with the mystery woman, and my heart twinges. Even with Michael's endorsement that nothing ever happened, I can't help but be skeptical. Another thought pops into my head. One that's dangerous in nature. If I do this, and things progress between us, maybe he'll be more trusting and forthcoming with information. I mull it over as he watches me.

"I'll try," I concede. "But on a couple of conditions."

He grins, triumphant. "Well, shit. This is a lot further than I thought I'd get. Lay them out for me."

"No other girls. If we try this, it's just us. If I even suspect there's another girl on the side, I'll walk."

"All I see is you. Other girls aren't going to come between us, no matter how hard they try. What's next?"

I pause before my next demand because I know this one might just void the deal entirely.

"I want you to tell me more about how Brent died. I want honesty, and I want answers. I know there's more to his murder."

He hisses and rips his arm away from me, stomping away from the bed.

Too far. I've gone way too far,

His hands rake over his smooth head as he spins on his heels and stalks back toward me. "You know why I can't tell you, but I promise you, if there's something I need to tell you, I will. I have some conditions of my own. Being with me when the shit hits the fan isn't easy. The kids are out of danger, but if I think for one second something may endanger you, you're out of the loop. I won't put your life on the line. Do you understand me?"

"Yes," I whisper.

Michael bends and embraces as soon as the words leave my mouth. He places a sweet kiss on my lips before pulling away as if testing the waters of our newfound agreement. A smile cracks on his face, showing off the deep dimples at the corners of his mouth, setting off an explosion between my legs. Who knew dimples on such a rough man could look so fucking sexy?

"What would you have done if I'd have said no?" I ask.

"I would have kicked down the door and thrown you over my shoulder, then hauled your ass into my room until you at least talked to me. It was fucking torture standing outside of this door." He pauses as a shit-eating grin forms on his face.

"What the hell is that look for?"

"This," he says, then he yanks me from the bed and hauls me over his shoulder. I kick and squirm, trying to break away, but his hand comes down and slaps my ass, then he walks us both right out into the hall.

"Where the hell are you taking me?" I squeal.

"To my room," he chuckles. "Must have forgotten to mention that part. If you're with me, you don't live away from me. I want access to you at all times, and no fucking door or other room is going to keep me from you. It'll save me a small fortune on doors if I just move you into my room."

Michael continues to chuckle as he carries me down the hall. At his room, he opens the door with his free hand and carries me across the threshold, depositing me on the bed. I watch as he returns to the door and flips the lock. Slowly, he turns to me and the large bed, his hands falling to the hemline of his shirt and pulling it over his head, then tosses it aside before moving to his belt. His hands work quickly, his eyes never leaving mine, while he unzips his jeans. They fall to the ground, and he pulls a foot from each leg before adding them to the pile with his shirt.

I watch as he stalks over to the bed, my teeth sinking into my lower lip so hard, I nearly draw blood. Using his knees, he parts my legs and trails his fingers down my back, before hooking up under my shirt and slowly pulling it up, exposing my naked torso to the chilled air of his room. He's very careful as he pulls it over my head and lays it down on the side of the bed.

"You are too fucking perfect, Darcy. I've never seen another woman so beautiful in my life."

A blush creeps over my cheeks as he leans down. I reach for him, pulling him into a heated kiss. His tongue swirls against my own, smooth and silky and hot. When he breaks away, I'm breathless.

"As much as I want to continue this, darlin', I don't want to rush." He scoops up my shirt and stalks around the bed, tossing it onto his dirty clothes pile as he passes. He pulls back the sheets and slides into the bed beside me without a word.

Confused, I watch him as he settles onto his side. What the fuck?

Annoyed now, I crawl under the blankets and

settle in. I'm laying just a few inches from him, but his hand reaches out, pulling me to his warm body. He nuzzles his face into the back of my neck and sighs, settling into position.

I thought being with him would feel so foreign and weird, but it's almost relaxing, and as the rhythm of his breathing begins to slow, I feel my drowsiness return.

"Tonight, we sleep," he whispers against my hair. "But tomorrow, I'll show you just what I mean when I say you're mine."

Chapter 20

RAZE

THE MORNING SUN pounds into my room as I stir awake from the first good night's sleep I've had in a long time. I try to stretch out my arm, but when I look over, Darcy's sleeping form is curled up on top of it, facing me. I watch her chest rise and fall rhythmically. She has never looked more beautiful than she does curled up next to me, cocooned in my sheets. Her long brown hair is fanned over my arm, and her legs are tucked slightly under the covers. She's so fucking beautiful, and for the time being, she's mine.

I'm damn lucky she didn't kick me in the balls for my proposal last night. I didn't expect her to agree to our arrangement so quickly, but I'm damn glad she did.

Those three days after fucking in my office, were

pure torture. It took every fiber of my willpower to not cut the damn hinges off that door and storm in there like a caveman, hauling her off to my room to be fucked into submission.

Well, I guess some of that did happen, but it wasn't as barbaric as it could have been. Though, dominating her like that would be kind of hot.

I watch her sleep for nearly thirty minutes before she finally stirs next to me. Her eyes flutter open, and shock registers on her face. She moves to scramble away, but I grab her and pull her tightly against me.

"It's just me, darlin'," I whisper, holding her close. "Bad dream?"

Her body relaxes, and she sighs and she finally settles against me. "I've been dreaming of Brent since I came to the clubhouse. I relive losing him over and over again until I finally wake up in a panic, but today was different."

"Different how?"

"He was smiling at me, and not lying in the casket. It was... weird."

I place a kiss on her forehead, and her eyes fall closed.

"That doesn't sound like a bad dream to me. Since when is smiling a bad thing?"

"That's not what startled me," she admits. "It's

been quite a while since I've woken up with a man in my bed."

"I can say the same thing for myself. Well, with a woman. If I found a man in my bed, I'd be shooting first and asking questions later."

"Yeah, the guys might be asking some questions about a man doing the walk of shame out of your room." She giggles and yawns.

"I have no issues with who a person loves, but that's just not my thing."

"Mmhmm," she mumbles. "The club whores would be very disappointed if you decided to bat for the other team."

She grins and rolls to her back. I follow her, rolling on top of her nearly-naked body and pinning her beneath my weight. Her eyes grow wide as I dip down to give her a proper good morning kiss, then her hand darts out to cover my mouth.

"I haven't had a chance to brush my teeth yet," she cries.

I lick her palm, which makes her pull her hand away. Taking the moment of opportunity, I press my lips to hers. She fights for a only a second before kissing me back. I suck on her upper lip, then break contact and grin. "Darlin', you were right. Those teeth of yours need a good scrubbing."

"Hey!" she cries, but I quiet her with a longer, deeper kiss.

"If that's your morning breath, you can expect far more morning make out wake-up calls in your future."

"You ass," she says, playfully shoving me away. "You made me feel gross. I was about to shove you off of me so I could go get cleaned up."

I laugh as I lower my head and place a kiss just below her ear. I make a little trail of kisses down to the base of her neck, loving the way she shivers. "The chances of you shoving me off are about slim to none. Besides, what's the point of getting clean when I'm only going to make you dirty again. I have a promise from last night to keep."

I kiss the opposite side of her neck, feeling her nipples grow hard against my chest. She whimpers softly as I prop myself up on my hands, trailing kisses along her collarbone, moving toward her sternum. I lower my head, drawing one taut nipple into my mouth, and her breath hitches as I swirl my tongue around the hard nub. Releasing it with a pop, I repeat my actions with her other nipple as she squirms under me.

"I've gotta say, darlin', I can definitely get into you sleeping naked. It makes morning sex so much easier."

I don't give her a chance to respond before I move down her body, fluttering kissing along her stomach. When I find a scar across her belly, just above her panty line, I pause. She tries to shy away, but I reach up and turn her face to mine.

"This is from Wesson?" I ask.

"Yes," she whispers with a hint of embarrassment.

"I remember that day," I admit. How scared he was. How scared I was. Losing her and the baby would have hurt more than one of us in this clubhouse, but admitting that right now, when she is still so fragile, would only hurt her more.

"I hate the scar, but I'd rather have it than to have lost him."

"Scars don't define us, Darcy. They're badges of courage that we should be proud to wear to remember the trials we've survived." I pepper a line of kisses along her scar. "Beauty is in the eye of the beholder, and you my darlin' are the sexiest fucking thing I have ever seen."

She rolls her eyes, as if I'm some drunken idiot trying to pick her up in a bar.

"Did you just roll your eyes at me?" I ask with a smirk.

"I might have."

"Well now, that changes everything," I say. "To

think I was going to let you relax while I go rustle us up some grub, but breakfast is only for well-behaved girls. You, Darcy, are definitely not in that category if you roll your eyes at my sincerity. In fact, I think I need to teach you how to properly respond to flattery."

Her eyes grow wide as I inch down the rest of her body, using my knees to part her legs.

"For starters, good girls know that clothes are not permitted once the door of this room is closed. So these, of course, have to go."

I pull her panties away and watch as she shivers. She's uncomfortable, but even in her discomfort, her body responds to mine.

"Now that we have that little barrier out of the way, it's time to start your charm school lesson."

I slide off the bed and pull down my boxers, my dick springing from them, already hard and ready for her. Her eyes grow wide as she takes me in.

"You like what you see, darlin'?" I whisper. "Because it's all yours."

She flips over and crawls toward me, watching me palm my dick. My hand pumps a few times before I stop and watch her move. Her body rolls seductively, making me wish I was on the other side of the bed to watch her round ass sway.

"I saw how you looked at my cock in my office,

Darcy," I say, my voice low and husky. "Like you were looking at the world's largest sucker, and you were dying for a lick. I want to watch you fuck me with your mouth, and then I'm going to flip your sexy ass onto your back and fuck you with your legs high in the air."

Darcy sinks her teeth into her lip and crawls closer, her face now inches from my cock. She licks her lips to wet them, then takes me into her mouth. I hiss, my hands falling to the back of her head, brushing her hair aside to expose her face as she bobs up and down on my cock. Her eyes meet mind as she slides my lips up and down, and it nearly unmans me.

"Fuck, your mouth feels so good," I groan. She hums and takes my hard length farther, nearing the edge of her throat. "Jesus Christ, how much of my cock can you take? I can almost feel your tonsils."

She grins and flicks her tongue along the sensitive area beneath the head, eliciting another growl from me before I use her hair to rip her mouth away. She looks up at me, licking her lips, savoring my taste inside of her mouth.

"Jesus, darlin', that is the hottest fucking thing I've ever seen," I growl. "I'd love nothing more than to have you suck me until I finish, but I wouldn't be a gentleman if I didn't make sure you got yours first."

Pushing against her shoulder, I guide her onto her back and crawl over her, placing my knees on either side of her waist, my dick resting against her belly. My hands slide along her smooth skin, cupping her breasts as I take each nipple into my mouth once more.

"Someday soon, I'm going to fuck these beautiful tits of yours until I come all over them."

Her body shivers beneath me, and I make a quick mental note before all the blood rushes from my brain to my cock. I want to try a little experiment to see how responsive she is to my words. I'm betting I can make her come with just the dirty shit housed within my mind. I should try it in a public place to see if I can make her come without anyone noticing, tough I don't want to share her orgasmic moans with anyone else. Plus, I'd have to fuck her as soon as it was over. Public sex could be fun.

I trace my fingers down her stomach, tickling and caressing at the same time. Darcy tries to squirm away, but her motion sends me falling forward, and I take the opportunity to pin her wrists to the bed. Leaning down, I kiss her again before pulling myself back up and centering my body between her legs. She watches my every move as I press the head of my cock against her clit, moaning when I rub up and down, reveling in the feel of her wet pussy.

Moving faster now, I tease her clit with my cock until I feel her pussy beginning to clench, her orgasm building inside her. Her moans grow louder as she gets closer to release, but I stop what I'm doing and move, plunging myself inside her, pulling out briefly to push her legs up in the air until they rest on my shoulders. I thrust harder and fast, the edge of my release growing tighter inside me. I watch, enamored as her hand slides down her stomach until it reaches her pussy. With one finger, she circles it around her swollen clit, moaning and panting, her hips rolling. And then her orgasm hits her.

Her pussy clenches around my dick like a vice, and when she bucks against me, my own release slams into me. My hips falter and slow as I ride out my release, pulsating inside of her, giving her everything I have to give.

As our bodies calm and our senses return, I drop her legs gently to the bed before falling to her chest and pulling her into a sloppy post-orgasm kiss. I roll onto my side, pulling her lax body next to me as we both heave, trying to catch our breaths.

"I think you just bypassed lessons and became the teacher, darlin'."

Darcy giggles as we lie there in silence for a few minutes, enjoying the peace of just being together until I know I need to get moving. Sliding from the bed, I head for the bathroom. I can feel her eyes on my ass as I walk .

Closing the door behind me, I turn on the shower and stand under the hot spray, begrudgingly washing her scent from my body. If I could bottle up the way she smells after sex, I'd wear it as cologne for the rest of my life. Her scent is intoxicating enough, but throw in the afterglow of good sex, and that kicks it up a notch completely.

A few minutes later, I emerge with a towel loosely wrapped around my waist, while Darcy watches me with hungry eyes.

"You keep looking at me like that, the only food you'll be getting today will be served in this bed."

"That a promise?" she fires back without missing a beat.

"Oh, darlin', that's a challenge I don't think you're quite up to yet. Now, go get that sexy ass of yours in the shower and get cleaned up. I'll run out to the kitchen to grab some grub and check in with the guys. I've got Church in about two hours, but I think we can fit in a repeat session and breakfast before I have to go."

Chapter 21

DARCY

THREE WEEKS LATER

THE PAST THREE weeks have flown by as Michael and I have settled into our relationship. It hasn't been easy with two strong-willed people like us trying to learn to work together. We've had our share of fights, but all couples have them, and I, for one, am glad we're getting them out of the way sooner rather than later. Each day, he opens up a little more about the club, himself, and his ex-wife.

Maj is always a touchy subject, and even mentioning her name will stop him dead in his tracks. I've learned to talk about her in small doses.

Just yesterday, I was shocked to learn that his divorce from Maj was only finalized a few months prior. He had asked her for a divorce the day before she disappeared, and without any information to where she could have gone, he had to take a different approach to ridding himself of his legal responsibility to her and obtain sole custody of the kids. It took months of attempts to track her down, and even an ad in the newspaper, before the judge finally granted him the divorce. He seemed exhausted by the process as he explained it to me, but I was glad he could tell me. He needs someone to confide his personal feelings in, and the men of the club aren't exactly emotional creatures able to give him solid advice that doesn't involve their dick in some form or another.

While sex is still a major portion of our blossoming relationship, we also talk more and more each day.

Each morning he wakes me up with his own special version of a wake-up call, and I have to admit, morning sex is by far the best. I may still be sleepy or drowsy, but feeling that raw connection and emotion leaves me feeling bonded to him throughout the day. Even if we don't get to spend much time together, I still feel the connection in his absence. It's addicting and scary all at the same time. It leaves me feeling like I'm gleefully floating in the line of a firing squad.

I spend most of my time away from Michael reading, talking to the boys, and now, working on my home business. It still makes me laugh when I think about how I spilled the beans to Michael about my job.

"You have got to be shitting me, right?"

I laugh. "I'm definitely not shitting you, Michael. You heard me correctly."

He paces the floor of my home office as I gather my things to take back to the clubhouse. After a week of wearing the same clothes over and over again, he finally relented and brought me back to the house to gather more clothes, get my business supplies, and grab my laptop.

"Why couldn't you have had a normal home business like make-up or those fancy pots and pans?"

"I sell sex toys and homemade lick-able body paints. What's wrong with a vibrator and some edible lube? I'm betting you'd try them out with me."

He scoffs at my joke and turns to face me. "It's something entirely different with you, but knowing that you know more about sex toys than I could have imagined is a little unmanning, okay? What if you find a monster cock rubber wiener that you like more than me?"

I throw my head back and laugh as he frowns. "It's not funny, darlin'. I can't compete with that vibrator shit."

"Don't worry, babe," I coo, using the nickname he hates. "I'll give you fair warning before the Monster Cock 8000 and I run away together."

I giggle as I think back to how shocked he looked

when I'd teased him that day. Poor Michael. I wonder what he would do if he walked in on me masturbating with one of these toys currently strewn all over the bed we share.

Just as I pack the last box to be shipped out by one of the prospects later, Michael walks through the door. Every time I see him, my heart flutters like a school girl daydreaming about her crush. Maybe it's the sex, or how we've bonded over the past few weeks, but every time he's gone, I miss him.

Michael takes a few strides and pulls me into his arms, greeting me with one of his knee-buckling kisses. "You finished with your rubber wiener party in here?"

I grin. "Yup. Just packed away the last one, and I have the shipping labels on them for Slider to take to the post office." I pause. "You know, it would be easier, if you just let me handle shipping them."

"Can't let you out on your own, darlin'. Even though things seem quiet right now, we're still on lockdown."

I sigh as he rubs his large hands down my back in his attempt to quell my dislike of being cooped up like this for weeks.

"I promise, as soon as we get the club business handled, you'll be able to frolic to your heart's content on the outside. But for now, it's safer for you behind these walls, and for the kids to stay at your parents."

"I know, I know, but it doesn't make missing the kids or a bit of freedom any less desirable. I'm not used to being ordered around."

His eyes soften for a moment, but his lips soon turn up into a devious smile.

"You wipe that shit-eating grin off of your face right now," I warn. "After three rounds of sex this morning, my pussy needs a break from you and Godzilla. Not every woman is built to handle the likes of you."

"Godzilla, huh?" he says with a laugh. "I don't think I've ever had someone give my dick a nickname, but fuck, I'll take Godzilla." He looks down at his crotch and just smiles.

Good lord. I have only stoked his ego more.

"But that's not what the smile was for," he says, glancing back up at me. "How about you and I get out of here today? I have a surprise for you."

I roll my eyes and push away from his body.

"It's not Godzilla, I swear," he says, throwing his hands up in surrender. "Though, we'll come back to that portion of the discussion later."

He's got my interest now. Whatever it is, it'll be better than marinating in this clubhouse for the rest of the day. "So, where are we going?"

"You'll see," he replies. "Meet me outside in ten minutes. I need to make some phone calls before we leave."

Ten minutes later, I walk out of the clubhouse to find Michael sitting astride his running motorcycle. He smiles as I walk toward him and grab my helmet before putting it on. I slide my leg over the bitch seat and hoist my body onto the bike. Settling behind him, I wrap my arms around his waist just before he peels out of the parking lot.

We ride for hours before he pulls into a rest stop just before the California state line. If this is his idea of a fun day out, he has another think coming. The bike ride was fun, but this place isn't exactly LEGOLAND. He turns off the bike just as a voice calls out to me.

"Mama," I hear, and I turn, my heart soaring when I spot both of my sons running full tilt toward the bike. Michael leans back and helps me slide off the seat. He takes my helmet and leans in close. "Surprise, darlin'."

"Mama," Wesson screams as he plows into me with open arms, followed by Colt. The boys squeeze me so tight, and as I look up through my tear filled eyes, I see my mom coming forward carrying Roxie. My baby girl coos and smiles as she gets closer to us.

Mom hands her to me, and for the first time in nearly a month, my family is complete.

The boys chatter along about the things they've done with my parents, and how Colt misses his friends at school. After missing a week, Michael had arranged for a tutor to teach Colt at my mother's place until it was safe for him to return to school. While I didn't like the idea at first, it's far better for him to continue schooling at home while the danger the club put my kids in still lingered. What Michael told the school to allow him to be temporarily home-schooled was never mentioned to me, but I'm okay that he did it.

"Look how big you've all grown," I exclaim. "What has grandma been feeding you?"

"Heathy stuff that tastes like cardboard," Colt pipes up. "I miss your cooking, Mom."

I ruffle his hair as I pull him in for another hug. "I miss having you all at home."

"'Uncle 'aze says we can't come home. Is that true, Mama?" Wesson asks.

"I'm sorry, baby, but it is. It'll be just a little bit longer, and then you'll all get to come home."

"That's right, buddy," Michael replies, tousling Wesson's hair. "The day you come home, we'll throw a big old party with anything you boys want."

"Rweally?" Wesson screams. "Can we have the

biggest bowl of ice cream you've ever seen, with sprinkles, Uncle 'aze?"

Michael looks to me with a smile and nods. While I normally wouldn't let the boys have a ton of junk food, their homecoming can be an exception to the rule.

If only it was going to be tomorrow.

We spend the rest of the afternoon at the rest-stop diner, eating and just enjoying our time together. Almost immediately, Michael had stolen Roxie away from me and proceeded to walk her around, showing her all the toys lining the walls in the gift shop. The duo returned with a hot-pink stuffed bear with huge purple eyes. Roxie just shoved the toy in her mouth as she peacefully played in Michael's arms.

While Wesson clung to me, Colt gravitated more to Michael, asking him question after question about his motorcycle, and if he'll teach him to ride when he's older. Just watching the exchange between them, as Wesson colored on the placemat in front of us, made my heart melt. Colt's curiosity reminds me so much of his father, and how he and Michael would talk for hours on our back porch back in the early days of our marriage.

Long before I'm ready to let them go, Michael checks his watch and reminds us of the late hour. I could have spent an entire month with my kids, and it wouldn't have been enough. Together, we help my mom pack the kids into the car, and Michael walks away to get the bike warmed up.

After I kiss each of my children goodbye, Mom shuts the door and gives me a knowing look. "Is he the reason you look so happy?"

I smile, knowing I could never hide anything from my mother. "You could say that. You probably think it's too soon, but we're still trying to figure out what we are to each other."

She pulls me into a tight embrace. "Just remember, Darcy, happiness doesn't always come in the package we expect it. I may not know him well enough to approve, but the kids like him, and that's a good sign. Just don't go head first into something until you're sure. I don't want to see you or the kids get hurt again."

I fight back a sob as the roar of a Harley engine fills the parking lot.

Saying a quick goodbye to my mother, I tell her to send my love home to Dad, then walk away, leaving three little pieces of my heart behind.

Climbing back on the bike, I make a decision. It's time to put my game face back on and help Michael end this club bullshit. I want have my family back, and if I have to wait much longer, I may just butt in and handle their business myself.

Chapter 22

RAZE

"MORNING, DARLIN'," I whisper, my lips pressed against Darcy's head. She doesn't make a sound, but instinctively snuggles closer to me. I've come to hate these mornings with Church because I have to leave her behind to sleep while I handle business.

Pulling myself away from Darcy's warm naked body after another long night of fucking and talking until the early morning hours has become my least favorite part of the day. Sliding from the bed, I peer down at her before heading into the bathroom for a shower. The hot spray hits me with a jolt that jars me awake, and my aching muscles groan as they relax. As the water flows over me, I think back to one of our conversations last night.

"How did you get your road name?" Darcy asks,

rolling over to prop herself up on her elbows. "Is it short for Razor or something?" I shoot her a glare, but she just laughs. "You didn't answer me," she challenges. "Is it embarrassing?"

"No, darlin', it's not. What you have to understand first is that things were different back when I patched in. The club was in shambles and involved with a lot of crooked, back door dealings. It was one step away from blowing up in our faces. The day the gavel got passed down to me, after my pops died, I cleaned house. I took everything bad and illegal about our club and burned it to the ground. I wanted to make this club what it should have been all along; a brotherhood and a family."

"So your road name is nearly in the literal sense?"

"Yes, it was actually Jagger who gave me my nickname. We were sitting outside the clubhouse after a particularly rough night of cleaning up a mess my father had left behind. We were just shooting the shit, when he got a serious look on his face. He gave me this big speech about honoring our brotherhood, and making sure things never went back to the way they were before. From that night on, he started calling me Raze."

She quieted down after I mentioned his name, and even though she put on a good show, I could feel her wet tears falling on my arm as she pretended to sleep. It pains me to know how much she still mourns him. Almost like he was killed just yesterday, but who am I to put a time limit on her grief?

Shaking her sadness from my mind, I think about how Darcy has become nearly insatiable in the bedroom. It's to the point that I'm sore the morning after a particularly hardcore fuck-a-thon. I caught myself wondering how the hell Jagger kept up with her energy and fire with their age difference, but I shut that shit down fast. I don't even want to think about her relationship with him. I know they were married, but there's a part of me that's jealous knowing that another man had claimed her before I could. Learning to live with someone's past, all while thinking about the future can be a bitch sometimes. Especially if you're the one who could be crossing the line.

Exploring my relationship with Darcy has helped the last few weeks pass by relatively easy as we wait for news from Irons and Thrasher. It has shocked me how well Darcy and I work together in our relationship. Where I'm hard, she's soft, unlike my ex-wife who was all hard. The ease I feel with Darcy is foreign to me compared to my past relationships. It's like she gets me on a completely different level, and understands not to push sensitive topics. Granted, it took her a few times to realize that talking about Maj wasn't something I enjoyed doing, but I find myself opening up more to her about the downfalls of my marriage.

During some of these deeper conversations between us, I feel guilty keeping her husband's, and now my, secret from her. She deserves to know the full truth about her Jagger's death, but I'm afraid once she finds out, I will lose her. She's smiling again, and telling her will only bring more pain and suffering. I keep telling myself I'm keeping her in the dark for her own good, but lately, I've been thinking that maybe I'm doing it for my own selfish reasons.

Stepping out the shower, I dress and quietly slip out of the room. Out in the main room, I can already smell breakfast cooking for us before our meeting.

"Morning, Prez," Voodoo mumbles, as he shovels a heaping pile of scrambled eggs into his mouth. I pull up a chair at the bar between Hero and Ratchet, just as Ruby slides a full plate in front of me, followed by Bubbles with a cup of hot coffee.

"Thanks, ladies," I mutter, as I pick up my fork and dig in. I get three bites in, before I notice Ratchet fidgeting, shoving his uneaten food around his plate.

"You all right over there?" I ask, watching him toss down his fork before turning to me.

"So, you and Jagger's old lady, huh?" Ratchet asks, his eyes wide.

"What about it?" I ask, nodding to Tyson as he joins us for breakfast.

"Just seems a bit odd you'd take up with your former brother's wife. Isn't that like coveting another man's property or some shit?"

"Anyone else have an issue with it?" I demand, looking around the room, making eye contact with single man here. "Now's the time to voice your concerns, because once this discussion is over, we won't be bringing it up again."

"I'm fine with it, Prez," Hero says. Voodoo and Tyson nod from behind him. "You're both lonely, and we get it."

"Doesn't mean it's right," Ratchet mutters under his breath.

"Just a few weeks ago, Ratchet, you stood outside and told me to 'either fuck her or fuck her out of my system'. Well, we did just that, and for the time being, we're trying out whatever this is between us. It may be temporary, or it may be permanent, but as it stands now, you will treat her like my old lady, and you will give her your respect."

"We just don't want you distracted by her when we have more important shit to deal with, Boss, that's all. Good pussy is good pussy, but it shouldn't cloud your judgment," Hero chimes in. "But I'm with Raze. She's been an old lady before, and she knows the ropes. It's not like she's some fresh-faced whore off the streets."

"Thanks for the glowing recommendation there, Hero," I mutter, shoving away from the bar. I hop off my stool and shoving it back into place, then thanking the girls again for breakfast, even if the eggs weren't fully cooked. Ruby really needs to take cooking lessons or something. I doubt she can properly boil water, judging by her lack of scrambled egg skills, but then again, those aren't the skills the guys keep her around for anyway.

"Church in five," I demand, then I spin around and head for the meeting room, ignoring the hushed whispers behind me.

"You know that if she stays with you, you'll only end up getting her killed just like Jagger, right?" someone calls out from the bar. A flash of Darcy lying in a casket hits me hard, but I shove it away. Nothing is going to happen to her. Not as long as I'm still breathing, even if these fuckers I should be able to call my brothers think otherwise.

Shoving open the door of our meeting room, I stomp to the head of the table and plop into my chair while I fume. Fuck them and their judgment. Maj may have been a shitty old lady, but Darcy hasn't given them a single damn reason to question her loyalty.

I continue to fume as the guys begin to shuffle into the room. Church usually only happens a few days a week, but with Irons and Thrasher in Mexico, we've ramped up the schedule to meet almost daily to keep everyone up to date as information comes in. It took the guys some time to maneuver themselves into town without drawing suspicion, but earlier this week, we finally started to get some decent reports back about the area.

The last few days, they've been radio silent. It makes me uneasy when our contact is limited. With the unrest in Mexico at an all-time high, they could both be lying dead for days before we'd even go down to look for them. Church starts off as it usually does, with updates from Tyson on our finances, and Voodoo with his surveillance footage. Hero shares the only uplifting news that the girls are finally settled in at home and doing well. While it's exciting for him to have his kids at home, it also means he'll need to be away more often to support Dani in their care. Not that I mind it, but the timing just sucks. He's the kind of guy you want by your side in a dogfight, but I won't keep him from his family if that's where he wants to be.

"Anything else we need to talk about?" I ask.

Just then, the phone on the center of the Church

table rings. I lean over and hit the answer button, accepting the call and putting on the speaker.

"What do you have for me, boys?" I say without a hello.

"Well, hello to you too, Prez. I see you're in a happy-go-lucky mood today."

"Can the cuteness, Irons, and give us your report."

"It's a quiet little town," Irons reports. "El Diablo doesn't have much to offer except a small cantina and a few scattered houses surrounding it."

"It's been a bitch to get cell phone service here, Boss," Thrasher chimes in.

The men around the table roll their eyes as Irons and Thrasher continue to bitch about the lack of amenities and modern day luxuries.

"You two done bitching like spoiled Malibu Barbies?" Hero pipes up. "We'd like to hear some actual information we can use."

"Shut the fuck up, Hero," Irons says. "You'd be bitching too if you weren't able to get air conditioning in the pits of hell they call Mexico. I think a new river is gonna start from the crack of my ass if the temperature doesn't start going up."

Hero slumps back in his chair with a huff, and folds his arms over his chest.

Who pissed in his Cheerios today?

"Did you find anything at the coordinates Voodoo gave you?" I ask.

Irons goes mute, and my stomach drops knowing it's probably just another dead end.

"Sorry about that, Boss. One of the locals walked up to the truck trying to sell us fresh fruit or some shit. Took a while to get rid of them. Can you repeat the question?"

"Did you find anything at the location?"

"There's nothing out there. Just rocks and dirt paths."

A collective grumble fills the room, but Irons keeps talking. " I did find a path leading from that spot, and we followed it up into the mountain range nearby. It took about two days, but we found a house nestled into the north side of the cliff."

Voodoo comes out of his seat to my right and leans directly next to the speaker of the phone. "Please tell me you got an approximate longitude for this place?"

"Sure did, V. We used those long-range binoculars you lent us. They are cool as shit by the way. Anyways, we got a visual on the place. It's heavily guarded, with several expensive fucking cars parked outside. Thrasher is texting you the coordinates now, along with a few pics he snapped of license plates in town."

Voodoo's phone chirps in his pocket. He pulls it out and looks at it before bolting from the room.

"What kind of security are you talking about?" Hero asks. "Can you give us specifics?"

"Standard issue assault rifles, and some pretty big dudes. Guns looked to be an AR-15, but without being closer, I can't be sure. The last count we have was about twenty armed guards."

"You see anything else? People or drug vans pulling out of the place?" I ask, hoping they could get us at least an idea of who's running the operation.

"No vans, but the guy in charge looks to be short and stocky, with curly brown hair. We've been up there a few times to check them out, and he always seems to wear the same damn white hat and pants."

My heart begins to race at the man's description. If I didn't know any better, they could be describing Maj's Uncle, Ricardo Manuel. She used to tell stories about him to the kids when they were little. She had a falling out with her family by the time we'd gotten together, and she had no desire to ever be considered a relative of theirs. Goddamnit. Even knowing now how much of a fucking liar she was, the story doesn't seem that far-fetched. I'm betting she practiced that sobbing shit for months before she sunk her claws into my dopey ass, who soaked up every single word.

I'm a fucking idiot.

I close my eyes and try to think back to all the times she described him to the kids. The white hat and pants could be anybody, but I need to remember some detail that would distinguish him from the rest of the cartel. Just as I'm about to give up, a thought hits me.

"Irons, did you get a good look at his shoes?"

"Jesus, man. This isn't some fashion show. Why would his shoes matter?" Ratchet mutters.

"Just humor me, okay?" I reply. "Were they lime green, Irons?"

I hear muffled mumbling in the background as he confers with Thrasher.

"They sure were, Prez. Thrasher said he could see them from a mile away."

My stomach drops, and I'm on my feet in an instant, barking out orders. "I need you to get extra eyes on my mom's and Darcy's parents houses in Arizona. I want them to have rotating watch detail of two or more until they hear otherwise." While I had just a single prospect watching each house, I'd feel better knowing that, when the shit hits the fan for real this time, they are better protected. The thought crosses my mind of sending Darcy, Dani, and Ricca out there until we get back, but that's a bridge I'll have to cross once I have the rest of the details.

"Call Trax, Mistral, and Hazzard. Tell them to get their crews, and get their asses to Mexico. Make sure they come ready for a fight."

The men around the table stare at me in silence, likely wondering why someone's shoe color would set me off into motion.

"When my ex-wife talked about her family, she always mentioned an uncle who was a drug dealer, and how he always wore these ridiculous green shoes. Ricardo Manuel, the fucking head of the cartel. If he's there, we found their base of operations. Kiss your old ladies and hug your kids, gentleman. This time, we'll be settling things once and for all."

As the men file out of the room, I know what I have to do to protect Darcy. What I have planned will not only destroy what we've built together these past few months, but me as well. There is no turning back once the decision has been made, and I know I have to end this before she becomes the next victim in this war. She'll be safer without me, but I'm not sure I can say the same for myself.

Chapter 23

DARCY

WAKING up to find Michael gone each morning this week has taken some getting used to. I know it's crazy to think that after only a few weeks, I have come to care so much about him. It might be too soon to throw the L word around, but even I can't deny he makes those feelings stir inside of me. I roll over onto my belly and pull his pillow under me, snuggling up to his scent that still lingers. I'll admit, at first I thought our bond came from our individual grief, but this connection we have is so much deeper.

I must have dozed back off because I wake up in a panic as the door swings open with a slam, and hits the wall. He stomps into the room and immediately goes to the closet with a bag in his hand. What the hell is going on? My stomach falls as I watch him place everything I have stored away in his room into the bag, including my home business laptop. His face is unreadable, yet I can feel the anger wafting off him in thick waves.

"Am I going somewhere?" I ask sheepishly.

"Yes. Out of here and away from me."

"But I don't understand," I choke out.

"This isn't for you to understand, Darcy. I told you from the very beginning that, when one of us needs out, that's all there is to it."

"Why are you doing this?" I plead. "I thought you were happy with how things were going with us."

He tosses my packed suitcase by the door and turns to face me. "I am. Well, I was, but shit changes at a moment's notice. You scratched an itch that needed scratching, but that shit's finished now. I need you to gather anything else you have left and be out within the hour. Slider is waiting to take you to your parent's house. Someone from the club will let you know when you can come back."

I slide from the bed and allow my legs carry me toward the man actively trying to break my heart. My stomach rises to my throat, nearly choking me as I try to understand his sudden change of heart. Last night, he was so sweet and loving, but today, the asshole he can be is standing here trying to throw us away, and for what? Fear of getting to close? Pride?

He can't be the asshole he was before. I've seen the real him far more than this side he's currently displaying.

"This isn't about us," I prod. "Something has you spooked, and it's easier to shove me away than it is to fucking let me in so I can help you."

He huffs out a humorless laugh. "Help me? Darcy, you couldn't help me even if you put a bullet into my brain and put me out of my misery. I'm done, and we're over. Time to move on before things get even any worse than they already are."

I try to reach up and touch him, praying he'll soften as I try to desperately hold onto our connection, but he brushes my hand away and moves to leave. I bolt for the door and slam it shut, narrowly missing his face. Michael stands stunned as I flip the lock and force him into the conversation he's trying to avoid. He growls, charging toward me and pinning me against the back of the door with his body, his hands pressed into the door on either side of my face.

"Tell me what is going on and where this is all coming from," I say softly. "Are you and the club leaving?"

"Yes, and that's all I'm going to say. Please don't make this any harder than it has to be."

His arms are tense, and the turmoil swirling in his

eyes tells me this isn't what he wants. He's fighting himself as he tries to keep his charade going.

"Where are you going, and why can't I come?" I urge.

"Because where I'm going, and what I'm about to do, could get you killed. I'm not going to put you in harm's way because I can't handle being away from you for even a second. This is for your own good. I'm too dangerous for you to be around anymore."

Anger coils in my gut, quickly extinguishing the sadness he's put there by trying to force me out. "That's why you're pushing me away? To protect me? Jesus fucking Christ, Michael. The most dangerous place for me is away from you, or have you forgotten about those promises you made to me?"

"You don't know what you are saying," he snaps. "If you knew the things I have done, you'd be running away from me."

"I don't know because you won't let me in," I yell, fury taking over.

"I don't let you in because it would fucking get you killed," he snarls. "Why can't you see I'm protecting you by sending you away?"

"How are you protecting me by keeping me in the dark?" I cry. "I can't see what's coming if you constantly act as my buffer from all the bad shit in this world."

Micheal's fist slams into the door, and he recoils realizing how close he came to hitting me. I know he's angry, and that he would never touch me in a hurtful way, but feeling the wind as his fist sailed past my face startles me enough to send fat, hot tears running along my cheeks.

Michael shoves himself away from the door and paces the room, his hand scraping over his bald head.

"Show me how bad it can get," I persist. "I can't understand what it means to be with you if you can't show me."

He stops mid-step and stomps over to me, grabbing me by the wrist and dragging me out the door wearing only his t-shirt I had slept in last night. He escorts me out of the clubhouse, where everyone watches in silence as he drags me to a shed on the back side of the property. Throwing open the door, he shoves me inside. The shed is empty except for a few ropes swaying from the rafters.

"You want to know what it's like to be around me? Let me show you where I found your husband. He was hanging from the rafters with those ropes tied around his wrists, just like Jesus Christ on the cross. They fucking left him hanging here, bloody and beaten, because of his association with this club, and because of me. *I fucking did this to him,*" he roars.

"No," I whisper, shaking my head in disbelief. "I don't believe you. You're just trying to scare me into leaving so you don't have to deal with me anymore."

"If you don't believe me, ask the man who found his lifeless body in here. Ratchet."

A scream rips from my throat as I launch myself at him, trying to hurt him as much as his admission is killing me. I claw and punch until he grabs me by the wrists and holds me steady. Indescribable pain rips apart my heart as I fight against his grasp, trying to take a swipe at him.

"You fucking killed my husband," I sob. "You killed him."

"Yes, darlin', I'm one of the reasons he's dead. I may not have pulled the trigger, but I'm just as guilty as the fucker who did."

"Who?" I screech. "Who killed him?"

"My wife."

Those words stop me mid-swing. I gape up at him in horror. "What? Maj killed my husband?"

"Yes," he admits, his head hanging in defeat.

"How long have you known it was her?" I whisper.

"Since Tijuana."

I can see how much it hurts him to tell me, but I

should have known this before now. He should have told me before we started down the path of being together. So many things would have been different, and right now, I hate him for lying to me. Had I known the ugly truth the day Brent died, I can't be sure I wouldn't have killed Michael with my own hands for his part in this. Him and his fucking wife.

"You son-of-a-bitch," I screech, charging at him again, but his body holds me in my place. "You've known this entire time. *The entire time we've been together.*" This bastard had taken me into his bed, knowing what his wife had cost me. "Has this all been a fucking game to you? Our relationship? The feelings we have for each other?"

"No," he snarls. "This was never a fucking game, Darcy. Maybe it was fucked to believe this could work out between us, but I never intended for any of this to happen. I just wanted to make you happy."

My rage burns me from the inside out. "You didn't make me happy, you bastard. You made me fall in love with you."

Micheal gapes at me, his face frozen in shock. When he takes a step closer, I back away, putting a few feet of distance between us. His eyes never leave mine as he tries to get closer.

"Stay away from me, you fucking bastard."

"Darcy, I—" he starts, but I throw up my hand to stop him.

"I don't want to hear your apologies, or some heartfelt declaration of your fucked-up version of love. Like you said earlier, it's over. You were right when you said you couldn't protect me, because you can't protect me from yourself."

Micheal takes another step, but I counter by stepping back.

"The man I loved died, hanging right where I'm standing, so I guess it's only fitting for the feelings I had for you to die here as well."

"Believe me, Darcy," he says. "I know how you feel. My wife betrayed me, just as she did you. She took a life that meant more to me than my own. I would have died a thousand times just to spare his life because I'm just like my fucking father. I bring on my own destruction, and it's by my own hand that I kill and destroy everything in my path. I promise you I will fix this."

"That's where you are wrong," I seethe. "You won't fix this. I will. I will kill the bitch for this. Track her ass down, and when you find her, I want her on her knees in front of me. I want to watch her beg for her life before I put a bullet in her brain. Only then will I be satisfied."

"She's already dead," he admits. "She died the

day she betrayed Dani. I should have known then that her treachery ran far deeper than just handing over Dani for fucking cash."

I blink, shaking my head in disbelief. "She's the reason Dani was kidnapped? Jesus, Michael, what else have you turned a blind eye to avoid having to deal with?"

He sighs and stares at me, sadness brewing in his blue eyes. "Maj was using me and our marriage to bring cartel members into the clubs and expand their drug territories. Jagger caught wind of what was going on and started tracking her. He'd been following her for a while before she arranged his murder."

"That's why you're leaving," I say, all the pieces of the puzzle now falling into place. "You're going to Mexico to settle the score."

"Yes, we're leaving in the morning. We have men there already. We're going to clean out their compound and end this before more blood is spilled."

I stand straighter, looking him straight in his face. "I'm going with you."

"The fuck you are," he spits. "I wasn't kidding about you getting the fuck out of dodge, Darcy. I don't want you anywhere near this shit storm."

"No," I say, my tone firm. "The way I see it, Brent

died because of his fucking loyalty to you. Simply knowing you seems to be why the grim reaper has marked us all for death. Now, because of the both of you, my kids are in danger, and quite frankly, I've had enough of this bullshit to last a lifetime. So either you fix this with my help, Michael, or you learn to live with more innocent blood on your hands."

"That a threat?"

"No, it's not," I reply. "It's a promise."

Chapter 24

RAZE

HAVE you ever had a moment in your life when you instantly regretted an exchange or an argument? I know I sure fucking have. I knew I fucked up everything the very second I decided to push her out to keep her out of harm's way. The words of my brothers had clouded my fucking judgment, and my need to protect her at all costs meant I had to break her heart, and in the process, my own. In the short walk from Church to my room, I made a decision that not only killed any chances I had with her, but of the future I had been dreaming about as well.

I told her the ugly truth.

Trust me, doing what I did was far from easy. My heart was screaming inside my chest. My mind begged for me to stop my idiocracy and just tell her the truth. But no, I stooped so low that I just packed her bags and told her to get the fuck out of my life. The moment my anger got the best of me, I landed a punch to the door, just inches from her beautiful face, and I knew I had crossed the line. I couldn't stop myself from continuing to torture her, though.

Taking her to the shed and laying it out for her the way I did was me hitting rock bottom. As she screamed at me in the shed, I wanted so badly to take her in my arms and admit she was right about everything. It was my shortcomings as a man, a husband, and mostly as a leader for this club that delivered pain to both her family and my own. I should have known what was going on with my wife, and I should have stopped it before it cost Jagger his life, but I was too blinded by trying to keep my family together for my kids.

Darcy should have never known that her husband had been hung so close to the room she'd been sharing with me these past few weeks. It haunts me every single morning to look out the window and see that shed, knowing damn well what its walls had hidden just a year ago. Her bright smile was ripped away, and all that was left was a stone-cold woman, hell-bent on killing the people responsible for her misery. It had killed me to explain the details, but what stuck the knife in even deeper was the sheer determination on her face when she demanded to come along and finish the cartel by the club's side.

I underestimated just how strong she is. I never expected to fight with her, or to hurt her so deeply. I believed she would cry and accept my bullshit excuse, but instead, she meet me blow for emotional blow, challenging me. Even with her newly-founded hatred for me, I will gladly lay down my life for hers if she demanded it for my penance for my role in Jagger's death. But much like me, I don't think she could pull the trigger on someone she once loved.

Yes, *loved*.

I'm not naïve enough to think the feelings we had will remain after I showed my ass. She will likely never love me again, let alone be in the same room with me once all the debts are paid. I tore down every fucking wall I had just to let her destroy everything inside of me, and it wasn't until the aftermath of my stupidity that I realized I had fallen head over heels in love with her. I don't know when it happened, but I fell hard. I just wish I had known how tightly she held my heart before I destroyed us both.

Explaining the truth of Jagger's murder to my men had been even harder. The details I had kept hidden to save my own pride were laid out in front of them during an emergency Church meeting. And then I announced that Darcy would be coming with us.

Many of them were pissed, but they understood far more than I could have ever hoped. They knew their old ladies would want retribution for such a crime, but they agreed that she should be kept away from the front lines at all costs. I'm permitting her to be there to appease her, but also hoping that maybe she can once again find some semblance of peace once the smoke clears. It's not a place for a mother and a good woman, but I won't allow a single drop of her to be blood spill because of me. If she is the only one to walk away unscathed, I will gladly fall into the pits of hell and burn for eternity.

I spent last night alone, pacing the floor in my room. I tried to sleep, but not having Darcy by my side felt wrong. Her smell lingered scent on the pillows, and I couldn't bring myself to stay in that bed. Just a few doors down, I could hear her rustling around inside. Though she would never admit it, being apart was just as maddening for her as it was for me. We both spent the night suffering in self-imprisoned silence and loneliness. Rather than fight the useless battle to win her back so soon, I use that time to prepare myself mentally for the fight ahead.

The morning light comes far too quickly as the quiet of the clubhouse becomes replaced with the buzz of men preparing for battle. Opting to keep the element of surprise, I order everyone to take plain cars down instead of our bikes. We had everything we need to make it look like we're just a few visitors passing through the small town and nothing more. While we needed every man for the job, Voodoo, along with Slider, would be left behind to keep an eye in the sky, and to dig a little bit more into the photos Irons and Thrasher had sent over to us. I had also tasked them with arranging our new home away from home while we were traveling down. They will prove to be far more useful here than in the field with us.

I put in some quick calls to the other three chapters supporting us before carrying my gear out to the waiting SUVs. I round the back of the SUV and stop when I see Darcy cradled in Dani's open arms, sobbing into her shirt. Dani looks up as I watch them, her eyes narrowed on me. She knows what I did, and she is just as angry with me as Darcy. Hero steps up behind the two women and politely steals away his wife.

Darcy sighs, watching them steal a quiet moment together as Hero kisses her and the twins goodbye. I hate myself for dragging him away from his family, but he insisted he needed to be there. I had made him a promise that once we got back, he would be going on an extended vacation so he can enjoy more time with his wife and kids.

Darcy moves in my direction, but as soon as our eyes lock, she switches sides. The pain in her eyes is enough to know I need to steer clear of her. She slips around the SUV and slides into the back seat without a word to me or anyone else. While she might have prepared to ride in the other car, I will not let her leave my sight, nor do I want to be that far away from her. Even if she doesn't want to admit it, she's safer with me for the time being.

"You ready to go, Boss?" Tyson asks, slapping me on the shoulder.

"Is everything loaded?"

"The prospect just tossed the last of our bags into the back," he says with a hint of hesitation. "You sure it's a good idea to bring her along? I get she wants to be here, but it's not exactly a walk in the park where we're going."

"I know, brother, but she would have just followed us down anyway. If she goes with us and sees justice is done, she'll get what she came for and go home."

"Understood, Prez," he says, then he turns away, heading back to the waiting car.

Slipping back behind the tail end of the SUV, I walk to the driver's door and slide into the seat. Hero climbs into the passenger seat, and Ratchet takes his place next to Darcy. She shifts over in her seat, putting as much distance between them as possible. I know she doesn't like Ratch, but she made her choice when she bypassed sitting up front with me. While Ratchet's not a bad guy, he's not used to softening his words or ideas about a woman's role in club life. The two of them have only ever said a few words to each other, but I know she can feel his disdain for her after Jagger. There's only been one person to see through his asshole façade, and that's Ricca. She knows how to take his bullshit, but she also knows how to chuck it right back at him without missing a beat. Ricca is his match, and he's a fool if he doesn't stop her from leaving like she's threatened.

Starting the ignition, I shift the vehicle into drive and pull out of the parking lot with Tyson, Dirty, and Hot Shot taking up the rear of our convoy. Along the way, I field phone calls on my Bluetooth headset from the other chapters, and Voodoo with the directions to our new humble abode. Hero and Ratchet banter back and forth between calls about motorcycles and Hero's new domestic status, while Darcy sits in silence. When given the chance, I sneak peeks of her in the rearview mirror, only to find her eyes either trained on the passing view outside the window, or jerking away from the mirror. Knowing she's watching me the same way I'm watching her gives me hope that maybe, after all is said and done, I can repair the damage. A little hope is a far easier pill to swallow than none at all.

The drive down flies by until we hit the border traffic. We idle for over an hour in the inspection lanes before finally making it to the front of the line.

"Passports, please," the border patrol agent barks.

I reach over as Darcy and Ratchet pass their passports to Hero, who in turn hands them all to me. He looks them over, his eyes scanning each of us to verify that our photos match. His eyes linger on Darcy just a little too long for my liking, before handing the passports back to me through the window.

"What's your business in Mexico?"

"Meeting with a client for our security business," I state.

"And the woman?"

"A little R & R, if you get my drift," I say with a wink. Darcy growls from the back seat. "She's been mad at me for working too much, so I dragged her along with me on the trip."

He peers over my shoulder and looks back at Darcy, who I can only assume is fuming behind me.

"Looks like you're in for a long trip, sir."

"Yeah." I chuckle. "She's gonna be the death of me, let me tell you."

The man nods. "Everything looks good. Have a nice day."

The border patrol agent steps back from the SUV and waves for the man at the gate to let us pass. Putting the car back into drive, we maneuver out of the line and across the border. I drive us up a few miles before pulling off and waiting for the others to make it through the checkpoint. As we sit there, I peek back at Darcy, who still looks pissed at my little joke.

"Relax, darlin'. It got us through the border. You can now go back to your regularly scheduled hatred until we go home."

"You're a bastard," she snaps. "You know that, right?"

Hero laughs from the passenger seat, and I pull my attention from Darcy to shoot a glare straight at him. "What's so fucking funny?"

"You two," he says with a belly laugh. "You're too busy being pissy to notice how perfect you are for each other."

"Shut up, Hero," Darcy snaps. "I didn't know being a lying, conniving bastard was my type, but I'll take your suggestion under advisement. I'll file it under the never going to fucking happen again tab."

"Oh, kitten's got *claws*," Ratchet jokes.

"I'm not a fucking kitten, asshole."

"I can hear you hissing and spitting all the way over here, but you and I both know when the time comes, you'll end up right back in his bed, begging for him to scratch your ears and rub your belly."

"More like scratch his eyes out and bite off his pecker."

All three of us hiss in unison, and my hand falls to cover my dick in an act of protection, knowing that if she wanted to do that, she would. Finally, the others appear and we head out. The rest of the ride is spent in silence until we pull up to Voodoo's housing arrangements.

"What the fuck kind of place is this?" Hero mutters as I park the SUV outside of a rundown mobile home park. "It's like hoarders meets trailer trash."

The doublewide trailer in front of us is a shit-brown color and looks like a strong gust of wind might blow it over. Creepy little garden gnomes line the walk-up, and what I can only describe as cinder block saw horses form the stairs up to a plywood porch. Several of the windows appear to have film lining the inside of them, blurring out the light. I can only imagine how bad the inside of this place is going to smell.

"I told him to make us blend in, so I guess this is either his idea of blending, or it's another one of his fucking jokes."

Stepping out of the car, I open Darcy's door without being prompted. She slides from the seat and hops to the ground with a huff.

"I don't need you to open a door. I can handle that, and so much more, on my own without you, *Raze*," she seethes, adding extra emphasis on my road name.

Before I can stop myself, I spin around and pin her body to the car. "You know the rules. Call me Raze again, I will brand my name right on your ass as a reminder. Got it?"

"Sure thing, *Raze*," she taunts, her eyes narrowed to angry slits.

A growl escapes my lips as I hold my last thread of self-control to keep from flipping her around and pounding into her from behind. That would remind her of my name. "I've warned you once. I won't do it again. Never call me that name."

I leave her pressed up against the side of the SUV without another word. She stands there in shock, but I can smell the arousal pouring off her. If I hadn't walked away, I would have taken her then and there, and she would have never forgiven me. Having her here is more dangerous than a nuclear warhead in the hands of a man with a hair trigger. One false move, and I will destroy everything before I even have a chance to repair it.

Fuck.

Chapter 25

DARCY

NEARLY FIVE MINUTES pass before I move from the spot Michael had pinned me to the car. My body is screaming for his touch, but my mind struggles with tight restraint on my hatred for him. I'm a fool for still wanting him, and my body tries to betray me every time he walks into the room. It takes every ounce of my willpower to stand my ground around him without crumpling to the floor in an emotionally-exhausted heap. I want to fuck him and kill him at the same time. My pussy doesn't know whether to be pissed or turned on.

I'm a fucking hot mess.

I knew by forcing him to bring me down here, I was only putting myself back in the line of fire of him and the shit we're facing. I sat in that shed and cried for hours after he shoved me in there and revealed the truth about his wife's involvement in Brent's murder. What shocked me more was that he could so easily kill the woman who gave him his children. Though, she did deserved her fate, it showed me just how cold and calculating he could be, and that scares me.

I stayed quiet most of the ride down here because I didn't want to draw his attention, but that was an epic fail. I couldn't keep my eyes off of him in the rearview mirror. With one glance in that fucking mirror, he made me feel alive again, yet his mistrust and anger still stabbed me directly in the heart. I wanted to reach around the seat and touch him to ease his pain, and then choke him. His lies have pulled my soul apart, and now, two different sides of myself live within. The ruthless side that wants revenge, and the soft side that wants to forgive and forget.

I'd be a fool not to know he lied to me to spare furthering my pain. I'd even go so far as to admit I would have probably taken the same course of action had the roles been reversed. That line of thought may make me a hypocrite, but I can't help the betrayal I feel . What stings more than his lies is how he just shoved me away when things got tough, like I was his some toy to be discarded and hidden away because he didn't want to share me with anyone else. With Michael, it's all or nothing, and I seem to have ended up on the latter side of the spectrum. Nothing like pain, fear, and being in love with a fucking monster.

"Welcome home, Darcy," Hero says, pulling open the door to the trailer. The putrid odors of urine, mildew, and neglect wafts from inside in waves that nearly make me throw up. Hero goes in first and starts popping open the windows in a feeble attempt to make the place smell more inviting. I let the place air out some before even stepping inside.

Trash litters the floor of this dump. I kick empty beer bottles out of my path as I walk to the back of the trailer. The bedrooms are a bit better than I thought they would be, but I think I'd rather take my chances and sleep in the SUV for fear of contracting some Mexican shitting disease. Scrunching up my nose from the smell of the nearby bathroom, I hear footsteps behind me.

"I know it's not the Hilton, but it's going to have to do," Michael's gruff voice whispers in my ear. His baritones make my body shiver, and his closeness sets my skin on fire. "We need to talk," he demands, taking me by the hand and leading me back outside into the sun and heat.

He leads me over to a tree with a shoddy picnic

table beneath it and waves his hand, motioning for me to sit. The old wood creaks under his weight as he sits down across from me. "I know you're fucking pissed, and that you want nothing to do with me, but I need to get this out before the rest of the crew shows up and we have to leave. If I don't come back, I will regret every single second in the afterlife if I don't tell you this." He speaks quickly, stumbling over his words. "I love you, Darcy. I think I've loved you from the moment you walked into our clubhouse on Jagger's arm."

His admission hits me like a slap to the face.

"How *dare* you," I his, jumping to my feet. "You love me? You don't even know what it means to love someone. Love means you trust them and confide in them. Not lie to them until you have no other choice than to be honest. You blew your chance with me. You couldn't fucking tell me the truth, and no 'I love you' is going to save this."

Not letting me have the upper-hand, he stands and plants his feet. "You're so single-sighted, you don't see what's right in front of you, Darcy," he snaps, his arms flying into the air. "I may be the devil you desire and hate at the same time, but I'm the man willing to be the single strand of barbed wire separating you from the evil in this world. No one else would be standing here about to go to war to keep you and the kids safe."

He takes a step closer, and the pull I feel toward him becomes stronger. I dig my heels into the dirt to keep myself from flying into his arms.

"Keep me safe?" I scoff. "How is this keeping me safe? Or my kids safe? Or your own fucking brothers *safe*? We're standing in the middle of the Mexican wastelands, about to charge a cartel compound."

His face grows dark, his anger falling away, only to be replaced with sadness. His arms fall to his sides like broken branches.

"I've made mistakes in my life that I can't go back and fix, no matter how much I want to. That shit's on me, but this is my chance to right the wrongs and end this thing. I'm tired of the bullshit and bloodshed. It's time to usher in a new era for this club. One where we don't have to keep looking over our shoulder for the next person to take a swing at us."

I shake my head. "That's just a pipe dream, and you know it. You talked about how you wanted to be different from your father, and you've ended up just like him. Knee deep in shit with blood on your hands. Changing the club's image isn't going to fix this, and neither is expanding that security business of yours. To change things, *you* need to change. You can't keep burning bridges and hope your enemies don't rebuild them. You have to live with the consequences of your actions, instead of burying them and hoping they never resurface again."

He shakes his head and scoffs. Taking a step toward him, I force him look at me. His eyes are so dull and lifeless now, compared to the light shining behind them before. He's in far more pain than he's letting on.

"Michael, you can't keep putting the weight of the world on your shoulders. You need to let someone in that can help distribute it. I'm not saying that's me, but someone needs to be able to help you."

He winces and moves closer to me. "What if I want it to be you?"

"I can't be that person for you anymore," I admit. "And as much as I want to forgive you, I just can't. Too much has happened in the short time we've been together." And with that parting blow, I walk away and head back into the trailer, leaving him behind, holding my bleeding heart.

"I can't promise you I won't end up like Brent, but what I can promise you is that even if I end up six feet under the ground, I will love you until we meet again," he calls out, before the door slams shut between us.

I know I lied to him, but I can't let him in again. Not until I know he wants to change, and that he'll fight for us. It's too risky to just fall to my knees and beg him to come back. He needs to feel the weight of the decisions he's made, and decide to change for the better without my influence. It has to come from him and him alone.

The rest of the afternoon, men from the other chapters ride into the trailer park, which apparently has been rented out in it's entirety by Voodoo. Each club has a cluster of mobile homes to bunk in. I was ordered by Michael to stay in the trailer while they had a combined Church meeting in one of the larger buildings on the property.

Bored, I open up the refrigerator in the trailer out of habit, recoiling as the foulest stench I've ever smelled seeps into everything. I bolt from the trailer, gagging and retching, trying my best not to throwing up.

I'm only a few feet from the door when strong arms wrap around me, pinning me to a hard body. Trax's sickening smile and hot breath bore into my neck. He tries to hold me in place, but I twist and struggle until finally tearing from his grasp. If there were someplace for me to take a scalding hot shower, I would sit in there for hours to wash away his touch from my skin. To say he gives me the creeps is a fucking understatement.

"Surprised to see you here, doll. I figured Raze would keep his little pet locked down back at home."

"The same could be said for you," I reply, crossing my arms and trying to remain calm. "I figured a man like you would be as far away from the fight as possible."

"Well, doll. As you said, a man such as myself has to protect his business interests. If this club bursts into flames, well that's bad for business. I'm here to make sure that doesn't happen."

Narrowing my eyes, I study him. "What's your interest in club business? You don't have a majority stake or claim to anything this club does. You're just a bitch player that does what Michael tells him to." I may not be an expert in all things motorcycle club, but in the hierarchy of the Heaven's Rejects, Trax isn't exactly a huge player in the organization. Michael holds all the cards to the club, and he plays them close to his chest. The only exceptions to that are the men who sit around his own Church table. Trax doesn't fit any of the criteria for being in Michael's inner circle.

"Oh, doll. I play a bigger role than you think," he chides. "Why don't you go back to your little trailer and play with that peashooter I see tucked into your jeans. Let the men handle the business at hand."

"This little peashooter," I say, tracing my finger along the butt of the gun hanging at my hip, "would be more than enough to put you out of your misery."

Trax throws his head back laughs, then turns and walks away. His mannerisms are troubling, and his words even more so.

Why isn't he with the others, hashing out the plan?

A short time later, the guys spill out of their makeshift meeting place and disperse to their various trailers. One man from another chapter, Hazzard, stops by with supplies a few hours after our arrival. He looks me up and down as he stands at the doorway of the trailer before just walking away.

Is he sizing me up, or looking over the woman who singlehandedly forced a man three times her size to take her along on this adventure?

As I put things away, a truck fires up outside and disappears down the drive in a cloud of smoke. Ratchet shuffles around the trailer, organizing the gear. I peek out the window and see a group of men cleaning their weapons beneath the shade trees. Hours pass, and Michael never resurfaces from that meeting. Something feels off about his absence, but I chalk it up to nerves, and wondering how I will play into this fight. I fully intend on participating in some way, yet I know he'll try to keep me away. That's far from what I want, but I get why he would try it. Safety seems to be his mantra when it comes to me, but sadly, for him, I'm not a watch and see kind of girl.

"You see Raze?" Hero asks, popping his head into the trailer as I attempt to make some sort of a meal from the meager rations delivered earlier.

"Nope," I say, popping a piece a fruit into my mouth. "The last time I saw him was before he whisked y'all off to Church. Why?"

"No one has seen him for hours, and Voodoo is calling my phone like crazy, trying to get ahold of him. You sure you don't have him tied down somewhere in the back?" he asks, worry clearly defined on his face.

"No," I bite back. "I haven't seen him."

Just when I go to repeat my unanswered question, my phone begins to ring. Another huge cloud of dust flies into the park as I slip my hand into my pocket and see Voodoo's number on my call display. Voodoo's words mush together in an incoherent sentence as soon as I swipe to answer.

"Woah, slow down, Voodoo. I can't understand a word you're saying."

"I need to talk to Raze. This is fucking important, and no one seems to know where he is. I figured if he was holed up with anyone, it would be you," he semi-yells into the phone.

"Like I just told Hero, I have no clue where's he holed up."

"Darcy, listen," he says, his voice laced with urgency. "I need you to find him and call me back. He needs to hear what I just found." A commotion erupts outside, and I watch through the window as men gather around the pick-up truck parked in the middle of the road.

"Voodoo, something is going on here. Can't you just tell me, and I will relay the message for him?"

"Shit, I shouldn't, but it'll take me longer to explain it yet again," he mutters. "Maj is fucking alive."

The phone falls from my hand and bounces on the floor. I can hear Voodoo calling my name as shock hits me, twisting my stomach into knots. I thought he said she was dead and by his own hand. Why the fuck would he lie to me again by hiding that she's still alive? It doesn't serve him any good to lie about something like that. What if... What if he wasn't the one who pulled the trigger, and he has been in the dark this entire time? Jesus, he probably doesn't know either.

I bolt for the door, suddenly desperate to find him, but I'm met with Hero standing in my way. His eyes are filled with rage, and I know in an instant that something has happened. He shakes his head as he tries to form words.

"What's happened?" I whisper, the pain in my stomach making me want to double over and scream.

"It's Raze," he rasps. "The fucking cartel have him."

Chapter 26

RAZE

IN ONE SPLIT SECOND, Trax and I were cutting up about some stupid ass joke he told me, and then everything went black. A chill surrounds my body as I try to force my eyes to open, struggling against the bonds keeping my consciousness from waking. It takes eons for my eyes to open, and the moment they do, my head pounds like a freight train had run over my skull and came back for round two. Every muscle in my body screams in pain. Silence surrounds me, making me aware I'm not on the road with Trax anymore.

"What the fuck is going on?" I rasp. "Trax, did we go off road or something? Trax? Where the fuck are you, man?" I try to shake away the haze surrounding my brain, but it continues to linger in my peripheral vision, making everything blurry.

"You're awake," a voice calls from the darkness. "Good. I was hoping you'd wake up for me."

"Who's there?" I call, trying to reach my hands out in front of me, but they won't budge. "Where the fuck am I?"

Shit, why are my hands bound? What the fuck is going on?

"Aw, babe. I'm hurt you don't recognize my voice," the voice says, laced with a familiar edge of evil. "It's only been a year. I thought you'd at least remember your own wife's voice."

"Maj?" I breathe.

A shadowed form steps into my line of sight. My eyes try to adjust, but it isn't until the person comes a few inches away from my face that their features become more defined and clear. Maj's former beauty has been replaced by sunken-in eyes and cheeks. I can smell the stench of the drugs on her pungent breath. I knew she had a problem when we met at the Sturgis bike rally. She was dabbling in cocaine back then, but judging by how raggedy as she looks now, I'm betting she's moved on to something a little harder, like meth or crack. Her ribs are clearly visible beneath her filthy t-shirt.

"That's right, baby," she coos. "Alive and well, no thanks to you, it seems."

I gape up at her. "You should be dead."

"That's the thing about death. You really should verify your kills before leaving the scene of the crime." Moving in, she drags her tongue along the side of my face. "Your blood is delicious, my dear husband."

I struggle against my bonds, trying to break free, but her cold hands slam onto mine, digging her nails into my flesh and drawing blood.

I stop moving and level her with a hate-filled glare. "He's in on it, isn't he?"

"Finally getting the full picture, aren't you?" she says, giving me another sick smile "He was never going to kill me. Unlike you, that bastard is in love with me, and you don't put a bullet into someone you love."

"Love," I scoff. "You don't know what that word means, you bitch."

"Of course I know how to love, baby. I just didn't love *you*," she replies. Sliding onto my lap, her bony ass digs into my thighs, as she grinds herself against me. "I used you to fulfill my uncle's wishes, playing the part of your loyal and dutiful wife. Well, maybe not the loyal part," she says with a laugh. She grinds against me even harder, a moan slipping from her chapped lips. A heavy door creaks open and weighted steps enter the room. Maj arches her body back and cranes her neck to see who had interrupted her fun.

"I see our prisoner is awake," a heavily accented voice says. Ricardo Manuel steps into the light and walks toward me. Maj kisses my lips before she dismounts and prances over to her uncle's side.

"Buenas Días, nephew. How do you like your new accommodations?"

"The chair could use some padding," I reply. "And the turn down service is a bit trashy. I'd like to speak to your manager."

Ricardo charges toward me and wraps his hands around my throat, effectively cutting off my air supply. I gasp for air as he chokes me, a twisted smile on his face. He squeezes my throat harder, until the pops and cracks of my trachea straining against the force of his grip can be heard. Finally, he releases me. I inhale a gasping breath, desperate to push oxygen back into my lungs.

"Such a smartass, you are. I can see why my niece took an interest in you," he says. Turning his back on me, he grabs a rag from a steel table in the center of the room. Reflections of light gleam back at me, bouncing off the tools littering the table.

"What do you want from me?" I rasp.

"I want your club, and its network," he plainly

states. "My reach is being shortened every single day by the Federales and border patrol. I can't sell my product if I can't move it. That's where you and your club come in."

"I won't be a fucking carrier pigeon for your drugs."

"Oh, but that's where you're wrong. I don't need you, and once I kill you, I already have someone in place to take over the club, and put my plan into action."

Rage courses through my body, and my muscles strain as I struggle to break free. My chest heaves as the rope tightly wound around my wrists tears into my skin. Trax. That fucking son-of-a-bitch has been maneuvering himself to take over as soon as Ricardo and Maj take me out. He's been the one spreading lies and stirring up shit with the other chapters. It started off as a simple disagreement, but it escalated once Brent was murdered. He will die one way or another. I will see to it.

"You putting two and two together, baby?" Maj coos while prancing around where she stands.

"It's been him all along hasn't it?" I snarl, my very being overwhelmed with hatred. "Where the fuck is he?"

"Well, duh," she flirts. "He's been the guy on the inside all along. How do you think Twisted Tribe got onto the property to dump Jagger's snitch body? He let them in, and as to his location... he's around. That's all you need to know."

"You fucking bitch," I sneer. "Why kill him and not me? I was the one you wanted dead."

Maj sashays over to me and bends down, putting her face directly in front of mine.

"That's simple, lover," she coos. "He was going to blow the lid off of everything, so he had to die. I couldn't have him spilling the beans before I had everything in place, now could I?"

"How did Twisted Tribe get involved in this?"

Maj laughs in my face. "Baby, I was fucking the VP on the side, and when I went to him with a sob story about how you had Jagger beat me when you found out about us, he put the order in to kill him. It was too easy. He played right into my hands. Right under your nose, and his."

"Fucking bitch!" I roar, my heart aching for all that Jagger went through because of this bitch.

"Dani and that little blonde bitch roommate of hers only helped to sweeten the deal. How are they by the way?"

"Both still alive, no thanks to you," I throw back in her face.

"Huh, I didn't see that one coming. That step-brother of Dani's was a bit on the loony side, but he paid me well."

She blows me a kiss and walks half way across the room before stopping and looking at me over her shoulder. "How're my kids? Do they miss their mommy?"

"They haven't asked about you once, you fucking whore. They don't need you. They have me."

Maj tosses her head back in a laugh, and a sickening feeling punches me in my gut. She can take my life and my club, but she wouldn't be so fucking evil to take my kids away from me, would she?

"Oh, baby," she giggles. "I knew you were stupid. The kids aren't even yours."

"You fucking *bitch*," I growl. "I'm going to get out of these ropes, and I will strangle you until your fucking eyeballs pop out of their sockets."

"Ooh, feisty. You keep that spirit alive, lover. You're going to need it when you watch me kill that new little bitch of yours."

Fear strikes me hard and fast. She's referring to Darcy. If it's the last thing I do, I will protect her. She doesn't deserve to be dragged into this.

"I don't have just one bitch. I have many. They're called club whores, a term you should be familiar with, since it's what I should be calling you."

For the first time, I see a different emotion flash in

her eyes. That struck a nerve. I need to keep pissing her off so she forgets about Darcy and puts her focus all onto me. That's the only way she'll survive this.

"That so?"

"With our sexless marriage? I had to get my dick wet somehow," I mutter. "I've gotta say, I'm a lucky man to have rid myself of you, Maj. I'd forgotten what good fucking felt like. You really should look into that pussy tightened up. The last time we fucked, I couldn't feel shit."

"That's enough," Ricardo demands. "You two bicker like fucking school children. It's time we get down to business."

He jerks Maj out of his way, and she slams against the table in the middle of the room. Ricardo is the kind of man that commands attention. His face is unreadable, and I know that kind of skill comes with years of practice and lack of emotions. Just looking at him, I can tell he's a stone-cold killer who doesn't give a flying fuck who he cuts down in the process.

"I want nothing to do with your brand of business."

"Well, here's the thing, Michael. You don't mind, if I call you that, do you? I detest the idea of those stupid fucking nicknames you bikers seem to think are cool," he says. "I had a feeling you wouldn't agree, so I have a little incentive for you."

"Nothing you could do would make me agree to be your bitch, Ricardo. My men will never accept Trax as their president. Your little plan will go to shit as soon as you pull that trigger."

"You say that so matter-of-factly, Michael, but I'm sure you'll change your mind once you see who I have coming to your rescue."

Panic grips my soul. He's talking about my brothers. They are walking into a fucking trap, and I have no way to warn them. I rack my brain for something I can use to get them out of this, but only one thing comes to mind; agree to his fucking deal, and try to fix it later. It's all I have left. I can't let them walk into this and lose their lives over something I should have stopped years ago.

"Fine. I'll do it."

Ricardo grins, his face devious as he nods to Maj. She stalks across the room, and my eyes trail after her every move. She stops on the left side of the room and reaches up to a sheet draped over a large object in the corner. Yanking the material off, she exposes a series of TV monitors with live surveillance footage. Dust clouds the air on the screens, and I strain my eyes, trying to focus through the dust, but my vision is still distorted from my capture.

"It's good that you agreed to our little business

agreement, Michael. Unfortunately, for your friends, it's already far too late."

Figures move into view on the screen, and Maj watches and laughs. "The party is just about to begin."

Chapter 27

DARCY

THE CARTEL HAS RAZE.

Panic and unbridled fear take hold of my body as I rush out of the trailer past Hero, hoping this is all some bad dream. This wasn't supposed to happen. What if I never see him again, or get to tell him that I do still love him? All the what ifs and whys send my head spinning as I stop dead in my path. The truck that flew out of here like a bat out of hell earlier sits parked in the drive, while a bloody and beaten Trax is being pulled from the driver's seat. Ratchet and a man I don't know haul him from the truck and lay him out on his back on the porch.

He sputters something as they lay him down, and Hero brings out a medical kit from the trailer to tend to his wounds. I watch as the men hover around him, asking questions he answers with intelligible replies.

Hero starts to stitch up the wound over his eye, and doses him with what I can only assume is an injection of pain medicine, before he begins to make any sense.

"What happened, man? Where's Raze?" someone yells out.

"We went into town for supplies," he sputters. "They must have seen us there. We got shoved off the road, and I blacked out from the impact. I woke up and he was just gone."

I listen to his explanation, but something doesn't add up. Why would they go into town for supplies, when Hazzard had already dropped some off hours earlier? Looking at the truck, I don't see any visible markings from an impact that would have caused that much damage to his face and body. Shouldn't there have been some kind of ding or scratch to go along with his wounds?

"We have to go get him," Hazzard growls.

"What do we do without Raze to lead us?" someone calls out.

Hero steps up onto the porch and throws his hands in the air to quiet the crowd. He looks at me, and then at Trax propped up below him before speaking.

"We stick to his plan, and we get him out. That's our number one priority. Even if we can't get to the cartel leader, we get Raze out, no matter the cost. Now, let's go get this fucker, and bring our president home."

The men yell to signify their agreement, all of them moving swiftly toward the vehicles. In Raze's absence, they are turning to Hero to make the decisions. While he has good intentions on bringing him home, he doesn't know the full story. He goes into the trailer to grab his gear, and I follow.

"I'm going with you," I inform him.

Hero spins around while doing up the Velcro on his bulletproof vest. "The hell you are."

"Michael brought me here to help," I remind him, trying to make him see reason.

"No, *Raze* brought you here because he'd rather you be here, where he could watch you, instead of you charging into this on your own."

"That's misogynistic bullshit, and you know it, Hero. You're taking me with you, and that's final," I demand, reaching for the small bag of weapons and protection equipment on the table.

"No, you need to stay here and look after Trax. We can't leave an injured man here. If they kill us all, you two can get the fuck out of dodge and live. Besides, if Raze is alive, he will kill me if I include you in this. You weren't brought here to fight, Darcy."

"You have to take me because Voodoo relayed information to me that you don't know."

Hero grabs two handguns and tucks them into the holsters under his arms, and then shoves a series of knives into his boots and wrist sheaths. He takes two steps toward me, trapping me against the sink in the trailer.

"You can either tell me and give me a chance to save him, or not tell me and possibly condemn him to death. Your choice, Darcy."

"Maj is alive, and at the compound," I stammer. "Voodoo saw her in some of the pictures Irons and Thrasher sent back. The bitch that killed my husband is still fucking alive." Hot tears spill over and trail down my face. In my attempt to win him over, frustration and rage has boiled over inside of me.

"Fuck," he whispers, just as shocked at the news as I was. "Was he sure it was her?"

"Yes."

"Darcy, listen. I know you want a piece of her, and frankly, I want to deliver her to your feet so you can kill her yourself, but if we have a chance to get him out, and it's between him and her, I'm choosing him. That's how it is. If I can get them both, you can pull the trigger. I promise you that. Now, I need to go and bring our guy home. Do what I say and stay here. Promise me you won't leave."

I wipe away the tears on my face, nodding my head in agreement. Hero walks over and pulls my head close to his face so he can press a kiss to my forehead.

"I'll bring him home," he promises, and then he disappears through the door. I stand by, watching as dozens of men pile into cars, trucks, and SUVs, then they kick up giant plumes of dust as they speed off after Michael. As they disappear from sight, I mutter a silent prayer that they bring him home to me.

Trax is still on the deck, and he's struggling to stand from where he'd been laying. He's moving a little too well for an injured man.

"Let me grab you a pillow," I say, then I head back into the trailer, going right for the bag of weapons. Trax may think he's fooling everyone, but I know something isn't right. If I have to put a few bullets into som non-life threatening places to get answers, I will. His role in all of this is far more than he is letting on.

Thinking ahead, I pull out two blades and tuck them into the tops of my boots. A small caliber hand gun fits perfectly into the padded portion of my bra. It's uncomfortable, but he be would less likely to look there, and he already noticed the one at my hip. Adding an extra magazine to my back pocket, I stroll back onto the porch with the pillow from the dingy couch.

Trax is standing now, leaning against one of the posts making up the trailer's porch framework, puffing on a cigarette.

"About time you got back out here. I need your help sitting back down," he barks. Setting down the pillow, I walk to his side and help him ease down on to the porch. His hand conveniently slides to my ass as he leans back onto the pillow. "Sorry, doll. My hand slipped."

I ignore him, and take a seat across from him, on the other side of the steps. Trax takes another drag off his cigarette before throwing it to the ground.

"They ran you off the road, right?" I ask.

"I didn't end up looking like the loser of a UFC fight by picking wildflowers," he snap, drawing in a ragged breath.

"So, why doesn't that truck have scratches on it?"

He glares at me, but then his expression morphs into laughter as he leans his head back against the pole behind him. "What's with the third-degree interrogation? Can't a man recoup in peace?"

"Well, that's the funny thing about accidents. There's always a mark, a scratch, or a ding somewhere on the vehicle."

"What's your point?" he growls.

I rise up and move to stand directly in front of him. I plant my hands on my hips, fingering the gun hidden in the waistband of my jeans. When he'd noted it earlier, I knew I needed to move it to a different spot. I don't feel comfortable with him knowing I'm armed.

"My point is, I don't think there was an accident at all. I think you led Michael into town under false pretenses, then handed him over to the cartel."

Trax chuckles, opening his eyes and looking at me once more. "Why would I do a thing like that?"

"Because I think you were the one who was supposed to kill his wife. I knew as soon as you told me you were here to protect your business interests that you weren't talking about the club. You were talking about the cartel. You're in bed with them."

Trax stands easily from the porch and steps toward me, but before he can come any closer, I draw my weapon and aim straight for his face.

"I thought you would have figured that one out when you paid me cash for club secrets. Tell me, does Raze know you went behind his back to find out how your husband died?"

"You sold me lies. It doesn't matter."

"Lies are a funny thing really. Some lies hurt, while others protect from pain. However, the real lies, the ones that gut you and strip you down piece by piece are something entirely different. Take your husband's death for example. Did you know Raze and his men annihilated an entire club for his murder. Innocent men. I'm the one who put that knife to your husband's throat and watched him bleed out all over the floor of that shed. In fact, I still have a piece of his flesh hanging from the wall in my clubhouse. You should come see what's left of him."

"You *son-of-a-bitch*," I scream, pressing my finger onto the trigger and putting a bullet into his leg. Blind rage pools inside of me. I could end this now. End him for what's he's done. It would be so simple. A bullet to his brain. That's all it would take. So why I am hesitating? Why, when what I want is so close? To punish who killed my husband.

"You want to kill me, doll. Why not do it?" he taunts, his smile still wide despite clutching his bleeding shin. "Too chicken, just like your dead husband. Do you want to know what he said to me before he died?"

"Shut up!"

Trax straightens up, his smile growing wider. "He mentioned you, you know? Told me how much he loved you, and those kids of yours. What would he say now that you're fucking his club president?"

Rage blurs my vision and I fire another round into his leg, slightly lower than the first one. He screams out in pain. "Bitch," he seethes. "You'll pay for this." His anger and pain rolls off of him in waves.

"The only one who's going to pay is you and that bitch." That's when the idea hits me. I could end this. I could end this for me, for my kids, and for Michael. And Trax had the golden ticket to get me there. "Here's what we're going to do. You, me, and that truck over there, are going to go to the compound. You're going to get me in the same room with Maj, so I can put a bullet in her fucking brain and end this."

"And why would I do that?" he rasps, spitting blood on the ground. "What's in it for me?"

I stare down at him, revolted by his very existence. "I'll let you live."

"Well now," he says, his sneer melting back into that disgusting smile. "That's an interesting twist. You'd let the man who killed your husband live so you can kill the woman who set it up? My dear Darcy, I didn't know you had that kind of hatred inside of you."

"There's more to me than you'll ever know," I mutter. "Now get moving."

I shove the gun into his back as he hobbles by me on his injured leg. I only nicked him on the second shot, so I know it's more for show than anything else is. He opens up the passenger side door, and as he climbs in, I remove his weapon from his holster, tossing it the ground outside the truck, then shut him inside. I keep the gun trained on him as I walk around the front of the truck and slide into the driver's seat. The keys jingle from the ignition, and I start it up with one hand, keeping the gun pointed at him with my other. Putting the truck into drive, I fly out of the trailer park and demand he give me directions.

A few minutes later, we come up on a T in the road, and Trax directs me to follow the dirt path up the side of a mountain. The ride is bumpy and narrow, and at times, frighteningly close to the edge, but several miles later, we pull up behind a large white house. A tall fence lines the property. Leaving the truck, I pull Trax from the passenger's side of the vehicle and use some discarded zip ties I find lying in the seat to secure around his wrists.

He walks up the path and gives me a code to punch into the gate. It beeps and unlocks, allowing us to pass. Trax takes us to a stairway at the back of the house just as gunfire echoes off the front of the building. I watch in horror as dozens of men run from the building below us, heading right for the gates, where Hero and his men stand. Two trucks are backed up to the gate, and men are wrapping iron chains around the bars, trying to pull them down.

Two massive explosions rattle the foundation, and smoke fills the courtyard below us.

I press the gun into Trax's back, forcing him to move forward, but not before I notice a smirk on his face. This sick fucker is getting off on the fact that his brothers are fighting below, and probably injured. Maybe I shouldn't have made that promise to let him live, because him being on this Earth another second is not good for anyone.

He leads me to a room on the far side of the building, and a woman's voice floats from inside.

"Can I kill him now?" the voice begs, and I know in an instant it's *hers*.

I lean down and pull a knife from my boot, shoving it against his throat hard enough to draw blood. With the gun still pressed against his back, I kick the door open and use him as a shield for what lies in the room.

We inch inside, and my eyes fall on Michael, who is tied down to a chair with Maj straddling his lap, a look of pure ecstasy on her face as he grimaces in disgust. It sickens me to see her in such an intimate position, but his pants are clearly still belted tightly to his waist. This is her way of torturing him. I don't know if I can handle seeing her raping him without losing my composure and compromising us all.

"Well now, who do we have here?" she asks with

a giggle. "I see my lover has finally joined us." She squeals, clapping her hands like a lunatic. "Oh, and he brought me something to play with."

Michael's eyes lock on mine and he struggles to break free of his bindings. His face is bloodied, and so are his hands. He doesn't appear to have any serious wounds, but I can't tell with Maj's body pressed so tightly against his.

"You're just in time, Darcy," she purrs, her hands dropping down onto Michael's crotch, pawing at his fly. "I was just about to enjoy one last goodbye fuck with my husband before I kill him. Would you like to watch?"

"You touch him, Maj, and I will put a bullet into your boyfriend's brain right here and now."

Maj tilts her head to the smile and gives me a phony pout. "Aw, sweetie. You won't be doing much of anything in just a few seconds."

I glare at her, the hatred in my heart ready to explode. "And why's that?"

"Because you're failing hostage situation 101, baby. Always check the room for other players."

As soon as the words leave her lips, a rope is thrown over my head and pulled tightly against my neck. The gun and knife in my hands drop to the floor, and Trax stumbles away and falls to the ground. I struggle to breathe as the person behind me pulls on the rope, making it tighter and forcing it to cut into my flesh. Darkness builds at edge of my vision as my air supply disappears. I'm on the brink of passing out, and there's nothing I can do but watch Michael's face twisted in horror. My body begins to feel weightless when a shot rings out, echoing throughout the room. The rope around my neck falls slack, and I fall to the ground, landing on top of the man behind me. My hands grasp for my throat as I pant and gasp for air.

Maj just laughs, and when I look up, Trax is right there, holding my smoking gun. He smiles and reaches down, pulling me from the ground by my hair. He wraps an arm around my waist, pressing the knife I once held to his throat, against mine.

"Look what you made me do, Darcy."

He points the gun to the ground behind me. There, on the ground where I had I landed, is an older man with the rope that had been around my neck grasped in his eyes. His brightly colored shoes laying motionless at my feet. Blood pools around the floor from the gunshot wound in his head. It's then, that I feel the warm stickiness coating the back of my shirt. His blood.

"Kill me," Michael pleads, drawing me back from the tilted reality of the dead man at my feet. "I'm the one that you want. Not her. She's innocent in this."

"That's where you're wrong, my husband. She's as much a part of this as you are, aren't you, whore?"

Michael looks to me with pleading eyes.

"You see," Maj continues. "She paid off Trax to get information about your club and how Jagger died. She paid him a pretty penny to get that information from us. It was false information, mind you, but she still didn't trust you enough to believe you would make the right call."

Michael's nostrils flare, the veins in his neck bulging as he thrashes in his chair.

"You didn't know that did you, husband? You both spin so many lies, you're almost the perfect fucked-up couple. And you thought I was a bad wife." She laughs maniacally. It's a sound nightmares are made of.

"I'm *nothing* compared to you, Maj," I scream. "It's true, I bought information about the club, but unlike you, I didn't use it to hurt them. I didn't use it at all because I realized that my husband would never do the bullshit you fed me. And I know Michael far better than you ever did. Even if you kill me, he'll keep on fighting, and eventually, you will die. For real this time."

Maj slips from Michael's lap and walks over to a table, picking up a gun and sauntering back over to him. She places her leg on his knee while leaning forward and pressing the barrel of her gun to the center of his chest.

Another explosion rattles the building, quickly followed by several more.

"Oh!" Maj exclaims. "Sounds like they're having fun outside." The sickening smile on her face spreads as she turns back to Michael. "That's the thing about people, Darcy. Everyone is capable of a little bit of evil, and in my case, a lot of it, but at the end of the day, it's how you live with yourself despite the actions and decisions you make. Say goodbye to Darcy, lover. It's time for our business relationship to come to an end. No harsh feelings, okay? I'll make sure that my kids remember you fondly."

"I love you, Darcy," he screams as she moves her finger to the trigger.

Suddenly, Michael's feet break free of his bindings, and he brings his knees up and slams them into Maj's stomach. She falls to the ground at his feet, and the gun falls into his lap. Trax flinches, both from Maj's fall, and another explosion outside. I take my opportunity and donkey kick him in the balls, sending him spilling to the ground, just like Maj. He tries to get up, but I press my foot into his throat, taking the fight out of him in an instant. He gags and gurgles, his wide eyes pinned on me.

"Stop," Maj cries out. "I need him!"

"So do I," I growl, biding time while Michael tries to break free from his confines. "Let me guess. He's your dealer. He got you hooked on drugs, so he could take over the cartel and the club."

"I have an addictive personality," she says with a shrug. It's as if she doesn't have a care in the world.

"You get the cartel, and he gets the club. Isn't that right? You both get what you think you deserve. A happily little after in hell. That sum it up?"

"Yes," she admits. "So please don't kill him." Maj scrambles to get up and take the gun from Michael's lap, but a snap echoes in the room from one of the zip ties on his wrists. Just as her hand touches the gun, I pull the one hidden in my bra, take aim, and fire. The sound of the gun silences the room, and Maj's lifeless body falls in a heap at Michael's feet.

"People like you don't get happily ever afters, *bitch*," I scream.

Trax reaches up and grabs my ankle, trying to throw me off balance, but I twist and shoot him in the chest.

"That's for my husband, you motherfucker."

Blood bubbles from the hole near his heart while he sputters for air and dies at my feet. I watch Trax draw in his last breath, and a sense of peace settles in my soul. It's over. The people responsible for my husband's death are finally dead.

Dropping the gun, I run to Michael as he gingerly rises from the chair and stares down at his dead wife's body. "Are you okay?"

"I've been better," he hisses. "Are you okay?"

"I don't know," I admit. "Michael, about what I said earlier…"

Michael presses a finger to my lips and pulls me into his arms. Forgetting about the dead bodies on the floor, his mouth slams into my mine, letting me know that he knows exactly what I was going to say.

"We need to get you out of here, and then I'll go get the guys," I say, pulling away from his lips.

A loud bang comes from outside the door, and I whip around, preparing for another fight. The door flies open, and men pour into the room. Hero and Ratchet enter last, the fierce looks on their faces morphing to smiles as they see the two of us together.

"Well, shit. I guess I didn't need to rescue you at all, Prez."

Chapter 28

RAZE

WE LEFT Mexico within hours of settling our business. After getting everyone out of the house, we left Ratchet to do his thing. The smoke from the fire would draw attention, so we made sure we left behind nothing that could tie us to everything that had just happened there.

We're lucky. None of us should have gotten out alive, but the only casualties came at the expense of the cartel. Darcy has remained quiet since killing both Maj and Trax. Not that I blame her. Extinguishing a life is something you never forget, and it will haunt you for the rest of your life, even if it was part self-defense and part vengeance.

I was shocked she came for me at all. Her words when I finally told her the full story still bite when I think of them. She was so angry, and I thought for sure that was the end of us.

She saved me. That's the damnedest thing of all because I was trying to save her. I was the one who put up the barrier between our world and hers, and it was her who ultimately chose the fate of Maj and Trax.

Just thinking his name makes me want to spit on his grave—if he had one. The only grave that fucker has are in the ashes of that house. I trusted him with the darkest secret of my life, and he broke the bonds of our brotherhood for his loyalty to my wife. She had offered him everything he wanted on a silver platter, but first he had to kill me. That betrayal is hard to accept.

Yet, the person I feel pity for is Maj. She had everything, and by letting her family rule her, she lost it all. She could have had a good life, but instead she chose a different path, a more painful one that, and it ended with the ultimate sacrifice. Her death brought a sense of relief to me that I should be ashamed to admit, but now she can't haunt me or the kids any longer. The ghosts of my past are now dead and buried, and I know for damn sure they won't be coming back.

My kids. That's the part that still makes me seethe in anger. I had thought they had a piece of me inside them. I had believed all along that they were mine. Over the last few days, I've struggled with my newfound knowledge. I hate Maj for what she did, and if I could, I would bring her back to life just to kill her all over again for lying to us.

Harley and Ky are my fucking kids whether we share DNA or not. But do I tell them I'm not their biological father, or do I just go on living the lie for their sakes? It's not fair to them that their mother was a two-timing cartel whore, and I would never treat them any different if I did tell them. The decision will take some considering, but right now, my mind is pre-occupied with Darcy and helping her come to terms with what she did.

She'd tried to isolate herself from me, but I walked into her room at the clubhouse and carried her to my bed. The first night back, I held her until she cried herself to sleep. I kept her in my arms until the morning. She apologized for all the things we'd said before I hushed her and made love to the woman I owe my life to.

Two more days passed before she finally opened up about her feelings. She's conflicted because she knows that killing them both should make her remorseful, but she's not. She's relieved the people responsible for Jagger's death are finally gone, but taking a life will always haunt her.

Today, as I left her in my bed to go address my brothers about the future of the club, I made a decision. One that would not only affect us both, but that of our club. Things need to change around here, and for the better. It's time I step up as their leader and make this club great again. After that, Darcy and I will be next on the agenda.

"Brothers," I say, rising from my chair at the head of the table. "I want to thank you for being by my side and showing me that, even in a hopeless fight, you support me."

"You are our brother and our president," Hero says, his voice firm. "We're all here because of you, and your loyalty to us."

"Yeah, Prez. You've always had our backs, so it was only right to have yours," Voodoo chimes in.

I look around at the men surrounding this table, and it makes me proud to call them my brothers.

"This is the last time we deal with this shit." I declare. "I'm tired of wars. I'm tired of looking over our shoulders. No more bullshit. We are a brotherhood, and I won't have someone trying to cut us down anymore."

My brothers clap and stand at my words. "Voodoo, I want you to take Slider and head up to Trax's chapter. I need to know if they had any clue what he was doing. If they did, take their patches and burn their cuts."

"You got it, Boss," Voodoo says.

"Are you going to patch Slider in soon?" Hero questions.

"If he does well assisting Voodoo, we'll take a vote. He's been loyal, and he's kept our clubhouse safe over the last few months."

"Agreed," Thrasher pipes up.

"Today marks a new era in Heaven's Rejects' MC history," I yell over the noise of their applause. "Today, we put the ghosts of our past to rest." They guys hoot and holler, the noise in the room nearly deafening. "We focus on our families. We focus on each other, and we for damn sure focus on ourselves. The time for peace is here, and it's here to fucking stay."

Everyone stands, moving to the head of the table and surrounding me. I hug each one of them before dismissing Church. Next, I order Hero to take a few weeks off to spend time with his wife and daughters. He thanks me and nearly runs me over on his way out of the door.

When he gets back, we'll sit down and discuss the changes I have in mind. Voodoo's nerdiness will give us an edge on the security world, and it's time we increase our presence in the business. I also want to start investing more in our garage and bike repair shop. We've all but ignored those during the past year. They were Jagger's babies, and when he died, none of us wanted to step in his place. The last business we need to make a decision about is Maj's salon. Twisted Tribe had burned it to the ground, but the insurance company had paid us well for the building. Perhaps it's time to look into another business entirely, but that would depend on if Darcy would be interested in making her business a full-time venture. Plus, can I handle knowing she's selling rubber monster cocks for a living?

As everyone shuffles out the door, Ratchet stays behind. I pull up in the chair next to him. He's definitely got something on his mind.

"She's gone," he mutters. "She left while we were away."

I nod, not surprised by this news at all. "What are you going to do about it?"

He turns to face me, his eyes worried and sad. "I'm going after her. I have no idea where to even start, though. She's never told me where she's from."

I stand and slap him on his shoulder. "Get Voodoo to track her down with his computer wizardry, and then, you go get your girl."

Ratchet rises from his chair and pulls me into a

hug. "Thanks, Prez. I think it's high time you go get yours, too."

"That's the plan, brother. I just hope she'll still have me."

We walk out together, and in the hall, we part ways, both on our own missions of the heart.

I stand outside of my door and exhale a breath before slipping inside. Darcy is curled up on the couch with her freshly-washed hair in a towel. Her knees are tucked tightly to her chest, her chin resting on top of them.

"Hey," she says softly.

"Hey, darlin'." At the couch, I plop down next to her.

"Church go okay?" she asks, her voice absent and drawn. It kills me to see the fire inside her extinguished.

"Yeah, it was fine." Reaching over, I stroke her leg. "How about we get out of here and go get the kids?"

Her eyes light up in an instant. I'm hesitant to bring them home already, just in case there's some blow back from the cartel. Voodoo's been listening to the news channels, both locally and down in Mexico, but the only thing to come up was a report on a local home being torched and suspected to be the result of a local turf war between cartels. Knowing it's been discovered and we haven't been arrested gives me enough relief to bring them home. Besides, the only time I've seen a smile on her face since we've come back is when she talks to the kids.

"I'll go get ready," she says, bolting off the couch with a renewed pep in her step. I flip on ESPN while I wait. She emerges just fifteen minutes later looking like she had spent hours getting ready.

I can't take my eyes off her. "Maybe we should go get the kids later. I'd like to pull up that little sundress and fuck you into tomorrow."

She just blushes, but says nothing as she grabs her purse from the dresser.

"All right, all right. Kids first, sex later."

I hop up from the couch and place my hand on the small of her back, leading her out the door. I had already sent Slider over to her house to get the van. It might be a tight squeeze, but we'll all fit.

Her eyes light up when she sees the van, almost like she didn't believe we were actually going. Slider tosses me the keys while she slides in the passenger seat. It takes some creative maneuvering, but I wedge myself into the driver's seat. This is the first thing that has to go. I make a mental note to make an appointment with my car guy to start looking for a vehicle to haul seven people as soon as we're back. Well, that is, if today goes as planned. I lean over to help her buckle her seatbelt and press a kiss to her lips. She smiles without a word and slips on her sunglasses as I start the van.

Turning out of the drive, I make an abrupt left, instead of heading toward the highway.

"Where are we going?"

"I have a little side trip we need to make first."

Darcy looks nervous as I drive to our destination. Just before I pull into the drive, she whips around to face me. "Why are we here?"

"It's time, darlin.' You need to talk to him."

"About what?"

Unbuckling my seatbelt, I reach over and take her hand into mine. Tears are already welling up in her eyes, which only makes what I'm about to say even more special.

"Before we can move on, you need to let go of him, Darcy. I know I can't replace Brent in your heart, and frankly, I don't want to. But I know he wouldn't want you to spend the rest of your life in pain and misery. I don't need promises of forever, or even you as my wife, but please just fucking let me in and let me love you like you are meant to be loved."

"You want me?" she whispers. "What about everything that happened? I killed your wife."

Reaching out, I stroke a finger along the length of her damp cheek. "I just want you. The bullshit of my ex-wife is in the past. I want to wake up next to you every day and see your smiling face. To know what your love feels like, and to know that you and the kids are safe."

"I can't do what Maj did, Raze. I can't be the queen next to the king." She turns her face away, staring out the window. With my finger, I gingerly touch her chin and turn her gaze back to mine.

"I'm not asking you to fill her shoes. I just want a woman who will be by my side, tell me when I'm fucking up, and hell, just love me the way I need to be loved."

"What if I can't? What if I mess all of this up between us?"

"That's a road we'll cross if the time comes, but I don't see that happening, darlin'. Go talk to him."

Her hand starts for the handle, but I stop her, only to give her a kiss and press the envelope I've held onto for months into her hand. "When you've said your peace, read it."

She frowns a little, but nods and then opens the door. Palming my own letter, I wait for her to walk out of sight before opening it. As I finish reading, I shake my head and look up to the skies.

"Thank you for giving her to me, brother."

Chapter 29

DARCY

AFTER EVERYTHING that's happened over the past few months, today seems more daunting than anything I've ever faced. I know I should have done this far sooner than now, but I couldn't bring myself to come here and face him yet.

Taking a deep breath, I grip the unopened letter and begin the journey. Each step is labored as I walk down the path and onto the dewy grass. Everything is so quiet and pristine here, and yet, it rattles me. I walk a few yards further until I stop in front of my destination. Kneeling on the grass, I wipe the dirt from my husband's gravestone and press my hand on its marbled edge. With the tip on my finger, I trace his name carved into the stone.

"Hey, baby," I whisper, then I pause, as if waiting

to hear his voice in return. I twist my hands on my lap as I try to find the words I want to say.

"I know you've probably got a lot to say to me after watching the shit storm I walked into on your behalf," I say, choking on a sob. "I know you're probably disappointed in me, and I hate that every single day I wonder how you feel about the blood on my hands. About how stupid I was for getting involved with the club. But I did it for you. I couldn't live the rest of my life in the dark."

I use the back of my hand to wipe a tear from my cheek. "I have been angry with you for so long. Angry at you for leaving us, and for choosing the club over your family, but I understand now. You did it *for* us. You protected us in the only way you knew how. With your life. I wish you had told me about the things you were wrapped up in. Maybe I could have helped you, but your stubborn ass had to ride in like the knight in shining armor to save the day, as usual."

More tears stream down my face as I choke out words weighing heavily on my heart. "You're going to miss seeing the boys grow up, and you didn't even get a chance to see your little girl come into this world. I named her Roxie Belle, just like we talked about, and she is so much like you. Even at nearly seven months old, she has your smile, and your attitude."

A gust of wind picks up, sending stray leaves scraping across the gravel road. The chill from the air tickles against my skin.

"Yelling at you isn't why I'm here today, Brent," I whisper. "This shouldn't be so hard to say to a stone, but I'm in love with Michael. I never meant for it to happen, but we just collided together after you died. We've been through so much already. I know I'll likely get my heart broken again, but I want to try with him. Nothing about our relationship, or how quickly I fell for him, makes any sense, but when we're together, everything just falls into place. It's fucked up, I know, but I can't even describe it in a way that would make you understand."

Looking down to the letter lying in my lap, I know it's time to read the last words written to me by my husband. Gingerly picking it up, I run my finger under the seal and rip it open. My fingers trace the edge of the envelope before slipping inside and pulling out the folded piece of paper. I take my time unfolding it, and finally, after a deep breath, I look down to read the words.

My beautiful belle,
Before I even get out what I need to

say, wipe those tears away from that beautiful face of yours. The time for tears is over, baby, and it's time for your face to shine with happiness again. I know that with Raze handing you this letter, you have finally found someone who deserves you. Maybe even more than I did.

I'm sure by now he's told you everything. I think I need to explain my reason behind my decision to step into the line of fire for the club, and more importantly for him. From the moment I met him, I saw something no one else did. A broken man. He fought so hard to make the club legitimate after his father's death. He rushed into a marriage to fulfill his dream of having a family. I watched as he went from a good man to a man teetering on the edge of slipping to where his old man had fallen.

Was it fair for me to give up our family and marriage for his? No, but I couldn't sit idly by and watch everything we've worked so hard for over the last several years to be set aside because his wife was a cheating, no good bitch. I wanted to grow old with you and our boys, but that was never in the cards. I knew I would eventually have to risk my life for him, and I did it gladly. He needed someone to go to bat for him, and with my death, I left him something even better to rebuild the man I know is still in him. You.

From the very first day, I saw how he looked at you. I knew he would be the one to grow old with you, and protect you after I was gone. He has the fire inside him to keep that sassy mouth of yours in check, and to raise the boys the way I want them to be raised. He'll be a good dad to them, and to our little girl.

Yes, belle, I knew. As much as you wanted to keep your little secret, I knew. I found the pregnancy test in the trash the morning I wrote this letter. I didn't want to spoil the surprise, so I didn't say anything. I know it's crazy, but I knew our Roxie was growing in your belly. I would have loved to be her father, but she was meant for you and Raze. A chance to have a child to raise together, and I hope for Raze, a little hell on wheels to worry about, when she gets older. Tell her that her old man says she can't date until she's forty or some shit like that. If I was wrong, and our baby is a boy, then his brothers will raise him to be strong like their mother.

Be good to each other, Darcy, and please love again. Life isn't as sweet without someone to love, and I'm leaving you with just that.

I love you.
Brent
P.S.

Please thank Matteo for delivering the first letter for me. I knew he would find it and deliver it when the time was right.

"You okay?" Michael approaches from behind,

stopping next to where I knee and laying his hand on my shoulder.

My tears are flowing as I reach up and take his hand. "Yeah, I guess so. You were right. I did need to come see him."

"I know it seems weird, but it helps far more than you know. Even if you look like someone who escaped from the loony bin talking to a stone in the ground."

"It does help," I mumble. "But it also brings back all the painful memories of the past year."

Michael kneels down next to me and takes me into his arms. "Sometimes, the most beautiful things emerge from the ashes of destruction, Darcy. We live through the pain as a reminder that each day we're granted on this Earth is something to cherish."

His words break what's left of my control, and I cling to him, uncontrollable sobs seeping from the healing wounds on my heart. He holds me tighter as I cry until I have no more tears left inside of me. Pressing a kiss to the top of my head, he rubs his hands up and down my back, trying to soothe my emotions.

Pulling back, I look up at the man who's knelt next to me, and suddenly I realize exactly what Brent was talking about in his letter. Michael has been through far greater hell than I have, and here he sits, holding me while I cry out my pain and frustrations. He is the piece that holds me together, and the man who has walked through the valley of the shadow of death by my side. He is my future, and it's time for me to let go of Brent's ghost and cling to Michael.

"Did you read the letter?" he asks, laying a chaste kiss to my forehead.

"I did."

"How do you feel after reading it? Better? Did he explain his reasoning to you?"

I sigh as I hand him the letter, watching as his eyes scan the pages. The corner of his mouth ticks up in a smirk as he reads.

"You never could put one past him, could you?" he mutters, referencing the bombshell of him knowing about my pregnancy. "He left one for the man you moved on with too, you know."

I blink up at him. "He did? Do you have it with you?"

Michael smiles and pulls a folded piece of paper from his pocket, laying it in my hand. He rises from the ground and dusts the dirt off his jeans before turning to walk away, giving me space to read his letter.

To the son of a bitch who's in love with my wife:

> Who am I kidding? I knew it would be you, Raze. I knew from the moment my expiration date was stamped that you would be the man to put Darcy back together. You needed her just as much as she needed you after I was gone. It's time you finally have something good in your life.
>
> Take care of her and my kids. Give them the life and love they all deserve, and if you don't, I'll kick your ass the next I see you.
>
> Jagger
>
> P.S.
>
> Lead the club, and keep the goals you had set in mind when you took over for your bastard of an old man. Give our brothers the leader they need, and put aside all the petty bullshit of the past. Too many of us have died righting the wrongs. It's time for peace.

Maybe it's the sense of knowing that he knew Michael and I would take care of each after his passing, or the love that swells in my heart seeing the sweet side of my badass biker, but a calming peace fills my heart.

Leaning forward, I press my lips against the cold stone, giving Brent one last kiss.

"I love you, Brent, and thank you for giving me Michael."

Epilogue

9 MONTHS LATER

DARCY

TODAY HAS BEEN a long time coming. The day we get our families together to celebrate the trials and tribulations of the past two years. The loss and pain in our lives has only been made manageable by the fact that in the darkness, we found each other. My parents, of course, think Michael and I are moving way too fast, but trying the dating thing from a distance was never going to be in the cards for us. To make us work, we need to be with each other, and it only made sense to rip off the Band-Aid, and blend our two families together.

I would like to say it's been easy, but change never is. The boys were ecstatic to gain two new siblings, while Ky and Harley had initially bucked at the idea. They were so attached to the memory of their mother, they couldn't look at me as anything other than a usurper. It took many months, and many nights of being around each other, before they finally relented and accepted our relationship. I doubt they'll ever call me Mom, and I'm okay with that. I may not have given birth to them, but I will raise them as my own, just as Michael pledged to do with my kids. Our family may be roughly stitched together and have frayed edges, but I wouldn't have it any other way.

"Are the burgers ready for the grill, darlin'?" Michael asks, popping his head through the patio door of our new home. We decided a few months into our relationship that having two houses associated with so much pain wouldn't be conducive to a new relationship, so instead, we bought one together. It took more than two months before we finally found the perfect one; a modest two-story brick home with six bedrooms, a large den for my home business and his, and a spacious yard with a pool for the kids. We paid far more than we should have without selling our two houses to compensate the purchase, but now it feels more like home than anywhere else.

"Here," I say, handing him a plate of formed patties. "Is Dad giving you any grief?"

"Nah, darlin'. Mitch has been wrapped up talking to my mom about how us living together without being married is a sin. They're keeping themselves entertained. And your mom is fussing after Roxie."

"You're kidding about Dad, right? I'm not exactly a virginal debutante anymore."

"He worries about his daughter, darlin'. They grew up in a far more traditional time than we have," he says with a wink. "I mean, if he knew what we did on that patio table the night we bought this place, he'd probably have burned it by now."

I smack his arm, and he just chuckles as he walks back out to the grill.

That man. Good grief. I could never have prepared myself for his brand of love. Even as much as Brent spoiled me, Michael is so much worse. Not a day goes by that he doesn't surprise me with some token or bring home something for the kids. Hell, the day he came home with a pink little Harley motorcycle scooter for Roxie, I nearly just melted. She squealed when she saw it, and toddled over to the thing, hopped right on, and made vrooming noises as she chased after Colt and Wesson.

Michael beamed with pride, watching her mimic him. He asks me constantly when she'll be old enough to go for a ride with him, but he knows she's still far too small to try that yet. He asks every day though, hoping I'll relent.

I think the strangest part of our relationship has been being his old lady. I'm so much more involved now than I was with Brent. Michael made sure that when he gave me my new property patch, that Brent was still represented on my cut. Just below the "Property of Raze" patch was a small patch that simply read, "In Memory of Jagger." Michael knew how much I had struggled with Brent's name no longer being on it, but he made sure he was still a part of it, even if I wasn't his property anymore.

The club no longer scares me, and it feels more and more like my extended family every day. They held me close while I dealt with the aftermath of killing Maj, something only a few members of the club know about.

I have my bad days, the guilt of having her kids under my roof, knowing her blood is on my hands weighs heavily on me. But Maj had her chance to be a good person. She gave it all up for drugs and money. She was held accountable for her actions, and that's how she went out of this world.

"Darlin'," Michael calls from the patio. "Can you come out here, please?"

Grabbing the plate of vegetable skewers for the grill, I step outside and stop dead in my tracks. My parents are sitting at the small patio table with Colt and Wesson flanking either side. Michael's mom, Mary, is standing on the opposite side of my parents with Ky and Harley. There, in the middle of all of them, is Michael with Roxie in his arms. He bends down and sets her on the ground, sending her toddling on her little legs to me.

Roxie takes small steps, something held tight in her little hands.

"What do you have, baby?" I ask, setting the plate on the and crouching down to her level. Her little hand opens up, and in her palm sits a ring with a cluster of eight diamonds. She grins as she it in my open palm.

My mouth drops in shock, and my hand flies up to my chest as I gasp. Michael's footsteps draw closer, and without a word, Harley steps between us and whisks Roxie away while Michael kneels before me. I shake my head in disbelief as he plucks the ring from my hand and holds it up in front of us.

"I know we talked about not getting married early on, but, darlin' I want you to be mine, both in my heart, and in the eyes of God. We don't have to get married today, or even a hundred years from now, but I want the world to know you belong to me."

My heart is nearly at it's bursting point as hot

tears fall to my cheeks. He wipes them away, and takes the ring, sliding it onto my finger as I remain frozen in silence.

"What about the—"

"The kids and I had a long talk while you were out grocery shopping for the party. I even asked the boys permission, darlin'. We all agree that this is our family, and it's time we're all bound together."

I look to the kids, and each and every one of their faces beam with a smile.

"Even if you say no, it doesn't change a damn thing. But just know, I'll ask you every day until you agree. So, darlin', will do you me the honor of making our family whole by being my wife?"

I nod my head, and Michael chuckles.

"I need to hear it, Darcy. A nod isn't going to be how you answer me."

"Yes," I whisper.

Michael envelops me in his arms while our family cheers from behind us. He plants a chaste kiss that lingers with the promise that we'll celebrate in our own way later, without the prying eyes of our families.

The rest of the evening, we spend enjoying our family and riding out the excitement of his proposal. Once the food is gone and the dishes are clean, Mary and my parents ask to spend more time with the kids before heading back to Arizona.

While I'm about to protest the decision, Michael instantly agrees and packs an overnight bag for each child before practically shoving them out of the door. The sounds of their cars haven't even faded down the street before he's spinning me around and pinning me to the back of the front door.

His hands reach up under my ass, and he hoists me into the air, my legs wrapping around his waist and his mouth slams into mine. His lips devour my own, before his mouth falls away from my swollen lips, kissing trails down the side of my neck.

"I need to claim you, darlin'. I need to feel you clenched around me right fucking now."

His hands move higher on my back as he pulls us away from the door and walks toward the sectional in the living room. He lowers me down on the chaise lounge, and stands before me, removing his shirt. My hands fly to his zipper, and I yank down on it before he presses his body on top of mine.

His hands roam my body, cupping my breasts, and tracing between the heated pool between my legs. I moan at his touch and my breath hitches as he fingers the hem of my shirt before ripping it from my body, exposing my black lacy bra underneath.

"Please tell me you have matching fucking panties that I get to remove with my teeth."

I grin at the idea, nodding my head.

He groans and lifts up my skirt, exposing my lace-covered pussy.

"Damnit, I love you, woman."

His mouth falls on my breasts, his tongue swirl around my nipples under the lace of my bra. He pulls me forward, his nimble fingers working to unclasps my bra. I finish undoing his jeans, and he steps back, allowing me to push them down his legs before he steps out of them.

I gasp as he tugs my skirt down over my hips, leaving me in nothing my panties, before he falls to his knees. Trailing kisses up my inner thigh and down the next, he completely skips over my aching pussy.

"You missed a spot you know," I tease with a hiss.

"I did, huh?" he mumbles, nipping at my thigh before looking up from between my legs.

"I think you owe me, in fact."

He sits back on his heels and takes in my exposed body with an arched eyebrow. "That so? Let me apologize for the oversight, I will remedy the situation as soon as you shut that pretty mouth of yours, so I can eat my dessert."

I laugh, inching away from him as he tries to dive

between my legs. "See, that's the thing. I have an idea in mind for you to make it up to me."

His brow furrows in confusion as he waits for my answer. "Hmm, what is my punishment for being so neglectful?"

"I want to sit on your face."

Michael's eyes grow wide, and after a moment, his smiles spreading with excitement. "Well, shit. Bring that pretty pussy to me, woman."

He rises from the floor, reaching out his hand and easing me off my back and onto the edge of the lounge. He climbs in behind me, then leans back into the corner of the sectional. His eyes grow wide as I plant a foot on the edge of the lounge and step up. I straddle his waist before lifting my foot up to the arm of the lounge. Before I even get a chance to position myself better, his hands move to my ass and he pulls my pussy to his face.

His tongue laps at me, locking onto my clit and circling it. His free hand drifts along my flesh, searching for my entrance and plunging two fingers inside of me. His tongue strokes slowly, firm and hot, massaging every nerve just the way I like it. I moan, throwing my head back and rocking my hips as Michael licks faster and harder, building my release into an impending tsunami.

"I'm so close," I gasp.

Michael moans, sucking my clit between his lips, his tongue alternating between flicks and circles. He hooks his finger slightly, hitting my g-spot, and I can't take it anymore. An explosive of pleasure takes over, and I scream, riding his face as electrical currents flow like a live wire throughout my entire body.

Michael doesn't wait for me to settle before sliding down the couch and pulling me down onto of his lap. His dick strains against the boxers, begging to be released. Reaching down, I work his boxers from his hips and free him. Michael puts a whole new spin on being hung like a horse. I think even a horse would be jealous of his equipment, quite frankly.

"I need to be in-fucking-side of you, Darcy."

He picks me up once more and settles me down on his cock. He hisses once he's fully sheathed inside of me.

I rock my hips as he pounds his cock inside of me from below. He moves faster, his eyes glassed over with need as I arch my back and place my hands on his knees, deepening his stroke inside me. He watches my every move, thrusts inside of me so deeply it teeters on the line between pain and pleasure.

"Say you're mine, Darcy," he growls. "I need to hear you say it."

I roll my hips, pressing down harder on his cock as I scream out, "I'm yours. I'm so fucking yours."

He thrusts twice more, and then he stops, his face a vision of ecstasy as I keep up with the ride. A few seconds later, my second orgasm takes hold.

As our bodies settle, I fall on top of his chest, both of us breathless and panting in unison.

Michael wraps his arms around me. "You are my everything," he whispers against my hair. "I love you more than anything in the world, Darcy. Well, except for my bike."

I smirk and bite down on his nipple.

Michael yelps, covering the area with his palm as he laughs. "Fine, I love you more than my bike. Happy now?"

I nod, biting back a smile. "Yes, now fuck me again before they decide to return the kids early."

SERIES READING ORDER

Did you enjoy Angels and Ashes?

Read more from the Heaven's Rejects MC Series.

Heaven Sent

Angels and Ashes

Sins of the Father

Absolution

Lies and Illusions

Resolution

Song List

"Call Me" by Shinedown

"Bitch Came Back" by Theory of a Deadman

"Call Your Name" by Daughtry

"Things My Father Said" by Black Stone Cherry

"Drunk Enough" by Angel's Fall

"All The Same" by Sick Puppies

"Trying Not to Love You" by Nickelback

"Hollow Man" by Rev Theory

"Thing for You" by Hinder

"Save Yourself" by My Darkest Days

"Broken Pieces" by Apocalytpica

"Familiar Taste of Poison" by Halestorm

"F*cked Up Situation" by My Darkest Days

"Careless Whisper" by Seether

"Monster" by Skillet

Acknowledgements

Holy Shit. This is book number three for me, since I started putting fingers to the keyboard in 2015. It literally leaves me a bit awestruck to think that there are enough voices in my head to come up with yet another story. Well, the right voices I should say. There are definitely plenty of voices that probably shouldn't be heard rambling away in my mind, but we'll keep those hidden away. I don't think I would be a good patient in a padded room. Too much bouncing around to be had. Anyway, now it's time for acknowledgements, which ironically enough is one of the hardest things to write outside of the blurb. Do you know how many times I just want to put "Read this shit. You'll like it," instead of a thoughtful analysis of the book? Be thankful, that I have people to talk me out of half the things I come up with. Okay, back to the acknowledgements.

To my husband. It's finally done, and you have

your bubbly wife back. I've stowed away the bat-shit-crazy writing mess of a wife for a few weeks, but she will have to come back out to play soon enough. I know that this book took me away far more than any other books I've ever written, so I want to thank you for giving me the freedom to do something I love. Thank you for being the love of my life, and the most supportive man on the face of the earth.

Shauna Kruse and Alfie Gordillo, thank you both so much for my beautiful cover and teaser photos. You both captured the image of Raze so perfectly, and it makes the cover fit so well with the story.

About Avelyn

Avelyn Paige is a USA Today and Wall Street Journal bestselling author who writes stories about dirty alpha males and the brave women who love them. She resides in a small town in Indiana with her husband and three fuzzy kids, Jezebel, Cleo, and Asa.

Avelyn spends her days working as a cancer research scientist and her nights sipping moonshine while writing. You can often find her curled up with a good book surrounded by her pets or watching one of her favorite superhero movies for the billionth time. Deadpool is currently her favorite.

Want to talk books? Join Avelyn's Facebook group to learn about new releases, future series, and to hang out with other readers.

ALSO BY AVELYN PAIGE

The Heaven's Rejects MC Series

Heaven Sent

Angels and Ashes

Sins of the Father

Absolution

Lies and Illusions

Resolution

The Black Hoods MC

Dark Protector

Dark Secret

Dark Guardian

Dark Desires

Dark Destiny

Dark Redemption

Dark Salvation

Dark Seduction

The Bastard Boilers MC

Property of Azrael

The Dirty Bitches MC Series

[Dirty Bitches MC #1](#)

[Dirty Bitches MC #2](#)

[Dirty Bitches MC #3](#)

Other Books by Avelyn Paige

Girl in a Country Song

Cassie's Court

Printed in Great Britain
by Amazon